The Lady's Yuletide Wish is part of
Marguerite Kaye's miniseries

Revelations of the Carstairs Sisters

*To find happiness, they must first
reveal their secrets...*

But can these spirited sisters be brave
enough to let go of their pasts in order to
remake their futures?

Read Prudence's and Mercy's stories in

*The Earl Who Sees Her Beauty
Lady Armstrong's Scandalous Awakening*

Dr. Peverett's Christmas Miracle is the
final installment in Bronwyn Scott's

The Peveretts of Haberstock Hall

*Meet the philanthropic Peverett siblings:
unconventional, resourceful and determined
to make a difference in the world.*

Read all about Victorian society's
most intriguing family in

*Lord Tresham's Tempting Rival
Saving Her Mysterious Soldier
Miss Peverett's Secret Scandal
The Bluestocking's Whirlwind Liaison*

All available now!

Marguerite Kaye writes hot historical romances from her home in cold and usually rainy Scotland. She has published over fifty books and novellas featuring Regency rakes, Highlanders and sheikhs. When she's not writing, she enjoys walking, cycling (but only on the level), gardening (but only what she can eat) and cooking. She also likes to knit and occasionally drink martinis (though not at the same time). Find out more on her website, margueritekaye.com.

Bronwyn Scott is a communications instructor at Pierce College and the proud mother of three wonderful children—one boy and two girls. When she's not teaching or writing, she enjoys playing the piano, traveling—especially to Florence, Italy—and studying history and foreign languages. Readers can stay in touch via Facebook at Facebook.com/bronwynwrites or on her blog, bronwynswriting.blogspot.com. She loves to hear from readers.

UNDER THE MISTLETOE

——

Marguerite Kaye
Bronwyn Scott

HARLEQUIN®
HISTORICAL™

PLEASE RECYCLE
THIS PRODUCT IS RECYCLABLE

Recycling programs
for this product may
not exist in your area.

ISBN-13: 978-1-335-72348-2

Under the Mistletoe

Copyright © 2022 by Harlequin Enterprises ULC

The Lady's Yuletide Wish
Copyright © 2022 by Marguerite Kaye

Dr. Peverett's Christmas Miracle
Copyright © 2022 by Nikki Poppen

For questions and comments about the quality of this book,
please contact us at CustomerService@Harlequin.com.

Harlequin Enterprises ULC
22 Adelaide St. West, 41st Floor
Toronto, Ontario M5H 4E3, Canada
www.Harlequin.com

Printed in U.S.A.

CONTENTS

THE LADY'S
YULETIDE WISH

Marguerite Kaye

Chapter One

Hackney, East London—Monday, December 1st, 1856

The thick fog, a classic London pea souper, had begun to disperse, revealing an iron-grey sky overhead. A sulphurous tang stung the back of his throat, overlaid with the sickly-sweet smell of decay from the detritus that flowed sluggishly in the gutters. Flakes of soot like black snow floated listlessly downwards from the plumes of smoke puffing from every factory chimney.

Eugene shivered, pulling his muffler up to cover his nose, and took shelter under the awning of a shop selling second-hand clothes. Several pairs of boots were lined up at the front of the window display, though when he looked more closely he saw that at least two of them were mismatched. An array of hats, caps, mittens and shabby bonnets was piled higgledy-piggledy behind them. It was hardly the height of elegance, but that wouldn't concern the people who shopped here. Inside, stacked on shelves, would be the mainstay of the shop's business, much-darned clothing that hadn't become too threadbare from years of washing. Acutely conscious of his own plain but well-tailored black suit and his thick woollen coat, Eugene hunched his shoulders, turning away as the shop door opened. His starched shirt collar and cuffs would be smudged with grime, but they had started the day brilliant white.

Across the road lay his destination, a maze of narrow streets. Not a place for the faint-hearted or unwary, but sadly familiar, given the slum conditions he had publicly exposed over the years. This time however, he was not in pursuit of a story to publish, but on a much more personal quest. He had made little progress in the last six weeks, yet his instincts told him he was getting closer and his instincts were usually sound. Somewhere in the warren of alleys across the road lay the key to the mystery.

He dodged the late-afternoon traffic and headed down the first street. Cramped and dark, it was lined with brick-built houses three storeys high which soared far into the gloom. The frontages were flat with mean windows, the bricks soot-blackened and crumbling. As he walked on, the silence began to envelop him, for the streets were too narrow for through traffic. He had the eerie sense of being watched, though the few people he passed averted their gaze. He felt every inch the outsider.

He turned and found himself in a courtyard that was a dead end. Retracing his steps, he turned into another street, the walls so close together that he could almost have touched both sides with his arms spread. His usually reliable sense of direction failed him. He had no idea where he was, or how to locate the church where he hoped to find the breakthrough.

At a crossroads he hesitated. Each street stretched straight and decrepit, and all looked horribly similar, but one looked slightly broader than the others. He followed it, his hopes rising as he spotted light emanating from the windows of a large building that looked like it might be a church or mission hall. Two shallow steps led up to a battered door. Hugely relieved, Eugene turned the handle and stepped quietly inside.

He found himself in a small square vestibule and from behind the door ahead of him came a subdued, contented murmur and a delicious smell that made his mouth water. He eased the door open just enough to peer through. The hall was not large, but the ceiling was double height, giving it a spacious feel. Gas sconces flared at regular intervals along the freshly painted walls and a fire blazed in the hearth at the far side of the room. Three rows of trestle tables took up most of the space and around each table sat a very eclectic mix of diners, men, women and children of all ages. Some wore rags, others working clothes, and he spotted a number of soldiers in tattered uniforms, though the war in the Crimea had ended in March. Dinner was well underway, with tin bowls filled with a fragrant stew, plates stacked high with bread and mugs filled with milk and ale. He was unobserved, as everyone was concentrating on their food.

Then he saw her. Petite, with a wild tumble of curly black hair pinned up in a top knot, clad in a dark dress with a white apron tied over the voluminous skirt. He told himself that it was merely the resemblance to a nurse's uniform that made him think it could be *her*, but his instant reaction was too visceral for him to be mistaken. He would never forget that one, fleeting memorable night.

He remembered the silky, springy texture of her hair when it tumbled loose over her shoulders. He remembered the olive tone of her skin, the voluptuous curves of her body. He remembered the roughness of her calloused hands on his skin. The tangle of their limbs, slick with sweat. The scent of their lovemaking mingling with the all-pervading smell of battlefield mud. The soft, muffled cry she made when she climaxed.

He remembered the flickering oil lamp in the makeshift wooden hut. The coarse sheets and inadequate blanket on the small bed. The open trunk, half packed with her belongings. He could vividly recall his last glimpse of her sitting up in the bed, the sheet clutched around her, as he picked up his clothing from the floor in the grey light of dawn. And that last, lingering kiss goodbye.

All this flashed through his mind in those seconds as he stood rooted to the spot, both entranced and shocked. He had never thought to see her again, though their passionate night still haunted his dreams, nine months later. What the hell was she doing here? He had barely formulated the question when she turned. Heart-shaped face. Huge brown eyes under fierce brows. Full mouth which formed into an 'oh' of shock when she saw him. She stood perfectly still, absurdly rooted to the spot just as he was, the colour draining from her cheeks, before returning, colouring them bright red, as she hurried towards him, pushing him out of the door and back into the entranceway.

'Hello, Isabella,' he said, as if there was any doubt.

'What the *hell* are you doing here?'

'I had no idea I would find you here. I swear I did not come looking for you.'

Her mouth firmed. 'What then, are you in search of a story? Did Father Turner send you snooping in an attempt to find an excuse to shut us down? I'm sorry to disappoint you but as you can see, there is nothing untoward going on, simply wholesome food being served without the supplementary sermon he insists upon dishing up. I would very much appreciate it if you would remind him we are not in competition. God knows, these people need all the help they can get.'

'Isabella, I *am* looking for Father Turner, but I'm not here at his behest.'

She folded her arms, glaring at him. 'His church is about five minutes' walk from here. Don't let me detain you.'

She wanted him to leave, but eating at the tables in the hall were precisely the kind of people he needed to speak to and Isabella had their trust. Besides, he didn't want to leave, not like this, without a parting word, just exactly as before. 'I *am* investigating a story, but it's a personal one,' Eugene said, 'and I think you might be able to help me a great deal more than Father Turner. Will you let me explain?'

'I'm in the midst of serving dinner.'

'Then what can I do to assist?' He took off his hat and gloves as he spoke, a manoeuvre that had proved extremely effective in the past. Presume that you're welcome and basic good manners would make it more difficult for you to be rebuffed. He unbuttoned his coat. 'At the very least, you must need help with the washing up?'

Isabella remained where she was, though she didn't reissue his marching orders. 'Are you honestly saying that your being here is a coincidence?'

'I swear, I had no idea. When I saw you I was dumbfounded.'

Her mouth softened a fraction. 'The feeling was mutual. I thought—I don't know what I thought. I still don't know what to think.'

'Fate?' Eugene suggested wryly. 'Let me stay, help with the dishes and hear me out afterwards. Though if you'd rather I left now I would understand. I'll go and ask for Father Turner's help as planned and I won't trouble you ever again,' he added.

She pondered this long enough for him to wonder whether he'd be able to act on such a promise, walk away without knowing anything more about her than he already did. Then, slowly, she nodded. 'Very well. If you were serious about helping with the dishes...'

'Lead me to the scullery,' Eugene said, smiling with relief. He followed her back into the hall and through a door at the rear into a well-equipped and obviously new kitchen, where an amply proportioned woman was removing huge basins of steamed pudding from the top of a stove.

'Maisy,' Isabella said, 'this is Mr...'

'Eugene.' Now was not the time for formal introductions, he decided, smiling at the cook. 'That smells absolutely delicious.'

''Course it does,' Maisy said, failing to be charmed. 'My spotted dick is famous in these parts.'

'And if you do a good job with the dishes,' Isabella said, 'you might even earn yourself a slice. Maisy also makes excellent custard.'

'There won't be any of that left. Never is. Excuse me,' Maisy said, pushing Eugene to the side. 'Scullery's in there.'

The room contained nothing but two sinks and several drying racks. 'We are fortunate enough to have the water supply switched on every day here,' Isabella informed him. 'You can hang up your coat and jacket on the peg there. The hot water comes from the kettle on the range, we haven't managed to have a boiler installed yet.'

Seeing him look with dismay at the stack of dirty crockery, pots and tin plates, she took pity on him. 'One for washing, one for rinsing, and then they go on the rack there. Start with the soup bowls. You'll be joined by two of the ladies when they've had their pudding.'

Her voice was low, cultivated, her plain clothes, like his, deceptively expensive. He guessed her to be twenty-five or so, five or six years younger than himself. She had gone to the Crimea at the start of the war back in fifty-three and left the day after they met, at the end of hostilities in March. She had been unmarried at the time and still wore no wedding ring. That was the sum total of what he knew about her. Eugene's innate curiosity, both his Achilles' heel and his driving force, was aroused, but he needed to keep it in check. He couldn't afford to be distracted from the task in hand. He began to pump water into the first of the basins. 'I'll get on then, shall I.'

* * *

Isabella returned to the main hall where she had been working on plans for the soup kitchen at Christmas in between helping out, but Eugene's presence made her menus and shopping lists a meaningless blur. The empty dishes were already being stacked on the tables in preparation for pudding. She never tired of the way the children's faces lit up at this treat, but as she set about helping to clear plates and distribute puddings, memories of that night kept intruding, flooding her cheeks with colour.

She had never behaved so wantonly before or since. It was triggered by the sense of a chapter ending and a new beginning, she had eventually concluded. The war was over, her life lay ahead, a blank canvas for her to paint. She was free, she was reckless and she wanted to mark the occasion, though when she had first encountered him earlier that day, a reporter in search of a war story, she had not imagined how it would end.

The attraction had been there, though, from the moment he shook her hand and introduced himself, Eugene Barnford, known in the press as The Torch. 'Shining a light on injustice,' he had said sheepishly, still holding her hand. They had talked, she recalled, of the war, of his work, of the story he had come to tell, tracking the men's homecoming, soldiers who had sacrificed so much for their country. What kind of reception would they get? Like her, he was alone and lonely.

Later, when he bumped into her in the dark, having left the going-away party, there had been no words. A kiss, which led to another kiss, which led to another. Searing, urgent passion and the knowledge that she was leaving for ever. The war was over, the future was undefined, she was returning to an empty house, an empty life, and there had only been that moment and that man. She hadn't ever expected to see him again, though she had read and admired his work. Now here he was, washing dishes in the scullery, and he needed her help. Once she saw him again, her next emotion after shock had been exactly as it had been that first time. Fierce longing.

He was not handsome, but he was memorable. His dark blond hair was fine, worn longer than was fashionable, curling at his shoulders. His mouth was full and sensual. A strong nose, a most decided chin, high cheekbones, and deep-set blue eyes beneath countered any trace of femininity about his appearance. And his body...

Isabella shivered at the memory of his lean body tangled with hers, the fine hairs on his forearms as he braced himself over her, the curve of his buttocks clenched at her touch, the dip of his belly that she had traced with her tongue, the way he had slid, smooth as silk, hard, inside her. And his mouth. Oh, dear heavens, his mouth.

'See you tomorrow, Isabella.'

She started. The hall was all but empty. Maisy was putting on her voluminous coat. Isabella had no memory of serving pudding, of anyone leaving. 'Yes,' she said, following the cook to the door, 'see you tomorrow.'

Another sixty people with full stomachs were returning to their homes and lodging houses, if they were the fortunate ones. For those who had nowhere to go, then at least hunger would not be at the top of their list of woes. They were easy to spot, the homeless ones, carrying their worldly goods in a heart-achingly small sack or bundle. She struggled, every day, to remind herself that she was making a difference, but it felt such a small act in a world where so much was needed.

She waved Maisy off and, heart beating fast, returned to the hall. Eugene was wating for her. His sleeves were still rolled up. His fingers, she noted, were prune-like from the water and there was a spot of grease on the front of his shirt. 'Did Maisy give you some pudding?'

He shook his head, grimacing. 'I have to confess I hate spotted dick. It reminds me of school meals.'

Now that, Isabella thought to herself, was a telling remark for 'school' must have been a boarding school. His clothes and his accent proclaimed him educated and well off. In another life, she would be breaking all the rules of propriety by being alone with him, but that world was long gone. 'Would you like a cup of coffee?' she asked him, striving for an ease she was far from feeling.'

'Thank you, that would be much appreciated,' he replied, unrolling his shirt sleeves.

In the kitchen she took her time, watching him through the open doorway as he put his coat back on and smoothed back his hair. That night had been an aberration, a moment out of time that was long gone. He needed her help, nothing more.

He stood up as she brought the tray into the hall, pulling out a chair for her and taking a seat opposite. Isabella poured the coffee and pushed a cup towards him.

Eugene nodded his thanks and took a sip. 'I was astonished to find you here, but on reflection not surprised. I remember when we talked, how concerned you were for the future welfare of the men you had nursed.'

'I followed your story in the press about the appalling treatment many of them suffered on their return home.'

'I'm not sure how much good it did. Those who concern themselves with such matters already knew what a scandal we were creating by abandoning them on their return, those who didn't want to know were unlikely to read what I wrote. This place, however, is providing tangible help. What charity is behind it?'

'It was my idea. I set it up and I fund it, though I rely entirely upon people like Maisy for the practicalities. Shopping, cooking, that sort of thing. There is a rota of helpers for each of the six days we are open.'

'Good lord! You mean you used your own money? That kitchen must have cost a fair bit and food for fifty...'

'Sixty, six days a week. You'd be surprised at how little that costs.'

'I could work it out and it's a substantial commitment to make, week in, week out.'

'How I choose to spend my money is entirely my own affair.'

Eugene held up his hands. 'Of course. I'm sorry, I didn't mean to offend you. What you're doing here is extraordinary. I'm extremely impressed by your dedication.'

'I'm not doing this to impress anyone.'

Eugene grimaced. 'You think I'm being patronising. I don't mean to be. It's none of my business, you're quite right.'

'It is your profession to ask questions, I suppose. You're a journalist.'

'Yes, but—look, this is a very odd situation, let's face it, and I'm curious about you. We met under extraordinary circumstances, we spent—'

'Please!' Heat rushed to her cheeks. 'There is no need to recall—to discuss—I see no point in raking over something that was—was…'

'Inexplicable.'

'Yes,' Isabella agreed gratefully.

'It was, you know, for me too. I am not the sort of man who—I mean I've never before, not like that.'

'Nor have I,' she said, relieved and reassured to see that his cheeks too were tinged with colour.

'The next day, I wondered if I had dreamt the whole thing. I went to the hut later but it was empty, you were already gone, and that only added to the feeling of incredulity. I simply couldn't believe it when I saw you here, though as I said, in a sense it's not surprising.'

'I had to do something. Three years nursing in the Crimea taught me that I need to be useful. It opened my eyes to the world, and when I returned to England I couldn't close them again,' Isabella frowned down at her ruined hands. 'I suspect all of us women who were there feel the same, those of us who were not qualified nurses, and who were in robust enough health to survive, I mean. We did not take up arms, but we have been through too much, in a different way, to simply step back into the humdrum lives we left behind. We were free, you see, out there away from family ties.

'I know my friend Honoria McGrath, another nurse—a real nurse, unlike me, she was a midwife before the war—she is now working in the Royal Hospital Chelsea for Soldiers. I can only surmise about the others. I haven't kept in touch with them.'

'What about your family?' Eugene asked. 'What do they think of your work here?'

Isabella stiffened. 'My mother is dead. As for the rest of them, they neither know nor care. It is none of their business how I use my inheritance.'

'So it is a legacy from your mother which funds this place?'

'That, as I believe I have already informed you, is none of your concern. I have no desire to have The Torch shine a light on me, thank you.'

'The title was my editor's idea, not mine, and I told you, I'm not here to write about you, though it seems to me your soup kitchen would make an excellent story. How many of the men here today fought for their country and yet they can't afford to feed themselves? And those children too, they weren't all here with parents, were they? Runaways, some of them, doubtless from orphanages, from workhouses, escaping from harsh masters. It's a scandal that no one wants to hear about. May I ask why you are so anxious to hide your light under a bushel?'

'I don't want to antagonise Father Turner any more than I already have, that's all. We have different approaches, but I am keen that we co-exist.' Isabella took a sip of her coffee. 'I have nothing against religion, I know it provides a great deal of solace to many, but Father Turner passes judgement before a person is even allowed across his threshold and will not feed those he deems undeserving, and that is what makes me so furious.'

'"Judge not, lest ye be judged"—isn't that what the Bible tells us? Perhaps Father Turner hasn't come across that particular passage.'

'Has he ever been starving? Desperate? Is it so wrong for a man to steal in order to feed his children, for a wife to sell her body in order to do the same? He has no idea what people will do when they are in dire straits, while I have seen—' She stopped abruptly. 'He is a fundamentally good man providing a much-needed service.'

'And you are trying to do the same, but he sees you as competition rather than complementary?'

'Even though most of the people who eat here would not cross his threshold.' She finished her coffee and pushed the cup aside. 'Which brings us back to what brought you here.'

Eugene sighed. 'I'm trying to find someone. A woman. It's not what you think,' he added hurriedly, seeing her expression. 'I've never met her.'

'Then what is it you want with her?'

'I think she may have been wronged, though not quite in the way you are imagining, and certainly not by me.'

'Then who?'

The silence went on for so long, she thought he wasn't going to answer. When he broke it, his voice was rough. 'My brother.'

'Why isn't he here, with you?'

'Because he died six weeks ago.'

Chapter Two

'Oh, Eugene,' Isabella exclaimed, 'I'm so sorry.'

'We weren't particularly close.'

Impulsively, she reached over to put her hand over his to comfort him, then thought the better of it, pretending to brush a crumb from the table. 'What happened? Was he ill?'

Eugene shook his head. 'He died in a train crash in October. Two trains on the same line, a head-on collision. It was in the papers. You may have read about it.'

'I did! A ghastly tragedy. Goodness, I remember it now, because one of the people killed was an earl, Lord Kingarth, and I remember—oh, it doesn't matter. What was your brother's name?'

'Wilbur,' he said, eyeing her strangely. 'Were you acquainted with Lord Kingarth?'

'Not really. He was a friend of my—my mother knew him. But the man who died must have been his son, because he was far too young.'

'Thirty-two.'

Isabella stared at him in shock. 'That was your brother?'

He nodded. 'He is—he was two years older than me.'

Her eyes widened as the implications of what he had said fell into place. 'Does that mean that you are now Lord Kingarth?'

He smiled crookedly. 'To my sister's dismay, almost as much as mine.'

'I thought you were a reporter.'

'I *am* a reporter.'

'Yes, but I mean when we met—I had no idea you were—and now you're an earl.'

'I'm still the same person though, it hasn't changed me, and if it comes to the bit, I thought you were a nurse, not someone whose mother moved in the same circles as my father.'

'I am. I mean, I was.' Flustered, Isabella pushed her chair back and got to her feet. 'Who exactly is this woman you're looking for?'

'You'll doubtless find this as unbelievable as I do, but I'm looking for Wilbur's wife.'

She dropped back into her chair. 'In Hackney?'

'I told you, you wouldn't believe me.'

'There are no countesses living in Hackney.'

He gave a snort of laughter. 'No, I didn't think it would be that easy, not after I discovered that there were none in Islington either.' He dropped his head on to his hands. 'These last six weeks have been a nightmare I wish I could wake up from. First Wilbur died and I find myself with a title and an estate and a host of responsibilities I've no idea how to deal with and never wanted. Then I discovered that he was married, but of his wife there is no trace and until I find her...'

'Wait! Wait a moment. You *discovered* he was married?'

He sighed again, straightening up. 'A misalliance, almost certainly, that to the best of my knowledge no one else knows about save myself and his wife. And now you. Whatever the truth is, I can't see how it can do anything but reflect badly on Wilbur and that would hurt my sister.'

'Were she and your brother close?'

'She is devastated by his death. Cecily is the eldest of the three of us, and she thought Wilbur was the sun and moon and stars, just as our parents did. She would have much preferred I had died in the train crash rather than him. She more or less said so.'

'Oh, no! People say terrible things in the shock of grief, but I'm sure she didn't mean it.'

Eugene shrugged. 'What I don't want is to be the bearer of further bad news. Cecily always imagined that I envied Wilbur, but she couldn't be more wrong. I wish as fervently as she does that he had missed that blasted train.'

Families, Isabella thought bitterly, her empathy for him increasing several-fold. The tragedy ought to bring brother and sister closer, but it seemed that Cecily was determined to drive a deeper wedge between them. He was in an appalling position, the younger and less popular son inheriting a title he didn't want and now forced to deal with a missing wife whom no one else knew about. Heavens, a wife who might not even know she had been widowed.

Isabella surrendered to the temptation to offer comfort, reaching across the table to cover his hand. 'Tell me what you know, and if I can, I'll help you.'

'Thank you,' Eugene answered, putting his other hand

over hers. 'I need to find her. Until I do, I can't think about anything else.'

There were dark shadows under his eyes, a rawness in his voice that spoke of grief and desperation. She had seen both so many times in Crimea, men clinging desperately to life, or desperately trying to hide their torment. She knew from experience that sympathy was of little use. 'Let's start at the beginning then, shall we?' she said. 'How did you find out about the marriage?'

Eugene tried to order his thoughts, but Isabella's touch was distracting him. Her hands were small, her fingers long and tapering, but the nails were cut very short and her knuckles were chafed. A nurse's hands. He remembered them smoothing over his chest, her lips trailing kisses…

He swore under his breath, pulling his hands free, pushing his chair back. 'The certificate was in his papers, in a drawer in his desk. A secret drawer,' he added wryly, 'or so Wilbur thought. I'd discovered it years ago, as a child. I didn't expect to find a real secret in it.'

'Your sister didn't know about the drawer, I take it?'

This hadn't occurred to him. Was it possible that Cecily knew? He shook his head. 'My sister has a very strong sense of what is right and proper. The desk was untouched, all Wilbur's correspondence, bills, invitations, exactly as he'd left them. What's more, finding Wilbur a suitable match has been Cecily's mission for God knows how many years. She was lamenting his single state only the other day. I confess, it's one of the things I wondered about myself from time to time. Wilbur was an extremely eligible bachelor with as strong a

'As to Rebecca's current whereabouts, the only tangible piece of evidence I have is the word of a neighbour, an old woman, who is adamant that she said she was moving here, to Hackney. And that,' he concluded, dismayed at how little it sounded in the recounting, 'is about all I know. It's not much to go on, is it?'

'It's not,' Isabella said, wincing. 'The last trace of her that you know of was—how long ago?'

'I don't know, no one seems to be able to be exact with dates. Three to six months after they were married, I reckon.'

'Barnford is an unusual name.'

'Exactly. I hoped someone in your clientele might know of her.'

'Ye—es. Though if she doesn't wish to be found, they may not talk.'

'Or if they imagine she's in trouble in some way. I can't very well come out and tell the truth, can I? The less people know the better. I considered saying that I was a lawyer with an inheritance to divest, which at least has the merit of being partly true, but then I'd be laying myself open to all sorts of fraudulent claims. In fact,' Eugene said despondently, 'aside from questioning priests and checking registers for her death, there's not much I can do. But as a woman, and one known around here, you can ask questions which I cannot.'

'She may have reverted to her maiden name.'

'Smith!'

'Oh, dear. Well, I'll ask about a woman named Rebecca, who is twenty-three. What about your brother's records?' Isabella asked, perking up. 'Bank details, accounts? Is there any trace of his paying the rent or an allowance?'

Eugene shook his head. 'No evidence of either, which suggests they were presumably paid in cash. I'm utterly certain his lawyer knows nothing about it.'

'I wonder what on earth happened. Is it possible that your brother sought an annulment? That he realised he'd made a dreadful mistake and paid her to disappear? I'm sorry, I know that puts him in a terrible light.'

'You're not saying anything I've not thought myself. An annulment is a lengthy process and complicated. Someone would have known about it—the lawyer at least. And there's the fact he kept the certificate too, so it obviously meant something to him.'

Isabella pursed her lips, studying him intently. There were flecks of gold in her big brown eyes. Her lashes were very long and thick and, with her glossy curls and olive skin, gave her an exotic look quite at odds with her setting. Nursing was a hard slog, cleaning and mopping up filth. What had attracted a woman like her, obviously well born, with independent means? He didn't even know her second name.

'If no one else but you knows about this marriage,' she said, dragging him back to the matter in hand, 'and Rebecca Barnford or Smith herself has, I presume, made no attempt to contact her husband in over two years, why are you so determined to find her?'

'Because whatever the circumstances, why ever my brother kept it hidden, the marriage was legal. His widow has rights, a legal entitlement to an inheritance.'

'There is no question of you quietly sweeping it under the carpet?' Quite unexpectedly, she smiled at him. 'Of course not! So this is another injustice that The Torch wishes to shine a light on?'

'Quite the contrary. I won't sweep it under the carpet, but if I can put the matter to rights and avoid scandal at the same time, I will.'

'I think that's a good idea. There are some skeletons better kept in the cupboard, even if it does mean concealing the truth.'

His instincts told him that she was speaking from experience. Who was she? For the first time in six weeks, he wanted to forgo his quest and take up a new one, to know the woman opposite him better, but questioning her would put her firmly on the defensive. 'My bigger worry,' Eugene said, 'is what I'll do if I don't find her.'

'It's a strong possibility.'

'I know. It's a mess, isn't it?'

'Yes, but it's not yet hopeless.'

'I can't put my life on hold for ever, though. Whether I want them or not, I have responsibilities. I've given myself until Christmas. If I haven't found any trace of her by then, I'll give up.'

'That's four more weeks.' Isabella nodded to herself. 'If she's here, we can surely find her in four weeks.'

'And you'll help me?'

'I said so, didn't I? You are doing more than many men in your position would do, but you can't do it alone, not here where no one knows you. Though I wouldn't go as far as to say that people would take me into their confidence, they do trust me and they are far more likely to talk to me than to you.'

'If I helped out here on a regular basis, they'd come to

know me too.' And he would have the opportunity to discover more about Isabella, Eugene thought, brightening.

'Have you discovered a penchant for washing dishes?'

He laughed, screwing up his face. 'If that's what it takes, then count me in.'

'You won't get to know people by hiding away in the kitchen.'

'I'll get to know Maisy and her washing-up coterie though.'

'Maisy will be a hard nut to crack.'

Eugene grinned. 'You don't rate my manly charms highly then?'

He meant it as a joke, but their eyes met and in that moment they were both transported back nine months to that March night in the Crimea. Then she broke her gaze, pushed back her chair and picked up the coffee cups. 'I am here every day save Sunday. If you are serious about helping out, then I will be very grateful.'

'I am serious.' Eugene followed her to the scullery. 'And as to being grateful, there's absolutely no need. I will be more than happy to help out and to see for myself how people live here.'

'If you wish to put your investigative powers to good use, you could find out where I can acquire a Christmas tree and some mistletoe to decorate the hall for our Christmas dinner.'

'I would be delighted to take that on. Are you planning a big celebration here?'

'It will be a fine balance between making the day memorable and not making everyone feel beholden, or overshadowing whatever they are doing with their own families.'

'You're right. Not too much, but just enough. I'd love to help if I may?'

'Won't your sister want you to spend Christmas with her, especially given the circumstances?'

His face fell momentarily, then he smiled. 'No reason why I can't do both. I can't tell you how glad I am that I lost my way today.'

'You may still discover that you are on a wild goose chase.'

'Goose! How many do you think we'll need? I would be delighted to track those down for you too.'

Isabella laughed. 'Several flocks, but seriously, Eugene…'

'Seriously, Isabella,' he said, giving in to the temptation to take her hand between his, 'I am very glad to see you again.'

She blushed faintly. 'You know what they say about a problem shared.'

'Not something I'm accustomed to doing.'

'Nor I.'

His fingers tightened on hers. Their eyes met and they took a step towards each other. Then she pulled her hand free, just as he let her go, and the moment was over. 'I'd better go,' Isabella said.

'You don't live in Hackney, I take it?'

'I get a cab from the main road every day.'

'I'll come with you, if I may? Then you can keep me safe.'

She smiled. 'Let me get my coat.'

Chapter Three

A cackle of laughter came from the kitchen, followed by several ripe and ribald comments. Isabella could not make out Eugene's response, though she could hear his low, amused tone, which gave rise to another burst of laughter. It was silly of her to feel left out, but she couldn't help being reminded of the early days in the Crimea when she and Honoria struggled to prove themselves, despised by the established nursing staff for their lack of formal hospital training and treated with suspicion by the others, army wives and working women, who considered them merely privileged young ladies playing at being useful. Even though Honoria was an experienced midwife and Isabella had spent a lifetime nursing. Even if she'd had only one patient, her mother. It was what had brought them together, she and Honoria, this sense of being outsiders, of being neither one thing nor the other, and what had kept them going, too.

Eugene had explained away his presence in Hackney to the ladies with vague references to philanthropic causes which he wished to understand for himself. It was absurd to feel that she was letting him down, but she had hoped to have been of more help. She tried to forget the night they met, but on the odd occasion when they had brushed against each other, when she caught him looking at her, thinking himself unobserved, she sensed he was still every bit as aware of her as she was of him. Their fleeting shared past, that one night she had thought consigned to history, kept intruding on the present, unsettling her.

A final rattling of pots, and with a clatter of boots and clogs on the scrubbed floorboards, today's washing-up party emerged from the scullery, bidding Isabella a friendly farewell, though several of them blew kisses at Eugene, standing in the doorway. 'If you're not careful, you'll have several husbands after your blood,' she warned him.

He grinned, shook his head and began to roll down his sleeves. 'It's just a bit of innocent fun. There's a line and I never cross it. You must know that, from being a nurse. Look, why don't you sit down, you've been on your feet for hours. Let me fetch the coffee. I've already made it.'

He was back within a few minutes, sitting down opposite her at the scrubbed table. 'Thank you.' She took a sip of the very dark, bitter brew. 'It's exactly how I like it.'

'Strong enough to keep you awake through a long night shift?'

'Yes, though it was a valuable trick I learned long before I went to the Crimea.' Ignoring Eugene's quizzical look, she took another sip of coffee. 'I'm afraid I still have nothing to report, save blank looks and shakings of heads. Did you speak to Father Turner?'

'I did. He's never heard of Rebecca Smith or Rebecca Barnford, and so he can only assume she has "gone to the bad". On the positive side, there's no register of a death that could be her. I asked him to do some discreet digging. I thought these men of God must stick together, you know, meet up and compare notes, but the impression he gave me is that he's far too busy to be socialising, so it looks like I've a few other calls to make now. The problem is that every time I speak to another priest, I'm forced to tell him at least some of the sorry story simply in order to allay their suspicions.'

'Men of the cloth are obliged to keep confidences, aren't they?'

'It's not that I don't trust them,' Eugene replied, 'but by the law of averages, the more people I tell, the more likely the story is to get out. I don't mention the connection, I'm as discreet as possible, but bandying the name Barnford about so much is making me nervous.'

'Did you get the impression from the priest in Islington that Rebecca was a regular church-goer?'

He shook his head, looking dejected. 'Not as such, but it's pretty much the only avenue open to me. It's like looking for a needle in a haystack.'

'Perhaps she's moved on?'

'Or changed her name, or died, in which case I'll find her eventually in another parish register.' Eugene drained his coffee. 'Enough of this for now. I don't know if you've noticed, but there was a glimmer of blue sky out there earlier and we've finished early. What do you say to taking a walk?'

'In Hackney?'

'I was thinking somewhere more scenic. I've been coming here four days and I barely know any more about you than when I started.'

'You're here to find Rebecca.'

'But I'd like to get to know you, too. I know, it sounds very strange, given the circumstances of our first meeting, but I still don't even know your surname.'

'Armstrong. You never asked.'

'I got the very strong impression that you didn't want me to. If you would rather I continued to curb my curiosity, then I will do my best.'

'Why are you curious about me?'

He laughed. 'You're not serious! You're a complete enigma, a woman of independent means who is clearly well born, yet seems to be entirely estranged from her family and any sort of society. You thrived in the Crimea, yet you're not a nurse. You're thriving here, too, for that matter. You are kind, generous, thoughtful. You are brave, bold and utterly self-effacing. And I know that we're not supposed to mention it, but I can't help it, Isabella. That night we spent together was one of the most passionate, extraordinary nights of my life.

'I thought I'd never meet you again, but now I have, I can't help but feeling that fate brought us together for a reason. Unfinished business. I don't know what the hell to call it and I've no idea whatsoever if you feel the same.' He stopped, staring at her helplessly. 'I didn't intend to blurt all that out. If I've misread the situation, tell me, and I won't say another word on the subject.'

He had said everything she'd been thinking, everything she'd felt, but she would never have had the courage to put any of it into words. She had no idea what that might entail, but as she met his gaze, she wanted whatever it was, fiercely. She felt giddy with expectation, that fizzing sense of possibility that had engulfed her the day she met him and, with it, the spark of recklessness. 'You haven't misread the situation,' Isabella said, smiling at him. 'I feel exactly the same.'

They took a cab to Regent's Park. By the time they arrived it was after two, but there were still some rare glimpses of blue in the sky and though it was cold it was not damp. They took the path that led around the perimeter of the park, rather than the more popular direct route through the plant nursery to the lake, which was usually thronged with nannies and their charges. The trees had shed their leaves, the grass was a dull dun colour, but the change in scenery was distinct enough for Isabella to feel that she could almost be in the countryside.

'Do you know this park?' Eugene asked her.

It was one of his typical leading questions, but since the point of their coming here was to get to know each other better, it would be churlish of her to say so. Instead, she decided to surprise him. 'I live about half an hour's walk away in Bloomsbury. It was my mother's house. She died four years ago. We had lived there for a few years. Before that, there were houses in Brighton, in Leamington Spa, in Bath and Cheltenham.'

'Spa towns! Was your mother an invalid? Is that how you acquired your nursing skills?'

'It seems to me you have already surmised a great deal about me.'

'I told you, you intrigue me. You're a puzzle and one of the reasons I'm a reporter is that I like to solve puzzles.'

'What are the other reasons?' Isabella asked.

'I have a curious mind. And, like you, I want to make a difference,' he replied, 'though that makes me sound like one of those do-gooders, which I'm not.'

'It's what I am, though. You know, Lady Bountiful, descending on the poor and dispensing charity.'

'But what makes you different is that you don't pick and choose those who benefit and I wonder—this is one of the many questions I've been asking myself about you,' Eugene said, smiling quizzically at her. 'I wonder how you come to be so open-minded and egalitarian?'

Isabella gazed down at her feet. She was wearing sturdy leather boots, as she did every day for her trips to Hackney. Her gown was dark grey serge, one of several almost identical outfits in her wardrobe, purchased for very practical reasons. Her uniform, though she hadn't thought of it that way until now, but that's what it was. Plain gowns, plain jackets in dull colours that masked the dirt and kept her warm and were easily cleaned.

In the Crimea, she had never been invited to the parties held by some of the more senior-ranking officers and their wives—she was never aboard Lord Cardigan's notorious yacht—and so there was no call for anything other than the serviceable nursing clothes she had brought with her.

Beside her, Eugene was silently waiting for her answer. He was very good at that, asking a question and then letting a person think about it, knowing that eventually they would feel obliged to fill the silence. Though his clothes were plain, like hers, he had the ability to make them seem to adapt to different environments.

In the park he looked like a gentleman, with his hat and gloves, his well-cut overcoat, his shoes which, she noted, were quite lacking the mud that clung to her boots. In the soup kitchen he always took his coat and jacket off straight away and rolled up his shirt sleeves, too. It wasn't only the clothes, though, it was his manner. He had a confidence that she lacked, that he would be welcomed wherever he went and, as a result, he was.

She caught his gaze. 'I'm still thinking.'

'Take your time. I'm happy simply to be in your company.'

The feeling was entirely mutual, though Isabella didn't have the courage to say so. Would he continue to think so if he knew her better? Would his interest in her wane if he knew more about her, if she was no longer mysterious, a puzzle? It didn't matter, did it? By Christmas, if not before, he'd have resolved his own mystery. Perhaps she should stop thinking and simply enjoy his company while she had it.

'I've never really considered myself particularly open-minded,' she said, finally returning to the question he had asked, 'but in the Crimea, what struck me from the very first was how very differently the men were treated than the officers. Food, clothing, boots, tents, and of course the treatment they received when they were ill or wounded. Not that anyone was treated well. When I first arrived conditions were utterly appalling, but even then, it was as if the officers were more deserving, as if they were better than the men, their suffering more—more important. No, that's not the word.'

'More noble?'

She frowned. 'Yes, and more—because they were better educated and of so-called better birth, they *felt* more, you know?'

'And their loss was more important, too.'

'Yes! Exactly! There was competition among the nursing staff to be on the officers' wards, too, because it was so much more prestigious to have nursed officers than men. Not that I had any chance of joining that elite,' Isabella said ruefully, 'thought that is what was assumed I wanted, when I arrived. I didn't go as part of a nursing party, you see, because I'm not qualified and I was pretty sure that I would fail Miss Nightingale's strict criteria.'

'Why did you go, then?'

'Because I knew I could help. Nursing my mother, as you have already deduced, provided me with a great deal of experience, though no one in the Crimea gave it any credence at first. We all had to prove ourselves, we volunteers, like myself and my friend Honoria. I can understand why, we came from such diverse backgrounds, had such varying levels of experience. There were some who fell into a fit of the vapours when they realised that nursing involved confronting the physical reality of wounded men. I hope I haven't shocked you.'

'No, but I do wonder—if this is not too indiscreet a question—how did you deal with such intimate contact? Nursing your mother can't have prepared you for what you—er, came face to face with.'

Isabella burst out laughing. 'My mother would have been shocked to the core of her very large being at the very idea of my being in the company of a ward full of semi-naked men, never mind actually nursing them.'

'She died before the war, I take it?'

'About six months before. I was twenty-three years old, my own mistress for the first time in my life, and I had no idea what I wanted, save that I was done with waiting for it to happen. I read the reports in *The Times* of the suffering and I knew I could help, so I went. Nothing prepared me,' she continued after a moment, 'for the sights I witnessed, I mean. Nothing *can* prepare you. Anyone who says they weren't sickened, that they never felt faint, that they didn't sometimes wish themselves far from the hell on earth there, is lying. But there is nothing to be done about it either, except get on with it.'

'You could have come home.'

'It never occurred to me to do so, not until it was over.'

'Then we met, the day before you left, the day after I had arrived,' Eugene said. 'Ships that pass in the night who could so easily have missed each other. I am very glad we did not.'

The air, it seemed to Isabella, crackled with tension. Possibilities. Excitement. Exactly like before. It didn't occur to her to prevaricate. 'So am I.'

'And now here we are again.'

'Passing more slowly this time, but still passing.'

'Yes,' he said wryly, 'I am very much aware of that.'

They had reached the top end of the lake, which was in the shape of the letter 'Y'. A few ducks were paddling in the shallows and several more could be seen nesting on one of the small islands, but at this time of year the boathouse was closed and there were little boys sailing their toy yachts.

'There's a bench here, with a bit of shelter,' Eugene

said, pointing at a seat resting against the boathouse. 'Shall we sit for a moment?'

He waited until she did so, then sat down beside her. It was quiet here, sheltered from the slight breeze which had blown up and ruffled the brackish water of the lake. Above them, the sky was copper-coloured. Isabella tucked her gloved hands into her coat sleeves. 'What made you become a reporter, Eugene? I presume it was not a need to earn your corn?'

'No. Like you, I inherited an independent income from my mother.'

She decided not to correct his assumption. His mouth was pursed in thought, his hands dug deep into his pockets, his legs stretched out in front of him. The second son, the second favourite. Taking a leaf from his book, she waited for him to fill the silence.

'No one has asked me that question before,' he said eventually, surprising her. 'Cecily thinks I do it out of some perverse wish to spite her—I'm a hack, as far as she's concerned. And Wilbur was one of those men who isn't interested in anything outside their own narrow world. Not selfish exactly, but blind, you know?'

'Only too well.'

'The voice of experience?'

Isabella nodded. 'Very much so,' she said. 'I'll explain some time, but I want to hear your side of things first.'

'Fair enough.' He angled himself to face her, his leg brushing against the cage of her crinoline. 'I'm a loner by nature. I always have been. When you have a brother like Wilbur, one of those people who are effortlessly popular, the type women and men gravitate towards whenever they enter a room—well, you don't compete. At least,' he added wryly, 'I never did.'

'Effortlessly popular,' Isabella repeated sardonically. 'I know exactly what you mean. The kind of person everyone assumes one envies, if one does not choose to be dazzled by them.'

'Ha! Yes, that is it exactly. I was never envious of Wilbur, though that was the standard assumption. We went to the same school and of course I was forever being compared to him, never in a positive light. It got my back up, needless to say, being told that I wasn't as popular, or I wasn't as sporting.'

'So you set yourself up to be the opposite, I'll wager?'

'I did, yes. I became a scholar.' His expression hardened. 'There's an assumption in a public school that being bookish means you're weak and weakness is frowned upon. The older boys are encouraged to toughen up the runts of the litter.'

Isabella inhaled sharply. 'You were bullied!'

'Not I, but some of the other boys who preferred books to rugby football were and I was forced into defending them. And that,' Eugene said, 'was a very long-winded way of explaining how I first became aware of the perniciousness of privilege and decided that things needed evening up. Though it was years later, at university, that I met another undergraduate from Glasgow who suggested that I put my pen and my nose together and become a journalist. A lot of water passed under the bridge after that, before I made a name for myself as The Torch.'

'So you've always been an outsider, in a sense?' Isabella asked, touched. 'It must have taken a great deal of courage and conviction to stick to the path you chose. No, don't shrug it off, I know, Eugene, what such families are like. There must have been times when you were tempted to give in, do the conventional thing?'

'Join the church, you mean?'

'Well, I can more easily see you as a clergyman than a soldier, which would have been the alternative.' They were sheltered from the path in their little nook and, while he talked, had drawn closer, so that their shoulders were touching. 'And now your sister thinks it's time to fill Wilbur's shoes and it's the last thing you wish,' she said. 'She has no understanding of the sacrifices you're going to have to make to the life you have chosen for yourself.'

'Most people would think me in an enviable position,' Eugene replied gruffly. 'A peer of the realm, an estate, wealth, houses, position.'

'Responsibilities, as you said, that you've never wanted, all the same.'

'You're the only person who understands that.'

'Have you tried to talk to your sister about it?'

He pursed his lips, then shook his head. 'It's only been six weeks since Wilbur died. Perhaps after Christmas.'

'Will she find Christmas difficult? Was it a family affair?'

He gave a huff of laugher. 'Heavens, no. My family never really celebrated Christmas when I was a child. Cecily has a tree and gifts for her three girls, but Wilbur was a bit like Scrooge, from the Dickens story. He hated it, refused to host the dinner and turned down Cecily's invitations to her home every year.'

'And you?'

'I've always thought of it as just another day, to be honest. This year will be different in so many ways. I'm looking forward to decking the Hackney hall with boughs of holly, just like the song. I'd sing it, but you wouldn't recognise it, I'm tone deaf.'

'Oh, me too! After she was widowed, my mother never celebrated Christmas. "It's only the two of us, why make a fuss," she always said.'

'And before, when your father was alive?'

Isabella's face froze. She tried to pull her hand free, but Eugene tightened his grip. 'What have I said to upset you?' he asked.

'I'm not upset,' she said, as much for her own benefit as his. It was ancient history. It didn't matter. She never thought of it. She never, ever discussed it. 'I don't know who my father is,' she said tightly. 'I never have.'

Chapter Four

A long silence followed her unexpected confession, then Eugene gently disengaged himself and got up. 'It will be dark soon and it's getting cold. Come on.' He held his hand out. 'Let's go and get something to warm us up. There's a coffee shop not far from the main gates which serves hot chocolate. If we take the direct route we can be there in fifteen minutes.'

It took them slightly less than that walking quickly under the darkening sky, their breath visible in the rapidly chilling air. By the time they arrived, Isabella was puffed out, her feet and hands icy cold. The blast of warm air that greeted them when Eugene opened the door was extremely welcome. Inside, she was surprised to see an eclectic mix of people, students and clerks, several men, heads down buried in a book or a newspaper, and at one table a group of middle-aged women conversing together in a conspiratorial manner. Eugene nodded to the proprietor and made his way to the back of the room, ushering her into an empty booth, taking the seat opposite, and pulling off his gloves. 'Would you prefer coffee?'

'No, hot chocolate would be delightful,' Isabella said, smiling at the waitress who had appeared. 'Thank you.'

'And I'll have coffee, thanks, Millie.'

Isabella quirked her brow. 'You come here often, then?'

'You could say it's my home from home. I've been drinking coffee and writing here since I was nothing more than a junior hack at *The Times*.'

'*The Times!* Did you know Mr Russell, the war correspondent?'

'I've come across him. It was reading his reports from the Crimea which gave me the idea of going out there myself, when the war was over. Did you ever meet him during your stint out there?'

Isabella shook her head. 'He wasn't remotely interested in us, he only had eyes for Miss Nightingale and her coterie.'

'While you and the likes of your friend Honoria rolled your sleeves up and got on with it?'

'No, that's not fair. I mean we did, but it was Miss Nightingale who really made the biggest difference to conditions overall. She was a formidable woman who had the power and the influence to make things happen. I was completely in awe of her.'

The waitress set down a large china mug in front of her at this point and Isabella smiled her thanks. The hot chocolate was rich, dark and not too sweet. She wrapped her hands around it and took a sip. 'Delicious.'

Eugene sipped his coffee. 'So how is it that your mother was acquainted with my father?'

Isabella took another reviving sip of her hot chocolate. She had thought of it as ancient history, a closed book, but at some point in the walk between the park and the coffee shop it seemed she had resolved to re-open it. 'Through her husband, Lord Armstrong. The man I thought was my father.' She waited for a moment, trying to decide what she felt, but it was odd. She felt almost nothing.

Across the table, Eugene was, to her relief, refraining from asking the multitude of questions this raised. 'I remember him,' he said. 'A diplomat of some sort? Shrewd, though not as shrewd as he thought himself, with a very inflated opinion of his own consequence?'

Isabella gave a snort of laughter. 'Yes, that is exactly how I remember him, too.'

'His son, the current Lord Armstrong, is cut from the same mould. Harry, is that his name? His wife is one of those society beauties with a very ill-suited name, isn't she?'

'Lady Armstrong's name is Mercy, but I've never met her,' Isabella said, stirring her hot chocolate. Eugene was being careful, giving her every opportunity to turn the subject, but she no longer wanted to. 'They were married about ten years ago, but I was cast out of the family along with my mother about five years before that.'

'Cast out? But you must have been a child at the time.'

'I was ten.'

His frown deepened. 'We can change the subject if you find it upsetting.'

'I've never talked about what happened to anyone. It made my mother a very bitter woman and she could have been a happy one, if she'd tried, but it really is ancient history now. It's done, I can't change it, but I don't have to let it affect me.'

'That's an excellent theory, though I suspect more difficult to put into practice.'

She smiled at him, then finished her hot chocolate with a contented sigh. 'Let's see if I can practise what I preach, then. One potted history of the Armstrong family coming up.'

Eugene finished his coffee, watching the emotions trace themselves over Isabella's expressive face, with no idea at all of what she was about to tell him. He knew this woman intimately, his body craved her body every time he saw her. Sitting beside her in the park, sitting opposite her now, he was acutely aware of every fleeting touch, aware of the voluptuous body beneath the practical, prosaic clothes.

Yet he knew next to nothing of the real woman. No, that wasn't true. He knew nothing of her history or her plans, but he knew the essence of her, for they were alike. Kindred spirits. Outsiders. It was what had drawn them together that night, though they had neither of them realised it at the time. It was why he had spoken so candidly to her earlier, too. She understood. She knew him, too, in the way he knew her, the essence of him.

He swore under his breath, taken aback by the surge of longing, desire mixed with a yearning that brought a lump to his throat. He was grieving, he told himself. His world was turned upside down and Isabella was a temporary refuge, someone completely alien to the world Wilbur's death was dragging him into. It couldn't last, this hiatus, but while it did, he was enjoying every moment.

Millie appeared to pour him a second cup of coffee,

but Isabella shook her head at the offer of another hot chocolate. 'Shall I begin?' she asked, waiting for his nod. 'Well then, Lord Armstrong had five daughters from his previous marriage. He married my mother in order to get himself an heir, just as every peer of his ilk does, I suppose. My mother obligingly provided him with four boys in quick succession, if you'll pardon the pun! She gave birth to James within a year. Harry, who is the current Lord Armstrong, arrived the following year, and then two years after that, the icing on the cake in the form of twin boys, George and Frederick. Are you still following me?'

'Raptly,' Eugene replied and with a horrible sense of foreboding, too, though he didn't mention this.

'Even Lord Armstrong felt that four sons was sufficient. My mother, having served her purpose as a brood mare, was relieved of their care, I gather, and left to fester in Killellan Manor, where she had nothing much to do to pass the time except eat. And then at some point after the twins went to Eton, she met the man who sired me.'

Isabella pushed her mug to one side, frowning. With difficulty, Eugene kept silent, letting her order her thoughts and emotions, knowing how important it was not to interrupt.

'I've pieced it all together over the years,' she continued after a few moments, 'since my mother would never discuss it. I have no idea who my father is. Until I was ten years old, I thought it was Lord Armstrong. Then he died.'

She laced her hands together tightly and caught his concerned look with a grim smile. 'Don't worry, I'm angry, not upset. At the time I didn't know what was written in his will. All I remember is that we left Killellan Manor and severed all ties with the Armstrongs. As I said, my mother refused to talk about it and it was years later that I found out about the legacy I'd been left. I was sixteen, and tired of trying to persuade my mother to tell me why I wasn't allowed to see my brothers—for as far as I was concerned then, they were my brothers. So I wrote to Harry—James had died by then—and Harry sent me a copy of the will. No covering letter, just the will.'

Eugene swore under his breath.

'I know,' Isabella said with another grim smile, 'it sounds like a melodrama, doesn't it? I bet you're sorry you asked.'

'I'm very sorry to be causing you to rake up painful memories.'

'You're not, quite the contrary. Recounting it makes me realise just how vile they all are and how badly treated my mother was. She broke her wedding vows and I know that's a terrible sin, but I can't help thinking she was pretty much forced into it. She must have felt so lonely, and completely pointless. She wasn't old, Eugene, not much more than thirty, yet as far as her husband was concerned she had served her purpose, her life was over.'

'It's not an uncommon situation for a woman in her situation to find herself, though.'

'No, it's not,' Isabella snapped, 'but that doesn't make it right.'

'I didn't say it was. I'm sorry, that was tactless of me.'

'You've never even considered it, have you?' Isabella glared at him.

She was right and he found himself, unexpectedly and uncomfortably, on the back foot, shaking his head.

'It's not your fault, you're a man,' Isabella said, rubbing salt unwittingly into the wound. 'You have broken the mould by becoming a journalist, but you were expected to have a profession of sorts, were you not? Women born into so-called privileged society, women like my mother, all that is expected of them is to breed, and when they are done breeding, they take up good works, or embroidery, or they wait for their grandchildren to arrive.

'Some of them don't mind being invisible and pointless, some of them mind a great deal but do nothing about it, and some, a very few, find a new purpose in life, But they have to fight for it, Eugene. You have no idea how hard it is to break the mould as a woman. Look at Miss Nightingale! I don't like her, but by God, I admire that woman's sense of purpose.'

She smiled suddenly, noting his surprised expression. 'Women like my mother and probably your mother, and very likely your sister, Cecily, don't necessarily realise they are being suffocated, starved of life, imprisoned in the marriages they make, but they are, most of them. Some of them, like my mother, become entirely dependent on their husbands in the process. When that prop is removed, they need another man to cling to.

'So you see, the affair she had was almost inevitable and to be honest, I don't think that her husband cared much, even when I was the result. If I'd been a boy it would have mattered, but I was a girl, so my mother persuaded him to acknowledge me. Legally, I am Lady Isabella Armstrong. The truth, however, is that I have no name and no father. Do you think I could have a glass of wine?'

'You wouldn't prefer a brandy?'

Isabella laughed shortly, shaking her head. 'I suspect you're more in need of it than I. I'm sorry to have been so vehement.'

'You have every reason.' Eugene waved Millie over and asked for a bottle of hock. 'It's not only women who are expected to marry well and provide an heir. Within a week of my brother dying, my sister started her campaign to marry me off. I know men are permitted to have a life outside the family hearth and home, but I've never considered marriage before and to do so for the sake of a title I don't want—' He broke off, surprised to find himself shaking, and took a draft of the hock, which was very good.

'I can't imagine how difficult you must be finding all these changes,' Isabella said. 'You have enough turmoil, without adding any more into the mix.'

'Precisely.' Eugene took another sip of the wine. 'I've tried to tell Cecily that, but she doesn't listen.'

'She's trying to take control, to put the world back to rights. It's what people do when they are suffering from the shock of loss.'

'I'm not Wilbur and she's not going to make me into some sort of second-best version of him!' Eugene took a breath and then another sip of wine. 'Sorry.'

Isabella cast a look around to check they were unobserved, before pressing his hand. 'You're grieving, too, and in the same way as she is, trying to take control by finding Rebecca.'

'You are very perceptive.'

'I've seen a lot of loss.'

'Of course you have, much more than most.' He was suddenly, mortifyingly, on the edge of tears. He wanted to hold on to her hand, but forced himself to let it go, clutching his wine glass, though his throat was too clogged to drink.

'You haven't asked me what was in the will, but I expect you're desperate to know, so I'll tell you. It was a denunciation. Lord Armstrong disowned me from beyond the grave. I was not his child. Neither my mother nor I were to have any further contact with his sons and, in return, we both received a substantial pay off. I came into my legacy when I was twenty-one. It's what I use to fund the soup kitchen. My small act of vengeance. Lord Armstrong would have been appalled.'

'Bloody hell! I do apologise, but…'

'Oh, no need. I have heard much, much worse language, I assure you. Are you feeling better now?'

'Yes. Thank you. I'm terribly sorry.'

'Don't apologise. Grief is like that. It always creeps up on one when one least expects it. Even though you were not close,' Isabella added pre-empting him, 'he was still your brother.'

'What about your brothers—half-brothers? They are grown men, able to make their own decisions.'

Her lip curled. 'They chose to have nothing to do with their own mother and, for that reason alone, I'm glad none of them has ever made any attempt to get in touch with me. When James died, I was only twelve and clueless about the situation. I was devastated, as I think I told you, and my mother could barely speak for about three months. I don't wish any of them ill, but I have no desire at all to see them ever again. When my mother died, so did my connection with that family.'

'And your father?' Eugene asked gently.

For the first time, Isabella's lip trembled. 'He knew of my existence from my mother, but has never made any attempt to make himself known to me.'

'Aren't you curious?'

'What difference would it make? I am almost twenty-six years old and my own mistress. I don't need parental guidance. I certainly don't want interference.' Isabella took a sip of wine, then began to turn the glass around and around on the table, staring down at the contents. 'The last three years in the Crimea were incredibly difficult, but also incredibly rewarding. I think everyone who was out there came back changed. I know I am. Until then, I had never before been my own mistress. Even when I came into my inheritance, my mother was still alive and took up all of my time.

'When I returned to England, back to the house in Bloomsbury, it took me a few weeks to realise that I was free to do anything that I wished. I wasn't bound by all the constraints and conventions that my mother had imposed on me, that are imposed on women who were raised as I was. I didn't need a maid to accompany me to walk in the park, I didn't need to pay any heed at all to the proprieties. I found,' she said, with a slow smile, 'that I simply didn't care what anyone thought of me and that meant I could suit myself. For the first time in my life, I can do exactly what I wish to do.'

'And what you wished to do was dispense food to the needy! What will you do next?'

'I have no idea. I've not thought past Christmas. I want to make it special. Not like my mother did, back in the days when we lived with Lord Armstrong at Killellan Manor, which was the family country estate. I remember, after church, all of the staff standing stiffly in line waiting for their gift and the maids having to curtsy and smile and look grateful for the handkerchief they received every year when they'd much rather have had some scent or chocolate or a few ribbons.'

'What do you want, then?'

She rested her chin on her hand, smiling dreamily at him. 'To bring a little joy and Christmas cheer into people's lives which are sadly lacking both for the rest of the year. Lots of mistletoe and a tree for a start, which you have so kindly agreed to find for me. We can put it up on Christmas Eve. The children will enjoy decorating it.'

'And so will I. We'll have those sugar canes and candied fruit, glazed cherries and sugar plums. And we'll have gingerbread men,' Eugene said, warming to the subject. 'And marzipan animals, maybe an angel or so.'

'Goodness, that will be a Christmas tree fit for Queen Victoria herself.'

He laughed. 'Actually, all of those things were on the royal tree last year. I read a description of it somewhere.'

'We shall have a royal tree and a right royal Christmas dinner for everyone who wants it.' Isabella beamed. 'It will be the family Christmas neither of us ever had— that is if you are sure you will be able to help? I can't help feeling that your sister…'

'I want to and I'm going to,' Eugene said. 'I've promised you and I'm not going back on that. Next year—oh, who knows what will happen next month, never mind next year?'

'My own feelings precisely. The past is the past. Who knows what the future holds? Let's simply enjoy the moment. How trite that sounds.'

'But it's true.' Eugene picked up the bottle, surprised to discover that it was empty. Outside, night had fallen and the gas lamps were lit. 'It's after six, how did that happen?' he said, looking with astonishment at the clock on the wall.

Isabella began to pull on her gloves. 'You'll be expected for dinner.'

'Unfortunately, I am. I hate to sit down in splendid isolation every night to a formal meal, but that was my brother's custom, and it's easier to go along with it for now, to keep his staff employed, to keep the house running, while I consider what I want to do. I know, that sounds as if I'm simply burying my head in the sand.'

'You're very hard on yourself. It sounds eminently practical to me. Why make more changes, when you are already in turmoil?'

'Sound advice. Again.' He paid the bill and opened the door for her. Outside, the air was bitter, making them both gasp. 'There will be skaters on the pond in Regent's Park before long if this keeps up. Can I get you a cab?'

Isabella shook her head. 'I'll walk.'

'Good God, you cannot—' He broke off, seeing her face. 'I beg your pardon, I am sure you're perfectly capable of looking after yourself, but I would spend the rest of tonight worrying if I let you do that. Spare me, if you don't mind, and let me escort you home.'

'I have no desire to be responsible for making you late for your dinner. If it will put your mind at rest, I won't walk.' Isabella stepped to the edge of the busy road and expertly hailed a hackney cab. 'Thank you for the hot chocolate and the wine.'

'Don't take umbrage,' Eugene said, catching her hand. 'I wish I didn't have to go.'

Her fingers curled into his and she nodded. 'So do I.'

He didn't want to return to his dead brother's house and eat a solitary meal at his table. He wanted to sit with her and to talk and talk. And he wanted the talking to lead to kissing. And the kissing to lead to lovemaking. He wanted to lose himself in her. He didn't want to let her go. He lifted her hand to his lips and pressed a kiss to her gloved fingertips. He felt her shiver, saw his desire reflected in her face.

'Oy! Are you getting in or not? I ain't got all night.'

They sprang apart. He opened the door of the cab. Isabella jumped in. 'I'm busy tomorrow,' he shouted, remembering his promise to his sister, 'but I'll be there on Saturday.'

She nodded, made to speak, but the driver had already urged his horses into motion and the door of the cab slammed shut.

Chapter Five

Mayfair—Friday, December 5th, 1856

'I always said to Wilbur that it was such a terrible waste to have this lovely big house inhabited by a bachelor,' Cecily said. 'The ballroom is small, I grant you, but to instal a billiards table! Honestly, I said to him at the time it was a mistake, for it was not only his own wife and daughters he should be considering, it was my daughters, too. As you know, our more modest abode does not have a ballroom. But Wilbur—dear Wilbur, how he loved to play billiards! And he was so very good at it.'

'Was he?' Eugene picked up one of the white billiard balls and rolled it over the green baize.

'Wilbur was good at everything he did, you *know* that, Eugene. He was a top sportsman. Everyone said so. He was also extremely considerate. I am confident that when the time came for your eldest niece, my dear Beverley, to make her debut, he would have sacrificed this billiard table and hosted her ball. She will be sixteen next year, you know.'

'Sixteen! That's not much more than a child.'

'It is never too early to start planning and you don't even play billiards.'

'How do you know I don't?'

'You are not in the least sporting. You never were. At school, I recall, they were so disappointed that you were so very different in nature from Wilbur.'

Eugene rolled the second white ball across the table. 'I still am different, Cecily.'

His sister dabbed her eyes and gave him a brave smile. 'I have decided that the best way to honour his memory is to help and encourage you to follow in his footsteps as best I can.'

She didn't listen. She never listened. She was grieving, he reminded himself, recalling Isabella's words yesterday, but so was he. 'I am not my brother.'

'No.' Cecily picked the two white balls from the table and put them back in the rack. 'It will be a challenge, I don't deny it, but don't be intimidated. I shall be by your side.'

Eugene gritted his teeth. 'You're not listening. I'm not going to be joining Wilbur's clubs, or riding his hunters to hounds. I might take up his seat in Parliament, but there, too, we shall differ, because I'll make use of it.'

Cecily paled. 'What for? You won't have time to pursue your causes. Tragedy has placed a heavy mantle of responsibility on your shoulders. Your first and foremost concern must be for the family, the estate. You won't have time for anything else. Wilbur never did.'

'I am not Wilbur!' He cursed under his breath, seeing her shrink at his tone, taking a firm grip on his temper. 'No matter what you might think, I've never envied him either. I've always been glad to have been the second son, because it freed me to be myself.'

'Oh, don't be ridiculous. Who would prefer to be a newspaper hack to when they could be an earl! A peer of the realm! I'm sorry, Eugene, but I find that very difficult to believe.'

'Then try a little harder. My work means a great deal to me. It's been my life, and now, thanks to circumstances beyond both our control, I'm having to rethink that. I wish that Wilbur had not been aboard that train. I know nothing about my inheritance. I've never been interested, and I never imagined it would fall to me to take care of it. You know more about it all than I do. If I could pass it on to you, I would happily do so. It's always seemed a great shame to me that women can't inherit.'

Cecily softened marginally. 'Well, I must say I agree with you. However, the law is the law. For better or worse, you are now Lord Kingarth.'

'I'll step up to the mark, but in my own way,' Eugene said firmly.

'I miss him terribly.' She forced a tremulous smile. 'I know I should be grateful that I still have you.'

His anger gave way to pity at the misery lurking behind those words. It must be costing her dear to keep the stiff upper lip she managed to maintain most of the time. He gave her an awkward hug. 'Shall we put the past behind us and start afresh?'

Cecily slipped from his embrace, pursing her lips. 'If you truly are ready to step up to the mark, then you should be considering marriage. Naturally, there can be no wedding for six months for we are in deep mourning, but a quiet ceremony in June would be perfectly acceptable.'

His sympathy for her evaporated, but instead of growing angry again, Eugene decided to turn the subject to his advantage. 'Why do you think Wilbur didn't marry?'

'He would have, sooner or later.'

'He was thirty-two and in every way, with this one exception, a very dutiful earl.'

'And he would have married, I am sure of it. As you say, he understood his duty to the family name.' Cecily drew a circle with her finger on the green baize of the billiard table. 'We should do as you suggested and put the past behind us. The loss of our dearest Wilbur is proof that life is fragile. If you die without an heir, the title and the estate will go to our cousin, for I have only my three girls. The matter of your marriage is now extremely pressing.'

'I've more than enough change in my life to deal with, without adding a wife into the equation.'

'I know of several excellent young women,' his sister continued, ignoring him. 'You are now extremely eligible. A good marriage will help establish you in society.'

'Help make them all forget my grubby job, you mean?'

'Precisely,' she agreed, oblivious as ever to irony.

'I'm grieving in my own way, just as you are, you know. I'm in no fit emotional state to choose a partner for life.'

'Which is why I will help you choose.'

'No,' Eugene said, louder than he meant. 'For heaven's sake, you don't know the first thing about me. I hate to think who you'd pick. And the time for this discussion,' he added hastily, 'is not now.' Or ever, he added, but only to himself. 'I have too many other things to take care of, don't you think?'

'I am glad to hear you say so. I have barely seen you since dear Wilbur was buried. I thought you would have given up on your precious journalism, but it seems to be consuming more of your time than ever.'

If she knew what he was investigating—it didn't bear thinking of, though if he found Rebecca he'd have to tell her. Eugene shuddered. First things first, he had to find her. Talking of which...

'You and Wilbur were as thick as thieves, Cecily. I can't help but think there must have been a reason for his having dodged matrimony. An unrequited love, perhaps?'

His sister gazed at him in astonishment. 'What woman would have rejected Wilbur?'

He managed to refrain from rolling his eyes. 'If she proved ineligible then? Wasn't there someone, about three years ago in the summer?' he asked, desperate enough to take a risk. 'I seem to recall him being moon-faced round about that time.'

'1853?' Cecily frowned. 'The only thing I can recall of note from that summer was that he was attacked in the street. You won't remember, you were doubtless away somewhere.'

'You're right,' Eugene said, astonished, 'I had no idea. What happened?'

'Wilbur was always very cagey about the details. I presumed,' Cecily said, looking pained, 'that he was in that rough part of town to attend one of those horrible cock-fighting events he was so keen on. It was one of the rare subjects on which we could never agree, for I cannot consider it a sport. A vile practice, and so cruel I cannot understand why gentlemen enjoy it.'

'Nor can I, to be honest. What part of town was it?'

'I don't know. East,' she said, waving her hand at the window. 'Hoxton? No, that wasn't it, and it wasn't Clerkenwell. Shoreditch? Limehouse? No, Islington, that was it. Yes, Islington, I'm sure of it. He was hit over the head and he had a dreadful bruise on his cheek and his shoulder, too, so badly bruised he had to wear a sling for days. I insisted on calling in the doctor, though he said there was no need, for someone had taken pity on him and bandaged him up.' Cecily smiled faintly, shaking her head. 'How odd, I'd forgotten all about it until now. But as to him being moon-faced—more likely he was simply in pain, Eugene.'

He had no recollection of his brother being moon-faced, and had merely been fishing, but it looked like he might just have landed something. 'Wilbur didn't ever mention who his good Samaritan was?'

'Never, but the attack affected him, I remember now. He was—odd, after it. Distracted. And now I come to think of it, he was often absent. In the country, he told me, away from the city. Well, I could understand that and the country air certainly improved him for a while.'

'And then? How long do you think it took him to—to recuperate?'

'Goodness, Eugene, it was three years ago, I don't know. Three months? Six? I have no idea, nor any notion why you are interested in it all, when you were not in the least bit interested at the time.'

'I wish I had been. I don't even recall him being injured.'

'You were always far too interested in your own worldly concerns to look close to home at what really mattered. You have responsibilities now, which brings me to reason I asked you to meet me here.'

'I have to go.'

'What! We were going to look around the house, take stock.'

'Another time. Sorry, Cecily, I really have to go, but please feel free to stay and—and plan the ballroom. We'll get rid of the billiard table. It's never too early, as you said. I'll see you later.'

Small steps, he told himself, as he hunted down a cab to take him to Hackney. He had taken a small step with Cecily today. They would never be close, but in time they might come to understand each other better and if—when!—he found Rebecca, perhaps between them they'd also come to understand Wilbur a little better too. Though as he jumped into a cab and gave the address, he shuddered at the very idea of that particular conversation.

The cab set off. He put Cecily to the back of his mind, and turned to the far more appealing subject of Isabella. The frisson of awareness that shivered through them when their eyes met, when their hands touched. Desire—yes, of course it was desire, but it was more than that. It was the way she looked at him and listened to him and challenged him.

As a reporter, it was his job to probe, to ask difficult questions, sometimes intimate ones, but it was a one-way process. No one was interested in Eugene, the man behind The Torch. He'd become so accustomed to that, it had taken Isabella to remind him that he existed. It was a solitary road he travelled and she had shown him that he was lonely.

What did that mean? The question was too huge to answer. The future loomed in front of him, a massive stone edifice he didn't want to climb. He closed his mind to it, recalling Isabella's words. The past was the past. Who knew what the future held? He was going to enjoy the present.

The four children seated around the table looked on in fascination as Isabella cut out another crudely shaped little horse from the fabric of her apron and began quickly to stitch the two pieces together. 'There you are now,' she said, handing it to John, 'you can fill up his tummy with scraps. Janet will help you,' she said, smiling encouragingly at the eldest child, 'and in the meantime, let's put some faces on the other ones, shall we?'

She re-threaded her needle with some black cotton and sat down between the twins, Kathy and Mark, deftly wiping their noses. Until she opened the soup kitchen, she'd had very little dealings with children, but they were a great deal easier and more rewarding to look after than her mother, whose attention span was considerably shorter than a four-year-old's. Her mother's tantrums were more spectacular, too. She grew bored with being read to, usually just at the point where Isabella herself had become interested in the story.

She had thrown herself into every new hobby she read about, but had no interest in mastering anything, abandoning every project she started in its early stages. Lamenting the wrongs which had been done to her and eating were the only two pastimes to which she remained true. Bella had been terribly wronged. The separation from her sons had been permanent. Pity and anger had kept Isabella with her, dedicating her life to her mother. But Bella was dead four years now and Isabella's life was entirely her own. She was free of the past and free to make her own decisions.

What was she going to decide about Eugene, then? Last night, alone in bed, she had imagined him with her. She knew he desired her every bit as much as she desired him. The passion that had flared between them in the Crimea had not burnt itself out, though it would eventually. After Christmas, when his quest was over, one way or another, he would take up the reins of his new life and she would reconsider her future. But until then?

Isabella re-threaded her needle, smiling at the two little faces intent on her handiwork. 'Now, what are you going to call your horses?'

'Kathy,' said Mark.

'Mark,' said Kathy.

'Excellent choices.' She set about stitching in some eyes, thankful that she always carried her etui with needles, scissors and thimble with her. She would shred a bit more of her apron to make tails and manes for the animals, she decided. It was a shame she had no wool, for then the children could do that task. Beside her, Kathy and Mark were watching wide-eyed as the first horse acquired eyes and a nose. Her heart contracted at how easily pleased they were. In Bond Street and Oxford Street, the shops were already full of fancy goods and toys for Christmas, but for these children…

An idea popped into her head and she stopped sewing. It would take a little organising, but there was still plenty of time.

'Kathy's nose isn't finished,' Mark said plaintively.

Isabella looked at Kathy, baffled, before recalling the horse. 'Two more stitches,' she said, making them and snipping off the cotton. 'Now for a tail.'

When the door opened, Isabella looked up, expecting the children's mother, but it was Eugene who entered, automatically pulling off his hat and gloves, then stopping short when he saw the four children. 'What have we here? Are these—cows?'

'No!'

'Elephants?' He grinned, crouching down at the table beside Janet and John.

'No!'

'Dogs?'

'Horses,' all four children cried out in unison.

'Ah, of course, silly me.' He cast Isabella a comical look. 'Seems to me they need some manes and tails.' Throwing his coat down, he pulled up a chair and sat down beside John, who was trying to stuff another scrap of cotton into his over-full horse. 'A Derby winner, if ever I saw one,' he said. 'Though he looks as if he's eaten too many oats.'

'I can't believe I'm going to say this, but that was fun.' Eugene picked up what was left of Isabella's apron. 'A worthy sacrifice, don't you think? Mrs Simpson certainly thought so. A whole two hours to catch up with her chores and four children with unique toys to take home. Everyone's a winner, as they say.'

'It takes so little to make them happy, doesn't it? I

was thinking, with Christmas coming up, that it might be an idea to do something like this for more of them. Bring in some felt and wool, let them make presents for each other. I had thought of buying gifts, but I worried that some parents might take that amiss. If the children make them, though—what do you think?'

'It's an excellent idea,' Eugene said, 'and I'm sure that the other mothers, like Mrs Simpson, would be very happy to have a few hours to themselves, too, though you'd need help, wouldn't you? I am of course happy to provide entertainment and moral support, but as you saw for yourself, I'm all fingers and thumbs when it comes to setting stitches. While you—that needle was moving so fast, I could barely see it.'

'One of the few skills a young lady is taught is needlework,' Isabella replied wryly. 'It stood me in good stead in the Crimea. I sewed my first sampler at five. I have had years and years of practice, embroidering fire screens and handkerchiefs, collars and cushion covers and slippers and all manner of useless, pretty tat. And as for my tapestry! Have you ever looked at the reverse side of a tapestry?' she asked, seeing his blank expression.

'I can't say that I have. What have I been missing?'

'A tangle of knots and different-coloured threads, that's what. My mother in her later years developed a passion for tapestry, but her eyesight was failing and her fingers were swollen. Oh, my goodness, the hours and hours I spent tying off the knots she made, unpicking and unravelling her work when she went to bed. Unless you have tried it for yourself, you have no idea how much work there is in creating just one tiny fragment of a tapestry.' She shuddered, recalling the grim determination with which she had worked on that last cushion cover which her mother was determined to finish. 'Tapestry is an endurance test, not a hobby, a pastime invented to keep women so mind-numbingly occupied that they don't realise they are bored to tears.'

'"She knows not what the curse may be; Therefore she weaveth steadily, Therefore no other care hath she, The Lady of Shalott",' Eugene quoted from Tennyson's poem.'

'Precisely,' Isabella said, smiling grimly. 'And the next line, "She lives with little joy or fear" I believe exactly illustrates my point.'

'Is that how you lived? "With little joy or fear"?'

'"Half sick of shadows…"' She paused in the act of folding up her apron. 'I was waiting for my life to begin, that's how it felt. And then my mother died and the "mirror crack'd from side to side", but unlike the Lady of Shalott I was set free, rather than cursed.'

'You could have escaped earlier, but you chose to stay after you came into your inheritance. That was a very loyal thing to do.'

'She had no one else. I couldn't leave her.'

'No, after what you told me yesterday, I understand why.'

They looked at each other and the past disappeared, ousted by the awareness of each other, the unspoken desire that flickered between them in every moment of silence. 'I didn't expect to see you today.' Isabella's voice was breathless.

'I can't keep away from you. I can't help myself.'

He meant it as a joke, she told herself. She could turn

the subject and he would follow her lead. She could offer him coffee, but she didn't want coffee. She was no longer that passive Isabella, waiting for life to happen to her. Life was happening now. 'I'm glad you're here,' she said.

'Are you?'

It was a loaded question and she knew it, from the way he looked at her, from the way her heart was thumping, from the stirrings of desire inside her in response to the rough edge in his voice. 'Yes,' Isabella said. 'Yes, I am.'

She dropped her butchered apron and stepped towards him.

'So am I,' he said, putting his arms around her.

She lifted her face to his and their mouths met. It had been nine months since they had kissed, but her body recognised him instantly, familiar and exciting, the taste of him, at the touch of his lips. It was the same, but different. This time he kissed her slowly, small kisses, as if he was tasting her rather than devouring her. His hands fluttered over her back, one settled on her waist, the other tangled in her hair. He sighed his pleasure as she looped her arms around his neck and kissed him back. Small kisses. Tasting kisses. She had never kissed like this before.

Longing, yearning, flooded her, but in a languorous, drugging way. His hair was silky soft. He smelled of soap and wool, and the London air and a faint spicy cologne. Different, but the same. Their kiss deepened, slowly, their mouths shaping themselves to each other, and she stepped closer into his embrace, relishing the otherness of his body against hers, the gentleness of his hands, cupping her cheek, fingers fluttering on her nape, making her shiver with delight.

When it was over they stared at each other, dazed. Then he smiled and she smiled back. Then he laughed softly, and she laughed, too. And they kissed again, one more time, before ending it of one accord, feeling no awkwardness, but knowing that was enough. For now.

'Coffee?' Isabella asked.

'Please. I have news,' Eugene said. 'I have some more investigating to do which will take me a day or so, but it's progress of a sort.'

Chapter Six

Bloomsbury—Sunday, December 7th, 1856

His investigations had taken Eugene all of yesterday. Since the soup kitchen was closed on a Sunday, Isabella had suggested that he call at her house to update her. It could easily wait until Monday, for what he had discovered merely confirmed what he already knew, but he had missed seeing her yesterday. Telling himself that it was because two heads were better than one, he arrived at her house at the prescribed time, a terrace in one of the older parts of Bloomsbury.

The street was extremely quiet, the sky an ominous pewter colour. Though the promise of snow had not been fulfilled, he was glad of his scarf and gloves. The knocker he rapped on the black-painted door was heavily tarnished. The shutters on all of the windows facing the street were closed. He was beginning to wonder if he had the wrong address, when the door was opened by Isabella herself.

'You found me,' she said, stepping aside to let him in.

She was dressed in a dark green silk gown that was

very different from her usual attire, the full skirts over her crinoline trimmed with black ribbons and braid. The bodice was tightly fitted, the sleeves three-quarter-length showing of her olive-skinned forearms and slim wrists, and the neckline, though modest, was lower than he had ever seen her wear.

'It's an old dress,' she said, seeing him staring. 'Four years out of fashion, though I think I've only worn it once. I am surprised it still fits.'

'It suits you. You look very different. Lovely, I mean. Not that you don't usually look—' He broke off, embarrassed. 'I'll just stop there, shall I?' What he was really thinking was that she looked ravishing. He would kiss her, if it were not for the fact that she might think he was taking advantage, and she hadn't invited him over to kiss her, and besides, there were servants.

'I don't have any servants,' Isabella said, reading his mind. 'I have a young woman who comes in twice a week to clean, but most of the rooms are closed up. I prefer to look after myself and I enjoy living alone. Come upstairs to the parlour and you can tell me if you've made any progress.'

'I can tell you now that I have not,' Eugene said, following her, distracted by her swaying crinoline and the tantalising glimpses of her slender ankles, her feet clad not in their customary boots, but in soft silk slippers and sheer silk stockings. He cursed himself under his breath as desire stirred, almost relieved to reach the first floor and to be ushered into a room at the back of the house, where he halted in surprise in the doorway.

'It was my mother's bedroom until recently,' Isabella said. 'It gets the best of what winter light there is, though, and it's much quieter away from the noise of the street.'

There was no bed, no chests of drawers or dressing table. No sign that it had once been a bedroom. 'Surely you didn't move all the furniture yourself?'

'Susan, that's the young woman who comes in to clean, helped me move the bigger pieces. There's a desk full of papers that I still haven't gone through, that caused us a bit of trouble, but I did most of it myself. Nursing requires a great deal of brute strength, you know. I'm much stronger than I look.'

Eugene joined her at the double window, which faced out on to a small, neglected garden. 'I know that it's not all soothing fevered brows, but brute strength?'

'Have you ever tried to put a dressing on a grown man who doesn't want his wound to be touched? Or tried to feed a man who's so fevered that he thinks you're trying to poison him? Or change the sheets on a bed while the man is still in it?'

He shook his head. She didn't look strong enough to do any of those things, standing beside him, staring out of the window, a full head smaller than him, the green dress showing off her slender frame as well as her curves. Though her hands told a different story, he thought, taking hold of one, turning it over to examine her palm, running his fingers over the callouses and the rough skin. 'Your battle scars,' he said. 'You should be proud of them.'

He lifted her hand to his mouth, pressing a kiss on the pad of her thumb. He heard her breath catch. His heart thudded. She made no attempt to take her hand away, standing wide-eyed and perfectly still, watching him. He kissed the thin skin at her wrist, feeling her pulse flutter against his lips. She tasted of lemon soap. Her skin was warm. There were two thin white scars on the inside of her forearm, one above the other.

'My own fault,' she said. 'Never try to catch a scalpel if you drop it.'

He imagined her, exhausted, in the chaotic aftermath of battle, rushing from stretcher to stretcher, the cries of the doctors to hurry, hurry. He kissed the scars, tracing the faint indentations with his tongue, feeling her shivering response, his own blood stirring. She was so strong and yet so fragile it made his gut twist.

'How did you bear it?' he asked, releasing her hand to run his fingers down the delicate planes of her cheek, watching the soft swell of her breasts rise and fall, pushing against the neckline of her gown, aware of himself as two people, the curious man touched to tenderness by what she had endured, the other one, growing harder with desire, wanting.

'There was no time to stop and think.' Her voice was breathy. Her eyes were fixed on his face, her hand mirroring his, fingers feathering over his cheek, pushing back the fall of his hair to touch his nape, smoothing her palm over the skin above his collar. 'No option every day but to carry on,' she said. 'Same as everyone out there. I'm no different.'

'You are…' A heroine, he meant to say. Admirable. Inspirational. But looking into her eyes, the flush of desire on her high cheekbones, her big eyes becoming clouded with the desire that was slowly engulfing him, he forgot what he was going to say.

'Isabella,' he said instead. She stepped into his arms. 'Isabella,' he said again, murmuring her name against her ear, nibbling at the lobe, kissing the delicate skin behind it, feeling her pulse flutter wildly, like his own. 'Isabella,' he said again, as her arms twined around his neck, and then words gave way to kisses.

Not like the kisses they had shared on Friday. Passionate kisses, similar to the ones they had shared in the Crimea. Kisses that made him forget everything but the woman melting into his arms, the taste of her, the softness of her mouth, the touch of her tongue on his, the rush of blood to his groin that was his response. The way she pressed herself against him, the way her crinoline billowed out behind her, making her stagger, making him pull her closer, tighter against him.

The soft murmurings of her response, her mouth shaping itself to his, her hands in his hair, on his back, inside his coat. And his hands, sliding over the silk of her gown at the indent of her waist, smoothing up to the curve of her breast, the sharp intake of her breath as he touched her, the layers of her clothing frustrating and yet intoxicating.

More kisses. His heart thudding wildly, her breath shallow and fast on his face, her hands on the silk back of his waistcoat, tantalisingly close to his skin, his erection pressing hard against his trousers and her crinoline the barrier between them. Dear God!

He lifted his head, his breathing ragged. He swore again under his breath, shocked by the strength of his arousal, by how quickly they had been swept away. 'I didn't mean—when I came here today, I didn't plan—not this.'

Isabella stared at Eugene, his face flushed and heavy-eyed, exactly as her own must be. One word from her and he would let her go, but she didn't want to utter the word. She wanted this. Now. Because ever since he had walked into the hall on Monday—just six days ago!—this is what their encounter had been leading to. 'Do you want to?' she asked.

He cursed under his breath. 'You really need to ask?'

She laughed softly. 'You would ask me.'

'I want to,' Eugene said. 'I want to make love to you. With you. I want to, like before, though more.'

Her thoughts. The words she would have chosen. 'Yes,' Isabella said. 'Like before, though more.' She heard his breath catch. She took his hand and, heart hammering, she led him up the stairs to her bedchamber. It was a spartan room with a small bed, bare boards save for one rug, bearing more than a passing resemblance to the wooden hut where they had first made love. She saw him take it in, make the connection. She drew the curtains. And stepped into his arms.

She had told herself that her memory had betrayed her, that she had exaggerated the intensity of that first encounter, but when their lips met, knowing where their kisses would lead, she realised she had been wrong. Her body thrummed with anticipation. The sweep of his tongue, the softness of his breath, the stroke of his hands made her ripple with excitement, made her breathless with desire. His mouth trailed heat down her neck, into the hollows at her shoulders, along the swell of her breasts, making her nipples hard, aching for his touch.

His coat fell to the floor and his waistcoat followed as her hands tugged at his clothing, seeking the heat of his flesh. Under his shirt his back was warm, the muscles rippling in response, just as she remembered but more, his breath ragged. More kisses, their mouths kept returning for more kisses, as if they would devour each other. He unlaced her gown and she slipped free of the bodice. He groaned, burying his face between her breasts, tugging the front lacings of her corsets, and she struggled to untie the lacing holding up her crinoline. So many clothes, she thought, as the cage folded on itself, falling to the floor. Too many.

His shirt was next. In the dim light, his skin was pale, his nipples dark in contrast, puckering as she touched him. She remembered the dip of his belly, smoothing her hands over it, and the arrow of hair directing her from his navel down. She slid her hands inside his trousers.

He groaned again, freeing her from her corset and her gown and her petticoats. His hands were hot on her skin through the last layer of her chemise. He dipped his head to her breast, sucking one nipple through the thin cambric, making her cry out, making her tighten and tense inside, urgent for him now, as they staggered towards the bed, mouths fastened once more, kissing, making urgent, pleading noises, touching.

He threw off the rest of his clothes. She gazed at him, remembering, so caught up in passion that there was no embarrassment, only wanting this, him, inside her. She touched him lightly, circling her hand on him, stroking the length of him, relishing the power of her touch reflected in his face. And then they were kissing again, lying on the bed, his erection pressing into her belly as he touched her intimately, stroked her, sliding over her, inside, making her writhe with desire, trying desperately to hold on, but her climax ripped through her and she was crying out for him, hands tugging at him, body pressed urgently against him.

'Yes?' he whispered, poised over her.

'Yes!' she replied, arching against him. 'Yes.'

He slid into her slowly, resting his weight on his elbows, his face taut with the effort of maintaining control. She shuddered, wrapping her legs around him, tilting herself to take him deeper, and he groaned and thrust. Higher. They quickly found a rhythm, wild kisses growing wilder as they moved together, clinging, tensing, tighter, until she came again and sent him over the edge with a cry, pulling himself free of her with a deep, shuddering cry. And then more kisses, slow and deep, sated, their bodies damp with sweat and lovemaking, as they lay together on the tumbled, tangled sheets.

The last time, the first time, Eugene had left at the break of dawn and she had thought she'd never see him again. This time, he propped himself up on his elbow and studied her, frowning slightly. 'This isn't like me. I'll be thirty next birthday. I'm not without experience. I've had lovers, but I've never felt so—as if I can't help myself.'

Isabella pulled the sheet over her breasts, though it was rather late in the day for modesty. 'It's not like me either.'

'I guessed as much,' he said. 'I thought that first

time that it was the war, the sense of every moment being precious, your leaving, my arriving.' He pushed a strand of hair back from her forehead, smiling intently at her. 'And you. From the moment I met you I felt—I wanted—no, needed. I've never felt that before.'

'Kindred spirits, that's what you said the other day.' She pushed herself half upright. 'And it's the same now, in a way, as the first time, isn't it? A turning point. A hiatus.'

'Is that what you think?'

She didn't want to think. She was heavy-limbed and blissful. 'It doesn't matter, does it? I don't have any expectations. I have no ties and no desire to acquire any either.'

'Until six weeks ago, I was in exactly the same situation. Now—oh, now, who knows what lies ahead? I don't want to think about it.'

'Then don't. This won't last, it can't, but for now…'

'For now!' He smiled then, leaning over to kiss her softly. 'We should make the most of it while we can, yes? Because if that's what you're suggesting then I have an idea.'

His smile had turned wicked. His free hand was cupping her breast, his thumb circling her nipple. She had thought herself sated. She was wrong. 'What?'

'Let me show you,' he said, pushing back the sheet and beginning to kiss his way down her body.

Later, much later, fully clothed, they stood in the hall. 'I should go,' Eugene said, though it was a question, not a statement.

'We haven't talked about Rebecca. But if you need to go...'

'No,' he said, relieved. 'You're right.'

They went down to the basement kitchen. Isabella set about making tea and he sat at the large scrubbed pine table feeling awkward, for the situation was utterly new to him, intimate, domestic.

'This was the one room that I decorated when I returned from the Crimea,' Isabella said, putting the kettle on to the stove. 'I am fortunate to have running water in the scullery and this stove is one of the latest designs.'

He was relieved to see the faint blush of colour on her cheeks that betrayed her own uncertainty. Her eyes weren't quite meeting his. 'Maisy is forever singing the praises of the contraption which you had installed in the kitchen in Hackney,' Eugene said. 'How did you become such an expert?'

'Oh, I'm not an expert, but I became acquainted with one in the Crimea. Monsieur Soyer, the famous chef, designed a stove especially for the field kitchens and made it his business to train up cooks for each regiment. It is thanks to him that we saw fewer cases of food poisoning and the men at least had fuller bellies before they went into battle. Monsieur is like an English caricature of a French man and set a good many backs up, but I liked him and he took a liking to me. He even taught me how to cook, though I have not Maisy's talent.'

She drew breath to pour the tea, taking several quick sips in succession, looking enquiringly at him. 'Rebecca?'

Eugene shook his head, sighing. 'I had hoped for some sort of lead, but I'm afraid I came up with virtually nothing. I checked Wilbur's household accounts from the time of the accident my sister mentioned. There were regular periods marked where he was absent and no meals required, but nothing corresponding in the accounts for the country house. The butler keeps both and he's meticulous, thank goodness. Wherever my brother went, it wasn't the country estate and he didn't take his valet.'

'It's pretty likely he was in Islington with Rebecca, then,' Isabella said.

'It makes sense. She was almost certainly the guardian angel who came to his rescue and presumably romance quickly blossomed between them. But that doesn't take us any further forward.' Eugene stirred milk into his tea and took a sip. Isabella took hers black, the same way she liked her coffee, he noticed. 'I'm still working my way round the various parish burial registers and so far there's still no trace of Rebecca Smith or Barnford, but it's slow work. If I could trust someone else to do it I would. I'm beginning to think it's a wild goose chase.'

'If you can't find her, will you still tell your sister about the marriage?'

'I can't make my mind up. Does she have a right to know? Do I have the right to keep something so important from her? But she will be deeply hurt and if we don't find the woman—' Eugene broke off, shaking his head. 'Let's cross that bridge when we come to it. We've still a few weeks to go until Christmas.'

Isabella looked as if she was about to press him further, then changed her mind, pulling her work basket towards her. 'I've been experimenting,' she said, 'trying to come up with ideas of gifts the children could make.'

He took the small piece of green felt she handed him, smiling when he saw the white beads and realised what it was. 'Mistletoe! This is clever. What else have you created? May I see?'

She handed him the items, one by one. A rag doll with red hair and a red dress. A selection of animals: a donkey, a horse, a cat and a dog, each with a bell around its neck. A Christmas tree adorned with coloured beads. 'They are made from felt and wool, mostly, cheap materials,' she said, finally meeting his eyes. 'The beads and the little bells I bought at a market stall as a job lot. What do you think?'

'These are wonderful,' Eugene said warmly. 'The children will love trying to make them.'

'If I cut the shapes out for the tree and the mistletoe in advance, then all they'll have to do is glue on the beads. And as far as the littler ones are concerned, I thought we could give them paper and coloured pencils. And I was also thinking that we could get them to make little gift bags and, if I bought a selection of sweets, then they could fill them up.'

'And fill themselves up, too.'

She laughed, pouring them both another cup of tea. 'Well, of course, that's part of the fun.'

'You've thought of everything.'

'They have so little and Christmas should be a special time for children. I would love to give them all proper presents.'

'No, this is a much better idea. It's the perfect balance of fun and giving, and you don't run the risk of being seen as Lady Bountiful, giving them something better than their parents, for those who can afford gifts at all. You can count on my help. When were you thinking?'

'Saturday? That will be just under two weeks before Christmas.'

'Just about enough time for me to organise a Punch and Judy show—what do you think?'

'That's a wonderful idea. They'll love it.'

'And their mothers will be grateful to have some time to themselves.'

'Unless they stay to watch the puppet show.' Isabella began to put the toys back in her basket. 'I have been wondering about setting up some sort of day nursery, a place where mothers can leave their little ones for a couple of hours at a time. I'd need help, I have no idea at all how to look after babies, but if we could train some of the older girls, it would give them gainful employment.'

'What about the soup kitchen?'

'I'm thinking of starting to delegate more to some of the volunteers.' Isabella stared wistfully at the little rag doll. 'I'd like to spend more time with the children.'

'Have you never wished for children of your own?'

'I'd require a husband for that and I don't want a husband. I have found my own family, a huge one, in Hackney.' She put the doll away and closed the lid of the basket. 'What about you?'

'Me? I've got enough on my plate without taking on a wife and a family.'

'Yes, now, but later, when you are more settled?'

He shuddered. 'I don't want to be settled. I can't think of anything more tedious, can you?'

She was obliged to smile. 'No. Do you want more tea?'

'I'd better go. I have a stack of paperwork gathering

dust and the lawyer is starting to make unhappy noises every time I tell him I haven't looked at it.'

Isabella pushed back her chair. 'I'll see you out.'

Eugene followed her up the stairs and pulled on his coat, but set his hat down before he had put it on. 'I can't simply wish you good evening.'

'Please don't ask me if I have any regrets. I don't.'

'Nor do I, if you don't.'

She smiled softly. 'I've already said so.'

He stepped towards her. She lifted her face to his and their lips met in a soft kiss. His body reacted immediately, urging him to deepen the kiss. He dragged his mouth away, but then she smiled and he kissed her again, and pulled her closer. This time it was she who broke the kiss, her breathing ragged.

Isabella held up the little felt mistletoe, her smile positively sinful. 'Three berries,' she said, shaking the beads.

'Three kisses? I think we can do better than that.' He swept her into his arms again, picked her up and headed for the stairs.

Chapter Seven

Hackney—Saturday, December 13th, 1856

The hall was full of children working on their presents at the dinner tables, which had been set up as soon as the day's meal was over. Stacks of felt in different colours and boxes of glossy beads and bells were set out at intervals. Where the smaller children sat, the felt shapes had been cut out and pots of glue with brushes provided. There were ribbons in every colour of the rainbow, hanks of wool and reels of cotton.

At one table, a group of the youngest children were painting, some with brushes, some with their fingers. Some were drawing Christmas trees and winged angels with the coloured pencils. Others were content to make swirls of colour. A few of the children were simply staring in quiet awe at the hum of industry going on around them.

Laughter filled the air and every face held a beaming smile, whether the child was scrubbed clean, streaked with dirt, grubby, runny nosed, or a combination of all of those things. The older children who had volunteered to be mentors and monitors wore the gold stars, which Eugene had provided, with pride. There were several of the girls, Isabella thought, watching, who would be excellent candidates to help in the nursery, if she set it up. No doubt well versed in looking after younger siblings.

As she watched the activity, hearing the laughter, the odd spat, the very occasional burst of frustrated tears or temper tantrum, her heart felt full. Some of the mothers had remained to watch, to help, to enjoy seeing their children having fun. Others had been delighted to have the time for other chores.

'It's everything I imagined and so much more,' she said to Eugene, who joined her in the doorway to the kitchen. 'Look how happy they all are.'

'Look how happy you are.'

She laughed. 'And you, too. The Punch and Judy show is already proving an enormous hit. Most of the mothers are planning to return in time to watch. The hall will be packed.'

'It already is,' Eugene said, surveying the mayhem before turning back to her. 'All your hard work is paying off. You are a wonder.'

'I couldn't have done it without you,' she said. When he smiled at her like that, it made her breathless. It made her forget where she was and what she was doing. It made her feel as if there was only the two of them. It made her body ache with wanting him. Though they had made love every day since Sunday, she could not have enough of his kisses, his touch. It was because they had so little time, she told herself. Knowing that after Christmas she wouldn't see him again, she was doing exactly what they had promised themselves they would do. She was immersing herself in the present. She was making the most of what she had now. And when he was gone…

As ever, when she asked herself that question, her heart lurched and she closed her mind to it. It was easy to do, when she could read her own desire in his eyes, when his hand was feathering down her back, hidden from view of the hall. When he was gently nudging her into the empty kitchen and murmuring her name urgently, and for a blissful moment their lips met and she sighed her pleasure, until someone called her name from the hall and she dragged herself free.

'Sorry,' Eugene said, looking not at all sorry.

'Later,' Isabella said. 'There will be plenty of time later.'

A roar of delight sent them both back to the doorway. The curtains of the puppet theatre had opened, but they were quickly closed again. 'Benny, assessing his audience,' Eugene said, grinning. 'This is his debut performance. I'd better go and reassure him. I think he was expecting a slightly smaller crowd.'

'You didn't tell me he's never done this before!'

'He's an actor. He inherited Punch and Judy from his uncle.'

'How do you come to know him?'

'Edward Blanchard introduced us—he's the newspaper drama critic. I had no idea, when I promised you a Punch and Judy, that it would be so difficult to find one willing to perform in a mere soup kitchen. Benny leapt at the chance though.'

'You didn't tell me any of this. I didn't realise you'd had to go to so much trouble.'

'That's nothing, compared to tracking down the flock of geese we're going to need for Christmas Day. I'm beginning to think I'll have to shoot them myself. I'm teasing you,' Eugene added. 'Besides, it's a pleasure. And I've been thinking, too, having spoken to Blanchard—'

A sudden surge of people entering the hall made Eugene break off. 'Looks like the rest of our audience is arriving.' He caught her hand briefly. 'I'll explain my idea later.'

He headed for the corner where the puppet theatre had been set up on the far side of the hall and Isabella made for a table where the children were sewing eyes and noses on to donkeys.

'Our Janet has been practising,' Mrs Simpson said proudly to Isabella, watching her daughter with an indulgent smile. 'Never shown an interest in a needle until she made that little horse, and now! Not that I'm complaining, mind, I've been teaching her to darn and she even enjoys that, would you believe.'

'She is a very patient girl,' Isabella said.

Mrs Simpson rolled her eyes. 'Oh, don't be fooled, she has her moments. Have you got a minute? I've been wanting to speak to you, but if you're too busy…'

'No,' Isabella said, worrying at the woman's change of tone. 'Shall we go into the kitchen?'

'It might be nothing,' Mrs Simpson said, after a few tense moments. 'My Ma, although she's getting on, still has all her marbles. But still, it might be nothing.'

'What is it? You know that nothing you tell me will go any further if you don't want it to.'

'No, no, it's nothing to do with me,' the older woman exclaimed. 'It's about that woman you're looking for. Rebecca Smith.'

Isabella clutched at the edge of the table. 'You know where she is?'

Mrs Simpson nodded. 'I think I do.'

It was late, after five when the hall was finally cleared and quite dark outside. 'I thought that went splendidly,' Eugene said to Isabella, who was tidying the last of the felt scraps and buttons into a large wicker basket.

'I was very pleased to see that Mr Punch did not murder his wife, in your actor friend's version of the story,' she said.

'Hmm. I'm not so sure everyone agreed with you. They're a bloodthirsty lot, kids. You're very quiet. Are you tired? It's been a long day.'

Isabella closed the basket, shaking her head. 'And a very rewarding one. Thank you.'

'Don't be silly. I have enjoyed every minute.' The hall door was closed. They were finally alone. He pulled her into his arms, resting his chin on the soft mass of her curls. She rubbed her cheek against his chest and wrapped her arms around his waist. His body, as ever, reacted to her touch, desire, which was only ever temporarily sated, spreading heat through him, but it was the longing that accompanied it which perturbed him.

He wanted to make love to her, he always wanted to make love to her, but it was becoming increasingly difficult, afterwards, to leave her and that worried him. He knew when the time came that he was going to find it painful to say goodbye, though he also knew that there was no alternative. Was that true? Could they continue as lovers? It was a possibility he had not broached, but his instincts told him it wouldn't work. After Christmas, he would have to step up to the mark. His time would no longer be his own. That new world and Isabella's world were separated by a great deal more than a few London boroughs.

But Christmas was still almost two weeks away. 'That idea I mentioned earlier. I was thinking…' Eugene said, half dreamily, enjoying the way her curls tickled his face. 'Blanchard, the drama critic, the man who put me in touch with Benny—he's actually more famous these days for writing plays and pantomimes. He has a pantomime at Drury Lane premiering on Boxing Day, but they will have full dress rehearsals before that. What if I spoke to him, asked if we could bring our pack of children along on Christmas Eve to watch?'

'That's a lovely idea, Eugene.'

Her voice was oddly flat. He held her at arm's length. 'What's wrong?'

'I was talking to Mrs Simpson.'

'Janet and John's mum? I saw her earlier—has something happened?'

'Not to her or to any of her family.' Isabella, looking deeply troubled, extracted herself from his embrace. 'Shall we sit down?'

There could only be one reason. Eugene pulled out a chair, sitting down heavily. 'Rebecca?'

Isabella nodded, pulling out the chair opposite him. 'I'm afraid so.'

'Is she alive?'

She winced, reaching for his hand. 'Nothing is certain yet, but I do think you have to prepare yourself for the worst.'

She spoke gently, but firmly. She sounded like a nurse. He curled his fingers around hers, feeling sick, bracing himself, dimly aware, as he had not been before, of just how much he had wanted to find his brother's wife alive. 'Tell me.'

'Mrs Simpson's mother, Mrs Wallace, lives in Bethnal Green, the borough just south of Hackney. When Mrs Simpson paid her a visit last week, the children were telling her about today and the puppet show and my name came up, and I gather there was some speculation between the two women about me, as there usually is, because as you know, I take great care not to let anyone know anything personal about me. Anyway, the long and the short of it is that Mrs Simpson mentioned that I was trying to trace a Rebecca Barnford and Mrs Wallace remembered her.'

'In Bethnal Green? You mean all this time we've been looking in the wrong part of London?'

'We assumed that what she told the priest in Islington was the truth. It never occurred to either of us that she would lie.'

'It should have occurred to me.' Eugene let go of her hand, pushing back his chair to stretch out his legs. 'If she wanted to disappear—and it's clear now that she did—then why would she tell her priest where she was going?' He swore softly under his breath. 'And I call myself a reporter! I can't believe I've been so stupid.'

'What else could you have done, though, save follow the only lead you had?'

'And it led me here, to you.' He reached for her hand again. 'For which I will always be grateful. Go on,' he said, letting her go again, folding his arms against his chest. 'Let's get it over with.'

'Rebecca Barnford, as she was known, passed herself off as a widow,' Isabella continued in the same level tone as before. How much practice had she had delivering bad news? he wondered distractedly. Thank God, for he could not have borne anything more emotional. 'She was a respectable young woman, she rented a room next door to Mrs Wallace and took in mending. "Kept herself to herself" is what Mrs Wallace said.' Isabella stopped for a moment. Her hands, he guessed, though he couldn't see them, were tightly clasped. He almost wished she would remain silent.

'Cholera,' she continued. 'It swept through the area not long after she arrived. She survived, but never fully recovered, and shortly after she arrived in Bethnal Green, she...' Her voice quivered for the first time. 'She went to the workhouse.'

'But why?' he asked, wretchedly. 'Whatever the circumstances of the marriage, whatever happened between my brother and this poor woman, Wilbur would have taken care of her. There was no need for her to put herself at the mercy of one of those institutions. If she was ill, why could she not have sent word to him?'

'Eugene, she was expecting a child.'

'My brother's child!' He had considered the possibility, but dismissed it. Now he stared at her, dumbfounded, his mind struggling to work out the implications. If Wilbur had a child, his brother's legacy was not entirely lost. Cecily would be delighted, regardless of the circumstances. *If* Wilbur had a child. Isabella remained ominously quiet. 'Did it survive?' Eugene asked.

Her gaze dropped. 'The infirmary at the Waterloo Road workhouse is reputed to be better than most, according to what Mrs Wallace told her daughter. Visitors are not permitted. Mrs Wallace was not a relative. I'm sorry, I'm so very sorry, but she did eventually get word from another workhouse inmate that Rebecca died.'

'What about the baby?'

'I'm sorry. Mrs Wallace doesn't know, but in the circumstances it seems highly unlikely it is alive. Even if it survived the birth, a child born into a workhouse with no mother—I'm sorry, Eugene, the odds are very much against it.'

His loss hit him then, like a punch in the gut. Wilbur was dead. His wife was dead. The child his brother probably didn't even know about was dead. Tears burned his eyes and clogged his throat. He dropped his head on to his arms and gave way to the grief he had not succumbed to when he heard of Wilbur's death. Sobs racked his body, for he felt as if he had lost his brother all over again.

When he sat up, there was no sign of Isabella, but from the kitchen came the familiar sound of a kettle boiling and coffee being made. He scrubbed his face with his handkerchief. His eyes were raw. His hands shook when he took the cup she poured for him, but after a few moments the strong brew began to revive him.

'I'm sorry,' he said, though he was too drained to feel anything, even embarrassment.

'*I'm* sorry to have been the bearer of such bad news.'

'You must have kept it to yourself for most of the afternoon.'

'Did I do wrong? I didn't want to spoil today for you.'

Her eyes were red-rimmed, he noticed. While he had given way to grief, she must have been crying in the kitchen. 'Thank you,' Eugene said. 'I appreciate the way you told me. I thought I was prepared for the worst. I'll go to the workhouse tomorrow. They'll be buried— oh, God, they'll have been buried in a pauper's grave.'

'It's Sunday tomorrow and you need to think carefully before you pay a visit,' Isabella said, looking troubled again. 'What are you going to say? Unless you admit to your relationship to Rebecca, you have no right to any information.'

'I must confirm the story you have been told. If Wilbur had a son, he would have an heir. If so, surely he would have claimed him? If by some miracle he still does have an heir—now that really would be a miracle, don't you think?'

'Most men would think it a great misfortune to have their inheritance snatched away from them.'

'You know me better than that. I'd be delighted, if it meant Wilbur's son had survived.' Eugene heaved a sigh. 'Do you know *when* Rebecca entered the workhouse, exactly?'

'Spring is what Mrs Simpson said. I can ask her to ask her mother if you like, but...'

'I know, I know, it's unlikely she can be more accurate. Besides, if there was a cholera outbreak, it will be recorded. The workhouse will have a register, too. I must see for myself that there is no hope of mistaken identity. I know, I said that I would want to avoid any scandal, I remember, but I think…'

'You don't know what you think.' Isabella got to her feet and collected the cups. 'You're in shock. Now is not the time to make any decisions. Take tomorrow to mull things over. Take even more time, if you need it. There's no rush.'

'No. No, I don't suppose there is.' He dragged himself to his feet, staggering when he pushed the chair back.

'You're exhausted.' Isabella appeared with his jacket and coat. 'You need to go home and go to bed.'

'Yes, Nurse.'

She smiled faintly. 'I mean it.'

He remembered their kiss earlier. A few hours ago, but it seemed as if days had passed, and all he wanted now was to be alone. 'Do you mind?'

'Mind? Oh!' She coloured. 'Don't be ridiculous. That is the last thing either of us wants right now.'

He had thought so. Yet when he wrapped his arms around her, feeling the familiar, delightful shape of her, he changed his mind. To lose himself in her and then to lie entwined, curled up in her bed, and to sleep, and to wake the next morning to have her face the first thing he saw.

What the hell! Isabella was his lover, nothing more. Wilbur's wife was dead, along with their child, in all probability. His quest was over. The future loomed horribly close, bleak and forbidding and lonely. The responsibilities he'd been avoiding for weeks weighed heavy on his shoulders. He wasn't ready. He had promised himself until Christmas. What's more, he had other responsibilities here in Hackney, responsibilities he had assumed of his own free will. He wouldn't let Isabella down. He wouldn't let all these local people down.

Eugene disengaged himself and pulled on his jacket and coat. Don't think about it, he reminded himself. Tomorrow and next week, and no further ahead than that. 'I'll do as you suggest, I'll think about it, but I'll be back here on Monday and I'll keep coming back here as planned, until Christmas.'

Chapter Eight

Bethnal Green—Monday, December 15th, 1856

Isabella had spent a restless Sunday unable to settle to anything, the story which Mrs Simpson had passed on going round and round in her head. It was not uncommon, she knew, for women in Rebecca's state to enter a workhouse, sacrificing their freedom for the medical care the infirmary would provide when they gave birth, but such women had no alternatives. Rebecca was an earl's wife. She was ill. She must have known that childbirth was likely to kill her. Why had a workhouse infirmary been preferable to telling her husband? Why had she not told her husband that she was expecting a child that could have been a son and heir? Or had she?

All of those questions and more must already have occurred to Eugene. Was he, too, pacing, restless, wondering? Almost certainly. He was a reporter. It was his business to enquire, to look for gaps in tales, reasons for discrepancies, and what they now knew of Rebecca and Wilbur's marriage added up to a story riddled with holes.

She wanted to talk it over with him. It was not that she was missing him, she was worried about him. He was in a fragile state, he'd had a terrible shock, but that didn't amount to missing him. They had probably spent too much time in each other's company, Isabella told herself sternly, wandering the house, through rooms that had been closed up since her mother died. She had grown too used to him. She had forgotten how much she savoured her own company, treasured her independence. She couldn't possibly be lonely.

In a bid to take her mind off him, she had decided to clear out her mother's desk, an overdue task. It was in the dining room with the other furniture from the bedroom which she had still to arrange to have taken away. Her mind only half on the task, Isabella opened drawer after drawer, sifting through ancient bills and receipts, shopping lists and endless, extravagant menus for dinner parties she never hosted, for meals far beyond even Bella's voracious appetite. There were miniatures of her children, Isabella's four half-brothers. Golden-haired, blue-eyed moppets who bore no resemblance to the men they had become. She stared at them long and hard before putting them to one side, trying and failing to feel anything.

There was nothing more personal in the contents. She had been about to gather up the papers to burn when she remembered what Eugene had told her about the secret drawer in his brother's desk. Feeling silly, she set about investigating. When the latch clicked and the drawer popped open she stared at it in astonishment. *I can't wait to tell Eugene*, had been her first thought. Then she assimilated the content. A bundle of letters tied up with a red satin ribbon addressed to Lady Armstrong, at Killellan Manor, in a spidery script. Her skin had crawled. She didn't want to touch them. There was nothing else in the drawer. She knew instinctively who had written them. There could only have been one person. Shaken, she had pushed the secret drawer back into place, grabbed her coat and headed for Regent's Park.

A second sleepless night resulted in Isabella arriving early at the soup kitchen on Monday morning, where there was mercifully always a great deal to do. Maisy had merely raised an eyebrow and surrendered her knife when she offered to peel the potatoes. Eugene arrived at his normal time, when the hall was already busy with helpers. On the surface, he appeared to be his usual self, joking with the ladies in the kitchen, but there were dark shadows under his eyes and, when he thought himself unobserved, a grim set to his countenance.

The strength of her desire to put her arms around him, to comfort, not to arouse, unsettled Isabella even more. She was a nurse, it was in her nature to provide succour, but she had never felt any need to hug any of her patients. Once again, she reminded herself that Eugene's presence in her life was temporary. Once again, her stomach lurched at the idea of never seeing him again. She reminded herself yet again that she had almost two more weeks.

He took her aside in a quiet moment, in the lull between having everything ready to serve and opening the doors, and told her that he had decided, as she had anticipated, to visit the workhouse after dinner was over. She had determined that she would accompany him, and when she said so, ready to put up a fight, he disarmed her by accepting her offer with alacrity.

'As a nurse, you will be better placed to speak to the infirmary staff,' he said. 'I want to understand how well or badly women in Rebecca's situation are treated.'

Isabella had no experience of childbirth and there was no time for her to consult Honoria, who would be extremely well placed to advise her, but Eugene looked so strained, she kept silent.

'What will you say to the authorities in the workhouse?' Isabella asked when they were finally seated in the cab heading south to Bethnal Green.

'Whatever I need to, to discover the truth. Cecily has a right to know, too. I was wrong, thinking to keep this from her. Wilbur kept that certificate. Rebecca mattered to him. We owe it to his memory to acknowledge that.' He touched her hand, very briefly, seeing her confusion. 'I don't know exactly what I mean by that. Take your lead from me. Trust me, that's all I ask.'

The cab drew to a halt. He leapt down, helping her out before paying the driver. Isabella shuddered, pulling her thick woollen cloak more closely around her. The wind was biting, the clouds above leaden. The Waterloo Road Workhouse was completely surrounded by a high wall, save for the main entrance where they stood, where an even higher gate guarded the premises, with a porter's lodge on one side, and an office on the other.

Peering through the gate, Isabella saw a modern building of red brick with an extensive frontage comprising three storeys with a large number of tall windows, set well back from the wall, with well-tended gardens to the front. At first glance it looked pleasant enough, very different to the Hackney Workhouse, but the separate entrances demarcating the different functional wings of the institution hinted at the pain of separation which underlay every such place.

Husbands, she knew, were parted from wives. Children were wrenched from their parents. Infants were separated from their siblings. The workhouse was a necessary feature of every one of the poorer London boroughs, but it was a place only for the desperate, a last resort for people with nowhere else to turn.

In the porter's lodge, they were received with a mixture of mistrust and deference and informed that the Master saw no one without a written appointment. Eugene handed over a visiting card and a folded note. 'Inform him that Lord Kingarth wishes him to spare a few moments of his time.'

The change was remarkable. The porter pocketed the money and made a bow. 'I am sure he will be able to accommodate you, my lord. If you'll follow me?'

Lord Kingarth! It was the first time he had chosen to use the title, as far as Isabella knew. As they followed the porter through the most forbidding and largest of the doors in the façade, she felt she was in the company of not one, but two strangers. Eugene was wearing a different coat today. Better quality, though still plain black. His gloves and hat, too, were different, but it wasn't the clothes that intimidated her, it was the set of his shoulders, the tone in which he had spoken, of a man who expected his wishes to be granted.

Inside the workhouse, the reception area was spartan but clean, smelling of bleach and beeswax, but while they waited, other smells permeated. Overcooked cabbage and suet pudding, the stench of unwashed bodies and overflowing latrines, mingled disconcertingly with the smell of freshly baked bread.

'It's so quiet,' Isabella said in puzzlement. 'There must be upwards of a thousand men, women and children here, yet you can't hear a sound.'

'Most of them will be working in the outhouses, out at the back. I doubt they'll be permitted in the wards during the day, which are at the front of the building where we are. I wrote a piece on a workhouse in Liverpool,' Eugene explained. 'It wasn't nearly as grand as this though.' The silence stretched. 'I used the title for a purpose,' he said quietly.

'I know. I understand. It was a surprise. I don't think of you as Lord Kingarth. And it was effective.'

'It's the first time I've used one of those calling cards, too,' he said wryly. 'The lawyer had them printed. I reckoned if I told them I was a journalist, we'd get short shrift.'

'I understand,' Isabella said, relieved to hear him sound more like himself. 'Eugene, have you asked yourself...?'

'Whatever you have been thinking, I assure you, it will have occurred to me,' he said. 'I've barely slept.'

'Nor I.' A vision of the letters, neatly tied, in the secret drawer, popped into her head, to be banished immediately.

'Lord Kingarth.' A portly man with a bald head and bushy whiskers, dressed in a shiny black suit, appeared, holding out his hand. 'This is an unexpected pleasure. I am Jeremiah Brown, the Master here. How may I help you?'

* * *

The Master's office was stuffy, packed with over-large furniture. Leather-bound ledgers filled the shelves covering one wall and a huge desk took up another. An elephant's foot held a selection of canes, walking sticks and several umbrellas. Jeremiah Brown ushered Eugene into the largest seat facing the desk, leaving Isabella to perch on one considerably smaller and shorter. A deep-bosomed woman in a black dress and white cap appeared in the doorway, clearly, out of breath.

'Lord Kingarth, may I introduce you to my wife, who also serves as Matron at this establishment?'

'This is Miss Armstrong,' Eugene said as the Matron made a deep curtsy. Isabella received the merest dip and, from the Master, barely a nod. Had he introduced her as Lady Isabella, it would have been a different matter. A very different matter—for a start, Isabella would have been furious with him. He had missed her ridiculously yesterday. Time and again, he'd found himself on the brink of heading for Bloomsbury, wanting to talk over his thoughts, discuss his questions, try to make sense of what he had learned. He knew in his heart it was an excuse, though, and that was what had kept him pacing the rooms of the house he still thought of as belonging to his brother. Christmas was looming and with it an ending he didn't want to face.

'You have timed your visit well.' The Master's voice interrupted Eugene's thoughts. 'I would not go as far as to say this is our quiet part of the day, but it is our least busy, with dinner over and our inmates productively occupied.'

Inmates. The word made him grind his teeth. For

so many of them this place was indeed a prison. 'It is the fate of one of your—your patients which brings me here,' Eugene said, managing to suppress his rage. 'A Mrs Rebecca Barnford.'

Mrs Brown had taken a seat by her husband's side behind the desk, allowing Eugene to study them both carefully, but the name evoked no reaction. 'She arrived here,' he continued, 'at some point in the spring of 1854.'

'More than two years ago!' Mr Brown exclaimed. 'We have, regretfully, a very high turnover of inmates, it cannot be expected that we recall a woman among so many, from so long ago.'

'But you keep records,' Eugene said.

'Meticulously.' Mr Brown's mouth firmed. 'They are highly confidential, however. May I enquire as to the nature of your concern for this woman?'

Eugene hesitated. Did the answer lie in one of those ledgers lined up in the bookcase? He and Isabella were relying on the word of an old woman they hadn't even met. Had he been too previous, coming here without speaking to her first? But he was here now. He leaned forward confidentially. 'I hope you will understand, sir, that this is a most delicate matter. May I trust you?'

It was one of his stock questions as a journalist, posed not with any expectation of a truthful reply, but in order to make the recipient feel privileged. As he expected, the Master and Matron leaned towards him, nodding. 'Of course,' Mr Brown said, 'of course, my lord. Nothing you say will go further than this room.'

Did he believe them? 'I appreciate that very much, Mr Brown, very much indeed,' Eugene said gravely. 'As indeed, both Miss Armstrong and I appreciate the work you and your good lady do in institutions such as this one,' he added. 'Miss Armstrong was a nurse in the Crimea and is now involved in making a study of how we can improve the care we provide for our indigent.'

'Indeed—' Isabella took her cue, to his relief '—I believe we can learn a great deal from infirmaries such as yours. Many women choose to have their babies here, I'm told, for the care they receive is—is a great deal better than elsewhere.'

'You are quite right, Miss Armstrong,' Mrs Brown said, vehemently. 'So few people understand that we provide a true service to the community.'

Eugene listened as Mrs Brown, aided and abetted by her husband, launched into a eulogy. He sensed Isabella's growing indignation, but a quick glance in her direction reassured him that her expression remained suitably bland, though he was sure her hands would be tightly clasped under the folds of her cloak.

'Naturally, such a service comes at great expense,' he said, when the couple finally finished speaking and sufficient distance had been placed between his request for information and the bribe he was about to offer. 'I shall be honoured to make a contribution.

Impatiently, he waited while the couple exclaimed over his generosity, then proceeded to expound at length on just how costly everything was in an effort to increase the value of his donation. 'And you put me in mind that Christmas is coming,' he said, when their thanks and protestations finally came to a close. 'I shall send you a draft from my bank tomorrow which will include a sum to be used for the occasion. Now, to return for a moment to the matter of Mrs Barnford.'

The couple exchanged a look. 'Is the woman a relative, my lord?'

'As I said, Barnford is the family name.' They waited for him to expand on this. Eugene forced his expression into one of polite enquiry and waited for the silence to make them uncomfortable. He didn't have to wait long.

'Spring 1854, you say?' Mr Brown got to his feet and ran a finger along the ledgers, extracting one from the middle of a shelf. 'Here we are.'

He set it down on the desk and began, painfully slowly, to examine the pages. Eugene fought to sit still, wanting to wrest the book from him. Isabella's foot nudged his. He nodded, not daring to look at her, but returning the pressure, grateful for her presence. When the Master paused and his wife peered into the ledger, he thought he might scream.

'What is your exact relationship to Rebecca Barnford?'

There was a sharp note in the Matron's voice which had not been there before. They had found her. Eugene decided the time had come to stop prevaricating. 'She is my brother's wife.' He extracted the marriage certificate from his pocket and spread it out on the table. He did not say that Wilbur was his elder brother. He did not say that Rebecca had been a countess. 'My brother died six weeks ago,' he said. His knees were shaking. He sank back on to his chair. 'For reasons beyond my understanding, he and his wife were estranged. It is my desire—I would very much like—I want…' He couldn't carry on. To his horror, his eyes were smarting with tears again.

'Lord Kingarth is naturally concerned for the welfare of his brother's wife,' Isabella said. 'His motives are entirely honourable. He wishes to ensure that his brother's widow is comfortably provided for, that is all.'

'I'm afraid it's too late, my lord.' Mr Brown was visibly shaken. 'I am extremely sorry to have to inform you that the woman died. She was in a most decrepit state when she arrived, it says here. There was nothing we could do.'

'I don't give a damn...'

Isabella kicked his foot. 'Lord Kingarth has no desire to apportion blame.'

The Master looked miserably at his wife. It was Mrs Brown who spoke. 'Rebecca Barnford died in the infirmary, three days after her arrival. Her death is certified here in the ledger. Since she stated upon entry to the workhouse that she had no relatives, we bore the cost of her burial.' The couple exchanged another look. 'There is another matter, my lord. Rebecca Barnford died while giving birth to a child.'

'Yes.' He was suddenly very, very tired. 'Yes, I know. I will attend to the matter of the burial. If the grave cannot be located...'

'She was buried a pauper, my lord,' Mr Brown said. 'I'm afraid that means it will be impossible to locate her mortal remains.'

'Then I will have them commemorated in another way.' He hauled himself to his feet and picked up the wedding certificate. 'You will have my bank draft tomorrow. I am sure I can rely on your discretion.'

'Yes, my lord, but you seem to be under a misapprehension.' Mr Brown turned the ledger round so that he could see it, pointing at an entry. 'The child did not die with her mother. She was a robust infant, of some eight and a half pounds, and is now resident here, with our other orphaned children.'

Chapter Nine

It had started to snow on the drive back from the work-house to Bloomsbury. Isabella turned up the gas lamps in the parlour and threw a shovelful of coals on to the fire. Eugene was sitting, staring down at the glass of brandy she had poured for him. He had not taken a sip. He had not said a word since they left the workhouse. She knelt down beside him, resting her hand on his knee.

'You don't need to rush into anything. Take your time to consider the implications. Mr and Mrs Brown won't say anything or do anything precipitate. They are almost as shocked as you are.'

'They wouldn't let me see her.' His lip curled. 'It seems like there are limits to the power of a title after all.'

'You'd have thought less of them, if they had been persuaded by your rank to break the rules. Their prime concern, as it should be, is for little Becky's welfare.'

'As always, you are the voice of reason.' Eugene took a sip of brandy and shuddered. 'I am sorry I was so rude to them. You're right, I should be glad that they stood their ground. It's a crime against humanity that such places exist, but they provide a vital service and they do so to the best of their ability. I want her out of there as soon as possible though, Isabella.'

She got to her feet and poured herself a small brandy, dreading what she was about to say, but unable to persuade herself, as she had tried to on the journey back, to say nothing. 'According to the workhouse register, Becky's birthday is in April,' she said, sitting down opposite him.

'And Wilbur and Rebecca were married in the August.' Eugene sat up, clutching his glass. 'She might have arrived early. Her mother's illness would have made that likely, wouldn't it?'

Honoria would know. Oh, God, if only she could consult Honoria. 'Possibly,' Isabella said. She took a sip of her own drink, coughing as it burned its way down her throat, then set the glass aside. She needed a clear head. 'A baby of eight and a half pounds is large, even for a full term. I asked Mrs Brown when you were trying to persuade her husband to let you see Becky.'

'I know what you're trying to say. I had my suspicions when Mrs Brown used the word robust one time too many. I saw her looking at the marriage certificate, looking at the ledger. It doesn't matter. I don't care.' He threw back his brandy, a smile dawning on his face. 'I simply don't care.'

'I don't understand.'

'Wilbur and Rebecca may have jumped the gun. Little Becky may have been the reason my brother proposed. It's possible, isn't it? Remember the circumstances of their first meeting. He was attacked, she saved him. It's highly romantic, don't you think? The most natural thing in the world for gratitude to lead to desire. My brother was extremely good looking and he could be quite charming. She wouldn't have stood a chance. So that's one scenario, isn't it?'

'Yes,' Isabella agreed, bewildered by his sudden change in mood. 'But there's another, Eugene, that you haven't thought of.'

'I have.' He joined her on the sofa, taking her hand, his smile fading. 'She may already have been expecting. She may have seen Wilbur as her chance to escape the shame of being a single mother. She may have come clean to him. She may have lied to him. She may have fled because her conscience wouldn't let her go through with it. Did she know that she wasn't Mrs Barnford but Lady Kingarth? We don't even know that for certain. It may be that she knew who he really was and realised how unsuited she was to the position. She may have loved him enough to do what she thought best for him, to disappear without a trace, to leave him free to marry a more suitable woman. Any or all of that is possible.'

'And where does that leave Wilbur, when she fled? Happy to have the whole problem solved for him? I don't think so. He kept the certificate, Isabella. He considered himself married and it doesn't appear that he made any effort to change that. You see, the journalist in me has analysed it from all angles, but I know enough about Wilbur to be sure,' Eugene said, touching his heart, 'that he would never, ever have abandoned his child.'

The journalist had analysed the situation from all angles, but Eugene was an honourable man who would make the decision with his heart and not his head. He was also the man, she could no longer deny, who had worked his way into her heart, despite her best attempts to prevent him. She didn't want to love him, but she did and she couldn't regret it.

She had never for a moment considered they would have a future together. Her fierce desire to remain independent, to make her own choices, to keep control of her own life, made her determinedly against marriage, even if she were considered an acceptable wife for an earl, and she was not much more acceptable than poor Rebecca. Lord Armstrong had given her his name. Legally, she was his legitimate offspring, but morally he had no claim on her and she was glad of that. She belonged to no one, though her heart was no longer her own.

She pressed Eugene's hand to her cheek. 'Your brother didn't know about Becky, but you do, that's it, isn't it? Becky Barnford is to become the new Lord Kingarth's ward?'

'And the acknowledged daughter of the previous Lord Kingarth. That will give Wilbur's lawyer something to get his teeth into.'

'And your sister?'

'Cecily will love the child, if she believes her to be Wilbur's. I'd like to say that she'd love her regardless, but I know that's not true.'

'But you will? Even though you haven't met her yet?'

'I hope so.'

'You're taking an awful lot on, Eugene.'

'I know I am. It's not that I feel I have no choice though—you know that with the title comes responsibilities. It's what *I* want to do, what *I* feel is right.' He rolled his eyes. 'Who would have thought that today would end like this? I feel as if I've been through a mangle.'

'You're exhausted.'

'I was.' He turned towards her, smiling slowly, in a very different way. 'I'm not now, though strangely enough the idea of going to bed is extremely appealing.'

Her heart skipped a beat as it always did when he smiled at her like that. Had it been love that drew her to him, from that very first night? She ran her fingers through his hair, leaning into him. She loved him so much. Their lips met and she told him how much with her kisses.

It was as it always was with him, making love made her body thrum with delight and anticipation the moment he touched her, yet tonight it was different. She loved him. Their kisses melted one into another into another, but they did not rush, by tacit agreement taking their time to relish every kiss, every piece of skin revealed as they slowly undressed in front of the fire. She feasted her eyes on him, stroked him, tasted him, learning every bit of him with all of her senses, and he did the same, his eyes and his hands and his mouth hungry for her, slowly devouring her.

Naked, they sank down on to the hearth rug, kissing. She loved him. She loved him so much. Lying on her back, she reached for him, wanting him inside her, but he drew back, kissing her breasts again, kissing down her belly and then lower, licking inside her, drawing a deep guttural moan from her, and quickly sending her spiralling over the edge.

She bit her lip in her effort not to speak the words she wanted to cry out. He pulled her towards him. She wrapped her legs around his thighs and he rocked into her, making her shudder, drawing his name from her in a low moan. Their mouths met again. She held him tightly, high inside her, feeling him pulse, hearing him gasp, his heart thudding hard, and then they lost control, urgent, fast in their need, and when it was over and they lay together, there was no need for words. She loved him. She would always remember this. Always.

Eugene awoke to find himself naked on the hearth rug, with a pillow under his head, a blanket covering him. He sat up, scrabbling for his watch, astonished to discover that it was almost nine o'clock. He had missed dinner. His butler would be wondering what had become of him. *His* butler? Was he finally beginning to think of himself as Lord Kingarth? He considered this for a moment. The name opened doors, he had proved that today, doors which would have remained closed to his alter ego, The Torch. He had always assumed that Lord Kingarth and The Torch were mutually exclusive, but was there a way to combine the two?

A question for another day. Right now, he had more than enough on his plate. He stood up, rolling his shoulders and picking his shirt up from the floor. Where was Isabella? Was it his imagination, or had their lovemaking tonight been different? More intense? Was that possible? Was it because the day had been so fraught?

He laughed softly to himself. That was something of an understatement. Had he leapt to a decision too quickly? Ought he to consider what he was taking on more carefully? He knew nothing about children and Wilbur's daughter wasn't even three years old. Wilbur's daughter? Yes, that was how he would think of her. Rebecca was Wilbur's wife. He *knew,* just as he had said to Isabella, that Wilbur would have cared for her child.

Good lord, Cecily was to be an aunt. Little Becky would have three cousins. He had never taken much interest in Cecily's daughters. That was one of many changes he was going to have to make. There would be a nanny to find, a nursery to equip. How long would it take for the wheels of bureaucracy to turn before Wilbur's child could be released from the workhouse and come home? It would be a slow and drawn-out process, even with title and wealth to urge it on.

And what of his own Christmas plans, with Isabella? Now that he had found Becky, he would have to devote himself to fighting her cause. Their affair, and his involvement in the soup kitchen would be over. No. Fully clothed, Eugene dropped on to the sofa. No, no, no. He could not lose her and he could not renege on the promises he had made either, to help out over Christmas. Somehow he'd have to find the time. But afterwards?

Closing his eyes, he leaned back against the sofa. Afterwards? They had known each other less than two weeks, for heaven's sake, and he had never in his life felt like this with another woman. It wasn't surprising that he didn't want it to end. Not yet. Not ever.

He sat up abruptly. What the hell! He could not possibly be imagining himself in love! Not in two weeks. Not to a woman who was determined to live independently, to make her own life, and who most certainly would not wish to take on a husband, let alone a child. He could not have been so stupid as to fall in love with Isabella, could he?

Did he love her? Eugene swore under his breath, but

then he smiled. It explained so much. The way he had
been drawn to her from the moment he met her. They
were kindred spirits, he'd known that, but he hadn't realised what it meant. He loved her. They were meant to
be together. They were meant for each other. He laughed
again, softly mocking himself, but it made no difference. He was in love with Isabella. Oh, God, but what
on earth was he going to do about it? And what did she
feel for him? In a single day, he had managed to turn
his entire world upside down again. He couldn't imagine his life without a child he hadn't even met yet, and
it was even more impossible to imagine his life without
Isabella. What the hell was he going to do!

Take Isabella's advice. Think. Take his time. Don't
rush into anything. Wilbur's death had upended his life.
Now that he'd discovered Becky, he was going to turn
her life on its head. The workhouse was no place for
a child, but it was the only home she had ever known,
a place where at least she was surrounded by familiar
faces. Cecily would see her arrival as the perfect excuse to push for him to find a wife. It would be easier
for him to take care of Becky if he had a wife, but he
was damned if he was going to marry for that reason.
Or for the title. Isabella would insist she was completely
unsuited for both and she'd be right, and he wouldn't
insult her, anyway, by suggesting it. He didn't want a
wife, he wanted what he had here, with Isabella.

He couldn't have it. Sooner rather than later, he was
going to have to, in his own stupid words, step up to
the mark and step into his new life. He would forget her
eventually. She would forget him, too. What he was feel-

ing was love right now, but it wouldn't last. Starved of
her company, it would wither and die, as such things do.

But he didn't need to starve himself of her just yet.
Now, more than ever, he determined to make the most
of the time they had. Where was she? Probably in the
kitchen. Picking up his jacket, Eugene made his way
downstairs. There was a light shining from the door to
the dining room where she had stacked the excess furniture. She had kindled the fire and was kneeling down in
front of it. Her hair tumbled down her back in a mass of
wild curls and she was dressed in a red silk wrapper pat-
terned with brightly coloured, embroidered dragons, tied
with a sash. The fabric clung, showing the curve of her
back, the indent of her waist, the shape of her bottom.
Desire and yearning flooded him. He wanted to hold
her, to whisper that he loved her, to make love to her.

'You were so soundly asleep,' she said, getting to her
feet. 'I had not the heart to waken you.'

She had been burning papers. The desk. He remembered now that it was her mother's, full of papers, she
had said, that she hadn't gone through. There was only
one drawer open, in the side of the desk, exactly the
same place where the secret drawer in his brother's desk
was placed. There was a bundle inside. Letters, tied up
with a red ribbon. He could tell by the way she looked
at it that it was significant.

'I found them on Sunday,' Isabella said.

'You haven't opened them.'

'I don't want to.'

They were addressed to Lady Armstrong. Killellan Manor. The country residence where Isabella had

spent her early years. He knew then that they could be only one thing.

'From my mother's lover.' Her voice had hardened.

'From your father.' He stared at the letters, mesmerised for a moment. How would he feel? He would want to know. 'You found these yesterday and you never said a word.'

'You had enough to worry about.'

'These letters will tell you who your father is.' He studied her now, puzzled. 'Are you afraid to open them?'

She shook her head slowly. 'I was at first. I didn't want to touch them. But what happened today made me think again. *You* made me think again with what you said, about little Becky. It doesn't matter, you said, what the truth of her parentage is. You are choosing to believe that she's your brother's child.' She blinked, her mouth trembling. 'It's such a wonderful attitude to take.'

He winced, thinking now how it must have affected her, the horrible parallel he had unwittingly drawn for her with the man she had believed was her father, who had rejected her so cruelly from beyond the grave, the brothers who had followed their father's lead. And this unknown man, who had rejected her from birth. He tried to pull her into his arms, but she shook her head, pushing him away.

'Don't feel sorry for me. I promise you, I don't need or want pity.'

'Neither of them deserved you,' Eugene said fiercely.

Isabella smiled faintly. 'That is precisely what I have concluded.' She reached for the letters, picking them up and holding them at arm's length. 'I am not Lord Armstrong's daughter. I am not this man's daughter. I am myself. I don't want to know who that man is. I don't want to know why he never claimed me. All that matters is that he did not. He made a choice. And now I am making my own choice, too.'

She turned, taking him by surprise by throwing the letters into the blaze. For a long moment the two of them stared motionless as the bundle smouldered, still retrievable in those few seconds. He had to fight the urge to pull them from the blaze. He had no right to interfere. Then the ribbon took light and the decision was made final. The papers crackled, then went up in flames, turning quickly to ash.

Isabella gave a deep sigh and pushed the secret drawer of the desk closed. 'Thank you.'

'What for?'

'For helping me to see that I had a choice.'

'Are you sure you've made the right one?'

'Oh, yes. As soon as I decided, I knew it was right.' She touched her heart. 'Just as you did, today, when you found out about Becky.'

And when I finally put a name to what I feel for you, Eugene thought. *It was love.*

He opened his mouth to tell her, despite his resolution not to, but Isabella pre-empted him.

'You came to Hackney to find Rebecca. You've found her now and her child, too, and the little girl must take priority with you. I think it's best that you focus your attention on her.'

She was right. It was what he had already concluded, but there was a finality in her voice that set alarm bells ringing. 'I won't be able to spend as much time in Hackney as I had planned, but I have no intentions of reneging on my promises to help. There's the pantomime to organise and the geese to buy and the tree to be decorated. I've been looking forward to that.'

'So are the children. They can talk of little else. Do you really think you will be able to persuade your friend to allow them to go to the pantomime?'

'Yes, I believe so.'

'I wouldn't want them to miss such a treat.'

'*I* don't want to miss the treat of seeing their faces. We planned this Christmas together, Isabella. The family Christmas neither of us ever had.'

She nodded, turning her face away. 'You'll have a family of your own next Christmas.'

'I want to be part of your family in Hackney this Christmas.'

'We knew that this—our affair—we knew it couldn't last. Christmas is still ten days away and you have found Becky.'

'Are you saying—are you trying to tell me that it's over?'

'After today, it's very clear that our paths are going in different directions and it's better that you start now, on the new life you are so anxious to embrace.'

'I can do both.' She turned, eyeing him sceptically. 'For a couple of weeks at any rate,' he added. 'What are you trying to say?'

'Nothing. It's been a long and eventful day for both of us.'

'That was a very brave thing to do,' Eugene said, looking at the empty grate.

'It was the right thing. The last remnant of the past swept away—or it will be, when I have had this fur-

niture cleared. And after Christmas, I have decided I
will push ahead with my idea for a creche or a nursery
while you—you will be starting a nursery of your own,
on a much smaller scale.'

What was he doing? All he wanted was to have her
arms around him, to lie together, not to make love, but
to hold each other and to sleep. 'I'm terrified,' Eugene
whispered.

'So you should be,' Isabella said, smiling gently.
'You'll make it work, in your own way. I have every
faith in you.' Finally she did as he had longed for her to
do—she wrapped her arms around his waist. She laid
her head on his chest. But then she let him go. 'It's getting late and I have plans of my own to make. You'd
better get back to Mayfair.'

Chapter Ten

Hackney—Wednesday, December 24th, Christmas Eve

The Christmas tree was so large that the top was almost brushing the ceiling of the hall. Someone had brought a set of stepladders along and Eugene was perched precariously on top of them, taking mirthful direction from two of the boys. Janet Simpson had organised the younger ones into groups and assigned them each a specific decoration to hang on the lower branches, while the bigger children stood on chairs to reach higher.

There were sugar canes and candied fruit, glazed cherries, sugar plums, gingerbread men, women and children, marzipan cats and dogs, and little bags of sugared almonds. About half of them made it on to the tree, with the rest consumed en route.

At the table in the centre of the room, Maisy was supervising the creation of garlands made with holly and bay, and bucketloads of mistletoe, which had been left on the doorstep first thing this morning. Eugene's doing, as was the tree, and the geese which were hang-

ing in the larder waiting to be roasted—a process which
Maisy was planning to start today, for they would have
three sittings at Christmas dinner tomorrow.

The room was filled with the sound of laughter and
squeals of glee from the children and the air was redo-
lent of the festive greenery. It was everything Isabella
had never had and all she had wished for. She was delighted and proud of what she had achieved here, which
was so much more than she had ever thought possible when she returned from the Crimea. But the clock
was ticking. She was dreading Christmas Day. She had
no idea how she was going to find the courage to say
goodbye.

Eugene was holding the angel up now, encouraging
the children to shout up, higher, higher, higher, and to
clap and stamp their feet when he finally positioned
the figure on the topmost branch. He made a sweeping
bow, garnering another round of applause. Their eyes
met across the room and his smile became fixed. Colouring, Isabella looked away. She knew he, too, was
counting the hours, though, like her, he said nothing.
There was nothing to be said. That night, after she had
burned Bella's letters, the day he had discovered Becky,
they had said it all.

She knew that a clean break would have been better, that it would have been wiser for her to insist, as
she had tried to do, on an ending, but her heart was not
wise. She loved him. That he cared for her, too, deeply,
she didn't doubt, but it changed nothing. Their lovemaking had had a desperate quality to it. Afterwards,
they'd clung together, their bodies twined, but she felt

increasingly cast adrift. At this most intimate of moments, she had felt utterly alone.

'He's behind you! *Behind* you!'

The children shouted and screamed and pointed from their benches in the stalls, their voices echoing in the vast space of the otherwise empty theatre. Blanchard had been waiting in the foyer to greet Eugene, eyeing Isabella and the swarm of children who had filled several tramcars with amused astonishment. His play, *See-Saw, Margery Daw*, relied a great deal on costumes and farce and not very much on plot, he had informed them, but it was not vulgar and the sort of thing that Christmas audiences seemed to like. Audience participation was encouraged apparently.

This particular audience didn't require much encouragement, Eugene thought, as the screams turned to laughter. His own pleasure, in the last few days, had become decidedly bittersweet. Working with Isabella in the soup kitchen had given him a new insight into the lives of people he had previously assumed to be enduring unmitigated misery and suffering. Kindness was their strength, caring for each other and sharing what little they had. Looking back at some of his well-intentioned reporting, he cringed now at how patronising his words had been.

He had changed. The need to tell a story, to rail against the unfairness of the world he lived in was still there, but he wanted to do it differently. The written word wasn't enough, Isabella's practical philanthropy appealed to him. He studied her, seated at the end of the row, seemingly engrossed in the pantomime. He loved her and he knew that it was not a fleeting passion, as he'd tried to convince himself. He loved her.

His world had been turned upside down, and the state of turmoil in which he existed was set to continue, but his love for her was the only certainty. The reason he had found himself unable, time and again, to imagine saying goodbye to her tomorrow was because it was impossible. He had no idea how they would make a future together, but he knew, he knew with absolute certainty, that he wanted to try and that any future together, on whatever terms, was better than none.

'It's behind you,' the children screamed and, smiling, Eugene joined in enthusiastically.

The pantomime had been an unrivalled success. Back at the hall, Maisy and her squad of helpers had gone home. The last of the geese were cooked. The puddings were steamed. The sacks of potatoes stood lined up, ready to be peeled first thing in the morning. The tables were set for the first dinner sitting, which would be at twelve. The tree was groaning with decorations. The walls were decked with greenery. The air was scented with roast goose and pine needles. There was nothing more to be done tonight.

Isabella pulled on her cloak as Eugene emerged from the kitchen, her stomach fluttering with nerves. She longed to be alone with him and at the same time she dreaded it. She yearned to make love to him, but she was afraid that it would be the last time and she wasn't sure she could bear it. 'Maisy is planning on being here by seven,' she said. 'I was thinking that…'

'Never mind Maisy. *I've* been thinking, Isabella.'

She felt sick. Eugene looked queasy. Was this good-bye? Perhaps it was better this way. Oh, God, let her endure it stoically. She nodded, unable to speak.

He opened his mouth, then closed it again, shaking his head. 'I've had all afternoon to think of how to put this.'

She closed her eyes, gripping the back of the chair. 'Just say it.'

'I love you.'

Her eyes flew open. Her mouth formed an 'oh', but no sound came out.

'I love you,' Eugene said again, taking her hand. 'I knew I loved you the night I woke up in front of the fire in your parlour and I came downstairs and found you burning those letters. I knew I loved you then, but I had no idea what to do about it, how you felt, whether we could even—there seemed to be so many barriers. So I kept quiet.'

Eugene loved her. Eugene loved her! Isabella fell on to the chair. Her heart had soared and now it plummeted. She shook her head, trying to tell him not to speak, but he had dropped on to one knee in front of her. No, no, no, she thought, dimly aware that a part of her was thinking, yes, yes, yes.

'I know you don't want to get married. I thought I didn't want to get married either. I don't—not for the sake of the title or in order to give Becky a mother. I would never marry for either of those reasons.'

'No,' Isabella whispered, a refusal, a denial, for herself as much to him.

'I thought I'd wait,' he said, still holding her hand, looking up at her earnestly. 'I thought I'd wait until I had made a home for Becky, until I'd decided what to do with myself as Lord Kingarth, until you had made your plans, until there was some sort of order restored. That's what I told myself. Too much change, so best to wait. But today, thinking about tomorrow being Christmas Day, the day we had agreed we would part, I was trying to imagine myself living without you—I simply couldn't do it, Isabella.'

'No. Eugene, I can't—I don't want to—think about what you're saying. It's impossible.'

'I knew you'd say so. I thought it was. If you don't love me, then you're right. But I love you and what I realised today is that you matter to me, more than anyone, more than anything. We have each other now. We have no idea what the future might hold. There might be another war. Life is fragile, we both know that. Look at Wilbur, cut off in his prime and he never knew the fate of his wife, never knew he had a child. I don't want that. We have each other now.'

His mouth trembled. He tightened his grip on her hand. 'I love you with all my heart, Isabella. It's the one thing I know. I love you. I will always love you. And if you love me, too, then I am asking you to take a chance on me. On us. To marry me. And together, we'll find a way to make it work.'

She wanted to throw herself into his arms. She wanted, to her astonishment, to say yes. She wanted to ignore everything she thought she knew about herself, about what she wanted from her life, and to give herself to him. She wanted to. She longed to. But her independence had been so short-lived.

She did not want to become part of Eugene's life as Lord Kingarth, as an adoptive father, or even as a newspaper journalist. She didn't want to become subsumed, to be a prop or even a support. She didn't want to become the clinging vine that her mother had been. Eugene meant it, she didn't doubt that, when he said he wanted to find a way to make their marriage work, but it simply wasn't possible because she wasn't prepared to sacrifice herself completely.

'I can't.' Her voice didn't tremble. The words were the right ones, she knew as soon as they were spoken. 'I'm sorry.' Gently, she pulled her hands free.

He stared at her for a long moment, then got to his feet. 'You think marriage is a prison.'

'Not a prison, but I would have to give up so much. My plans, my dreams.'

'I would never put you in chains, Isabella. I love you. I don't want to change you.'

'But I would have no option but to change. I'd be your wife. Becky's mother. I'd be Lady Kingarth.' She shuddered. 'Can you imagine what they'd say about you, if my brothers ever chose to broadcast the truth about my heritage?'

'I don't give a damn about that.'

'But your sister would.'

'I don't care what Cecily says. I only care about you.'

'You are going to need your sister on your side, when Becky comes to live with you.'

'I don't *need* my sister. I want you by my side. I cannot imagine why your brothers would rake over those old ashes and I know you, Isabella, you don't actually care about them either. Please don't use that as an excuse. If you don't love me, then say so.'

It would be the easiest thing. The kindest thing in the long run. 'I—I can't,' Isabella whispered. 'I do love you.'

His face lit up. He took a step towards her, then stopped. One word and he would sweep her into his arms and she could lose herself in him. He would make love to her. He would love her and she would love him. And then…

'I do love you,' Isabella said, 'but it's not enough.'

Eugene flinched. He stood, his throat working, his fingers clenching and unclenching. Then he nodded. 'You're right. It wouldn't work because you won't give it a chance.'

'I would be the one making the sacrifices,' Isabella said, relieved to give way to anger. 'I would be the one who would have to change. I would be the one forced to move house, to change my name, to give up my work here, to play mother to a child I've never met.'

'You have no issue with playing mother to the children who come here every day and you'd never met any of them until a few months ago.' Eugene pulled on his overcoat. 'You're not listening. We would both have to make sacrifices, we'd both have to adapt, but think of the reward! A life together. Not the life I have or the life you have, but a different life. A better life, simply because we'd have each other.'

He waited, but she had nothing more to say and her

throat was clogged with tears. Eugene picked up his hat and gloves. 'I won't try to change your mind. I don't want to persuade you, but if you ever change your mind, you know where to find me. I'll wish you happy Christmas now, as I won't be here tomorrow. Good luck, Isabella—I hope all your Christmas wishes come true.'

Chapter Eleven

Hackney—one year later
Friday, December 25th, 1857, Christmas Day

The last sitting of Christmas dinner was finished. The hall was empty. The children had stripped the Christmas tree of its decorations. The boughs of holly and bay and mistletoe were beginning to droop. The day had been a huge success, as had Christmas Eve, when the tree had been decorated, and the Saturday before, when the children had once again gathered to make presents.

There had been a return visit to the pantomime for the dress rehearsal yesterday, too, to see *Little Jack Horner*, organised by Mr Blanchard, the playwright, though she suspected Eugene had played a part behind the scenes. She assumed he had sent the geese for dinner, too, and the tree, though they had been delivered anonymously.

Isabella pulled on her cloak and dimmed the gas sconces before locking the main door of the hall. Outside, the streets were deserted. Everyone was home with their families. She had never felt so alone. Even Honoria had, to her astonishment, married—and was deliriously happy, too. It had been exactly a year and a day since she had last seen Eugene. A year and a day since his proposal. A year and a day since he had left her alone, as she had asked him to, to get on with her life. To be her own woman. Independent. Answerable to no one. Free to live as she chose.

She hadn't wasted her time. Mrs Simpson had taken over the day-to-day running of the soup kitchen, delighted by the small wage that went with it. Isabella had established the Hackney crèche, delighting more mothers by providing a precious few hours' freedom. There had barely been a day in the last year which she had not put to good use, planning or working. And barely a day had gone by without her wondering, what was Eugene doing? Did he miss her? Was he happy?

Wearily, tipping the cabby and wishing him a Merry Christmas, she unlocked her front door and stepped into the hallway, almost tripping over the small parcel that lay on the floor. She picked it up, frowning. It must have been pushed through the letter box, for there was no address. Hanging her cloak up and taking off her hat, Isabella hurried up the stairs to the parlour. It was cold—she had been out since six this morning and had not bothered to stoke the fire.

She turned up the gas sconce and sat down on the sofa, pulling the blanket she kept there over her shoulders. The package was wrapped in red paper, tied with a green ribbon. Inside was small leather box. Her heart began to pound as she opened the clasp. Nestled on a pillow of velvet was a necklace on a gold chain, made of enamel in the form of a sprig of mistletoe, with three pearls for berries.

'Three kisses?' She closed her eyes, remembering Eugene's wicked smile. 'Three kisses?' he'd said, sweeping her into his arms. 'I think we can do better than that.'

Under the necklace was a card.

I hope all your Christmas wishes have come true.

She had not permitted herself to cry over the loss of him. The choice had been hers and it had been the right one. She had no regrets. It would have been a mistake to accept his proposal last year, but in the year which had passed, she had changed. She had proved herself. She had learned a great deal about her resilience, her determination. She had learned to trust herself. Last year, she had only just begun to discover who Isabella was. Now she knew. She was content, she was free and there were times, many times, when she was happy. But there was never a moment when she didn't miss him. Now she finally understood what he meant by a better life. A different life. Together.

Was it possible? She fastened the necklace around her neck. Tomorrow, she would send him a note, ask him to call. Tomorrow, she would ask him if there was still a chance, if it wasn't too late to change her mind. She got to her feet to draw the curtains. The snow which had been falling in brief flurries all day had become heavier. The little garden she had created was covered in a white blanket. Restlessly, she picked up the box again. She read the note again.

'Life is fragile,' he had said to her that day. She had waited a year and a day. Why wait another moment? Because it was Christmas Day. What if he was hosting dinner? Or a party? He might not be at home. He might be with his sister. And then there was Becky. She didn't even know when he had won the battle to remove her from the workhouse, but he would have won it, of that she was certain. She checked the clock. It was after nine. The little girl would be in her bed. It was far too late for her to call. And it was snowing. And she would never get a cab on Christmas Day.

Eugene was staring out of the window into the garden at the back of the house. The snow was falling thick and fast. Tomorrow, he had promised Becky that they would build a snowman. The day after, he had an appointment with his lawyer to finalise the purchase of the newspaper he had been trying to buy for the last six months. After the Christmas recess, he had decided to take up his seat in the House of Lords. It was an ideal platform for him to espouse the causes closest to him. He had already drafted his maiden speech.

Weather permitting, the following week he would take the train to Yorkshire, check on the renovations which were underway at Kingarth House and the progress on the deed to set it up as an orphanage. Then there was the matter of the work he was trying to fund at Waterloo Road workhouse. Cecily said he took too much on. Now that they were out of mourning, she said, he ought to socialise more. This had, as usual, been accompanied by a meaningful look. Eugene sighed, closing the curtains.

The doorbell clanged. It was almost ten o'clock at night. He had given the staff, including Becky's nurse, the day off. Frowning, hurrying lest the bell ring again and waken her, he unlocked the door. The figure standing on his doorstep was slight, clad in a cloak that was almost covered in snow.

His heart leapt. 'Isabella.'

'I couldn't get a cab,' she said, 'so I had to walk. If I'm disturbing you... I wasn't sure if you'd have guests or even if you'd be here.'

'I'm here alone save for Becky and she is sound asleep.'

She pushed back her hood, smiling up at him. 'She's here. I knew she would be.'

'Since February.' He opened the door wider. 'Are you coming in?'

Isabella made no move, but her hand went to her neck. 'I found your gift when I got back from the soup kitchen. Thank you, it's beautiful.'

Eugene reached into the pocket of his waistcoat and pulled out the felt mistletoe. 'I couldn't bear to send the original.'

'Oh. You kept it.'

A wave of longing swept over him. He had missed her so much. He wanted to tell her that he loved her. He wanted to pull her into his arms, but he was afraid. She was here. It could only mean one thing. But what if he was wrong? A gust of wind blew a flurry of snow over the pair of them, but still they stood, transfixed, on the doorstep.

Then finally, she spoke. 'I've changed my mind.'

Her words took the breath away from him.

'You said that if I ever did—you said—' She broke off, misreading his silence. 'I'm too late, aren't I?'

She turned away, just as he found his voice. 'No! No, no, no.'

'No?'

'Never, my love.'

'I'm still your love?'

He gazed down into her heart-shaped face, into those big brown eyes that had captivated him one night in the Crimea almost two years before. 'Always and for ever.'

A tear trickled down her cheek. 'I love you so much.'

'And I love you, my darling.'

'Will you marry me, Eugene?'

He laughed softly. 'Yes, please.'

'I don't want to wait any longer.'

'I'll arrange a special licence in the morning.'

She smiled at him. The smile that sent the blood rushing to his groin. 'Your card…it said that you hoped all my Christmas wishes would come true. They have now. I only have one left. And it's still Christmas Day for two more hours. Do you think…?'

'I do,' he said, sweeping her up into his arms and carrying her over the threshold. 'Your wish is my command.'

Epilogue

It was late when Lord and Lady Kingarth's town carriage finally brought them back from Hackney to their Mayfair town house and Becky, snuggled between them, was half-asleep.

'I think you need to go straight to bed,' Eugene said, smiling down at his beloved niece. 'It's been a very long day for a little girl.'

'The angel!' Becky and Isabella cried out in unison.

Eugene laughed, opening the front door and ushering his family inside. 'How could I have forgotten? Come on, then.'

Becky led the way, clutching the angel from the Hackney tree, making eagerly for what had once been the formal drawing room at the back of the house, but which was now the room where the family spent most of their time together, and where the three of them had decorated their Christmas tree the night before. By the time Eugene and Isabella arrived, she was standing, her little face uplifted, her arms outstretched. 'Up, up, up, please, Nuncle.'

He had long since stopped trying to correct her. It had been Isabella's idea to suggest that Becky called her Nant back in January, when the two had first met, and that name, too, had stuck, the little girl becoming more stubborn when Eugene's sister persistently corrected her.

'*Aunt* Isabella, Rebecca dear,' Cecily had insisted once more, at breakfast this morning.

'Nant,' his niece had persisted, slanting Isabella one of her still-rare little smiles.

'And it is *Becky*, Mama, not Rebecca,' Cecily's eldest daughter had added, beaming across the table at her little cousin, earning herself a firm nod.

'Ready?' Eugene held his niece up to the tree, smiling down at Isabella's upturned face, concentrated hard on Becky as she struggled to position the angel. Isabella was biting her lip to stop herself from trying to help. The two women in his life, he thought, amused, were fiercely independent and neither took instruction well. Finally, the angel was in place and as he let Becky go, she gave a huge yawn.

'Bed,' Isabella said firmly, scooping her up in her arms, adding over her shoulder, 'I won't be long.'

'I'm not going anywhere,' he replied. They hadn't been alone all day. First there had been breakfast with Cecily and her family, then there had been the pantomime and Christmas dinner in Hackney. It would be a step too far to say that Cecily approved of Isabella's work in the borough, but since all three of her daughters were slightly star-struck by Isabella and now helped out at the new crèche, she kept her feelings to herself— for the most part.

He had stoked the fire and taken off his jacket by the time she returned, having changed out of her gown into a frothy wrapper.

'She was asleep as soon as her head hit the pillow,' Isabella said. 'Still clutching that little horse that Janet Simpson made for her. "The best present ever," she said.'

Eugene laughed, recalling the huge stack of presents which Becky had opened this morning. 'I hope she doesn't repeat that to Cecily. Come here,' he said, holding up the felt mistletoe. 'I've been waiting all day for my kiss.'

Isabella stepped into his arms. 'One,' she said, kissing him lightly on the lips. 'Two,' she said, wrapping her arms around his neck and kissing him again.

'Three,' Eugene murmured, forgetting everything as she melted into him. Their lips met, their kiss deepened and the outside world disappeared as it always did when he was in her arms, leaving only the two of them, in their own world. 'I love you so much,' he murmured. 'This has been the best ever Christmas.'

'I haven't even given you your present yet.'

'Every day with you is a gift.'

'You say the most delightful things.'

'It's the truth,' he said, kissing her again. 'We've had our moments, you and I and Becky, but we're happy, aren't we? More than I had ever dreamed of.'

'We are. Very happy. More than I ever dreamed of,'

Isabella agreed, 'but I think my present might make all of us even happier.'

'What do you mean?'

'This time next year, our little family will be four, not three.' Her smile was tender as she took his hand to place it over her stomach. 'Happy Christmas, darling.'

* * * * *

If you enjoyed this story, check out the other instalments in Marguerite Kaye's Revelations of the Carstairs Sisters miniseries

**The Earl Who Sees Her Beauty
Lady Armstrong's Scandalous Awakening**

Historical Note

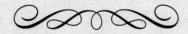

As usual, there's a ton of research embedded in this book—way too much to cover in this note—and, as usual, any mistakes in the research are entirely my own.

There's so much written about Florence Nightingale and nursing in the Crimea that I won't give recommendations here. Suffice it to say that women like Isabella, with a vocation and the money to fund themselves, did work as nurses, providing much-needed care separate from Nightingale's hospitals in Scutari. Mary Seacole is probably the most famous example.

The area where Isabella sets up her soup kitchen takes inspiration from the notorious slum called the Old Nichol, which was pulled down in 1889. It is described in very vivid detail in Sarah Wise's excellent book *The Blackest Streets*. Father Turner is modelled on the real-life Father Jay Osborne, who established a Men's Mission in the Old Nichol, an ambivalent character with very strong feelings on who would, or would not, benefit from his charity.

The French chef Alexis Soyer transformed the kitchens for the British in the Crimea and patented a field kitchen stove which was used for over a hundred years. He was an eccentric, endearing and flamboyant genius and if you're interested in finding out more about him I can recommend Ruth Cowan's biography *Relish*.

Waterloo Road Workhouse served Bethnal Green from 1842. It was purpose-built and provided a much-needed service, but an 1866 report describing the conditions makes shocking reading. Master and Matron in such institutions were often man and wife, but Mr and Mrs Brown are my own invention.

E. L. Blanchard was a drama critic and is often attributed as the inventor of the modern-day pantomime. His pantomimes were put on at the Drury Lane theatre from 1852 to 1888 and the two I've mentioned were performed on those dates.

And finally, just for fun, I'd like to give a shout out for Janet and John and their successors, Kathy and Mark, the heroine and hero of the children's books which were used when I was at school and which the late Terry Wogan revived on his morning radio show, entertaining me years later on my drive to work.

DR. PEVERETT'S
CHRISTMAS MIRACLE

Bronwyn Scott

For my family. Merry Christmas to you all.
I love knowing that wherever you are, you are
living your dreams, and I look forward to
having everyone home for the holidays.

Dear Reader,

Welcome back to Haberstock Hall! William's story brings
the series to an end. Once again, Christmas features in
the Peverett story line, as do healing and social justice.
In William, both of those callings align but they present
a dilemma for him. Now that he's been to war, he's not
ready to come home and take up the mantle meant
for him because he fears disappointing his father. He
must resolve the classic dilemma of duty and personal
happiness.

Honoria, like her counterpart Isabella Armstrong in
Marguerite Kaye's story, is looking for a home and
family to call her own. She, too, is newly home from the
Crimean War, where she served alongside William in the
field hospital of Sevastopol. But unlike William, she is
bereft of a family and home of her own. Where William
has too many choices, she has none. Alone, she is
tempted by the world William shows her when he takes
her home for the holidays. But dare she believe such
things are within her grasp?

William and Honoria's story is set against the backdrop
of the season of hope and love. Christmas is a
perfect season against which to explore the power of
homecomings, reunions, family and friendships. I hope
you enjoy their story and having your own reunion with
previous Peveretts and catching up with their lives.

Enjoy,
Bronwyn

Chapter One

London—December 19th, 1856

Dr William Peverett leaned against the rail of the ship as it docked and waited for the elated feelings attached to the joy of homecoming to fill him. But none came, despite the knowledge that he had much to celebrate. He was home from war after three years away, unscathed and whole, at least physically, which was more than he could say for the men being carried up on stretchers awaiting transport to the soldiers' hospital in Chelsea.

He was in London at the festive season, when the city was at its bustling best, its shops full of little delicacies he could only have dreamed about for the past three years, and he would be shortly reunited with his family at Haberstock Hall—a family that had grown in the years he'd been away. His four sisters had all married, the latest wedding just being a week ago. Two of his sisters had children. He was an uncle now to a niece and a nephew he'd never even met, with another on the way.

There was indeed much to be thankful for, much to

look forward to, not the least being that he was home and could step into the future that had been mapped for him since childhood, a future that had once appealed to him greatly—to take over his father's practice in Hertfordshire and be the next healer at Haberstock Hall, where there'd been a Peverett as healer for nearly three hundred years.

Some might say he led a charmed life, his purpose clear, his path straight. Once, he might even have said that, too. These days, he wasn't so sure. The joy he ought to have felt at being reunited with his family was displaced by anxiety: anxiety over a future he no longer craved, anxiety over fitting in to family that had shifted and changed, reshaping itself without him. If he didn't intend to be the healer at Haberstock Hall, where did that leave him? What would his place in the family be, then? Would his father forgive him for the familial desertion if he took his calling elsewhere? Would Thea, his twin?

A young, smooth-cheeked private found him at the rail—Charlie Wall of Painswick, Gloucestershire. William had made it a point to learn all their names on the journey home because sometimes a man's name was all he had. 'Dr Peverett, we're ready to disembark the men. There's this for you as well. It was waiting for us from the hospital.'

'Thank you, I'll be down directly to oversee the disembarkation.' Disembarkation and delivery of the wounded to the soldiers' hospital was the last duty required of him as an army surgeon. He'd stayed in the Crimea until the bitter end and beyond.

In many ways, he'd been the last man out of the

Crimea. The armistice had been signed in February, the treaty finalised the end of March, nine months ago, peace being conceived along with his soon-to-be-born newest niece or nephew. But the end of the war on paper wasn't necessarily the end of the war for the men he cared for. He'd remained behind as the last men to be wounded and those who needed more time to recover in order to make the long trip home convalesced until he could put off his return no longer.

William unfolded the note and scanned it hastily. The hospital was going to need him. The note enquired whether he would be able to stay on a few days and see the men situated? The hospital was short-handed at the moment for dealing with an influx of new arrivals given that it wasn't truly a hospital in the strict medical sense, but a pensioners' estate for those in the military who were of limited means. Many of the doctors who voluntarily came in to offer care to those who needed it were away with their families for the Christmas holiday, including Dr Lord Ferris Tresham—his own brother-in-law, someone else William had yet to meet.

William didn't mind the delay in his own return. In some ways, he was more than glad to spend a few days in the city. It would be his reprieve from the unavoidable, a chance perhaps to come to terms with being home before facing his family. Like the Russians at Kars last year, it seemed he, too, was merely delaying the inevitable. He tucked the note into his coat pocket and hurried to the gangplank. It was time to go to work.

The ship had been allowed to put in at the newly opened Victoria Docks just below Blackwall because of the dock's ability to accommodate passenger ships and access to a railway that would transport the wounded into the city more efficiently than loading them into wagons. That didn't mean it wouldn't be a laborious process, William thought as he issued instructions to soldiers and offered reassurances to the injured men.

'We're almost home.' He smiled and squeezed a man's hand as the man passed on a stretcher, looking pale and worn. What a journey it had been for these men who'd already suffered so much. Two weeks of travel from Sevastopol to London and in nearly every kind of conveyance: ships by sea, wagons overland and trains where they could be had. All of the jostling endured in order to arrive 'home' in London to a care facility that would be temporary, requiring one more move on most of their parts.

Some might choose to stay at the facility if they had the finances, but most would go home to their families. For those who did leave, what were they going home to? Their army careers were over. How would they provide for their families? Would Britain take care of its heroes? William was a pessimist on both accounts.

'Dr Peverett!' a man's voice rasped as another stretcher passed him on the way to the railcar. A hand fumbled for him and William grasped it. Peter Falkner. A man who'd nearly lost his life but had lost both legs instead. That had been William's doing.

'How are you, Peter?' William smiled warmly at the man. This man was lucky to be here, one of those who had needed every day of the last several months to recover. Had he done him any favours? Perhaps death would have been kinder. Such were the dark dilemmas that plagued him at night when the work ceased and the ghosts came.

'Happy to be home, Doctor.' Peter grinned. 'Thank you, I wouldn't be here if not for you.'

William fussed with the man's blanket, tucking it about him, uncomfortable with the praise. Would Peter Falkner thank him in two months? Would Falkner's family thank him for sending home a broken man who couldn't earn a wage? What was to be done for men in Peter's position? Had he done the man a disservice in saving his life? The old guilt gripped him even as he gripped Peter's hand. He should have done more, should have been able to do better than this for Falkner, for all of them. 'The best thanks is you continuing to get stronger. I'll look in on you once we reach the hospital,' William promised.

It was a promise he made several more times as the ship was emptied and the railway car loaded. William ran through the tasks needed today: there would be the train into town, then the loading of wagons to convey everyone to the hospital, then settling into rooms, visits to make sure everyone was comfortable and meetings with the nurses to apprise them of the patients' care. The last he would start tomorrow. It would take a couple of days. He'd want to personally introduce the hospital staff to each of his patients as he eased the staff into their rounds with the newcomers.

It would be a long few days. There was plenty to do between patients to see and reports to write. Just the way he liked it. More work meant less time to think. As the last of his patients were loaded, William took a final look back at the ship and waited once more for a sense of homecoming to fill him. There was still nothing. Perhaps it was because he had come home, but he'd brought the war with him. Until he could be free of the war, free of the guilt, he'd not truly be home.

Royal Hospital Chelsea for Soldiers

Honoria McGrath looked up from her roll lists as the first wagons rolled on to the grounds, dismayed by how many there were. General Sir Colin Haklett, the hospital governor, had left her in charge and with very little help. To be honest, he'd not directly left her in charge, but rather in charge by default. As the holiday approached, the responsibility of settling the last wounded from the Crimea had devolved to her because there was no one was else. Everyone was gone for the Christmas holiday, away with their families.

She had no family. No one was counting on her for Christmas. Her two acquaintances in town, Mary Seacole and Isabella Armstrong, who had also nursed in the Crimea, had their own businesses to attend to now that the Crimea was behind them. She missed them. But they were women of independent means and independent choices. Unlike her.

Honoria straightened her shoulders, refusing to wallow in the self-pity that might follow such a recognition. Regardless of how the responsibility had come to her, she was more than capable of handling the latest challenge. The men arriving were counting on her to make their transition a smooth one. They had served their country nobly and deserved the best she could give.

A man leapt down from one of the wagons, tall, hale

and whole, a rare sight for her these days which were filled with old men, broken men. His movements carried an athleticism that drew her attention, not only because they were conducted with a certain fluid grace, but because they were also…familiar—movements she'd memorised, spent her days working beside for a year and yet they belonged to someone she'd not thought to see again once she'd left the Crimea. Honoria's breath caught in recognition and in hope. Could it be? Was it really him?

His long-legged stride covered the ground between them until there was no mistake. She smiled in surprise and disbelief. Dr William Peverett was home, months after his fellow doctors had returned to their lives. But, of course, it would be him. He wouldn't dare let any of his treasured patients make such a journey without his care any more than he would have left their sides at the field hospital until he was assured of their recoveries. Dr Peverett was tenacious that way. It was a tenacity that had kept men alive through long hopeless nights, a tenacity she'd had the privilege to work alongside in Sevastopol.

Dr William Peverett was tireless when others flagged, steadfast when others gave up. It was a quality she admired in a man—such resilience showed a man's character. And he was kind, always ready with a smile and an appreciative word acknowledging the efforts of others regardless of rank, something many of the other doctors didn't take time to do. But William Peverett had time for everyone and a knack for making others feel special, valued, even her—Honoria McGrath, an insignificant young woman of no family, who lived her life in the background caring for others.

It was no wonder the French and British nursing sisters in Sevastopol had been fond of him, herself included. Nothing serious on her part, of course, just the standard battlefield infatuation that might occur between nurses and doctors when they worked together, an infatuation that took place mostly in the mind as a product of intense proximity and time spent in close quarters.

Honoria hurried forward to greet him, a little thrill at the prospect of re-encountering him firing her blood. She was glad she'd taken time to change her apron. Dr Peverett valued cleanliness and competence above all else when one was on duty and he was always on duty, she'd learned. Being 'off duty' was a luxury he extended to others, but not to himself. In that way they were not unalike. 'Welcome home, Dr Peverett,' she said with brisk professionalism.

He turned from giving instructions and favoured her with one of his famous smiles that the local women and nurses had sighed over. 'Nurse McGrath, what a pleasure it is to see you again. Now I know these men will be in the best of hands.'

Nurse McGrath. She'd forgotten how good he was with names even as delight flickered at being remembered after nearly a year since he'd last seen her and at his praise of her work. 'I'm here to help the men get settled. Governor Haklett regrets he cannot be here to greet you and the men himself,' she made the requisite explanations. 'Where would you like to start?' She gazed down the long line of wagons, careful to hide her dismay. Dismay was not professional. She'd not thought there'd be so many. She'd so desperately wanted to leave the war behind when she'd returned, but the war seemed to insist on lingering.

'Start with the first wagon,' Dr Peverett instructed. 'I loaded them by severity. Those in need of the most care are in the early wagons.' Of course he had organised it that way. She'd seen him use the same strategy bringing wounded in from the battlefield. He wouldn't want those men to suffer discomfort any longer than they needed to, compounding the long journey with the delay of being unloaded from the wagons.

Their gazes met, a moment of connection passing between them. He was remembering, too, the awful days of summer when wounded men bound for the British hospitals in Constantinople or Therapia were carried down to the beach and left to wait for hours until they could be loaded on to hospital ships for transport, the hot sun adding to their misery.

She gave a curt nod, dispelling the memory of helplessness, of being unable to do more. That wouldn't be the case here. 'My staff are ready and waiting at your disposal.' That sounded better than it was. Her staff consisted of orderlies who'd drawn the short straw, forced to work over the holiday, and a few good-hearted volunteers who lived nearby.

'Very good, Nurse McGrath. As always, I can count on you to have everything well in hand,' He flashed an appreciative smile and she felt his gratitude to her toes. What had been a task she'd looked upon as something of a burden she'd been saddled with was suddenly a privilege, a pleasure. That was the magic of William Peverett.

* * *

It took most of the afternoon to unload the men, her staff carrying stretchers to and fro while she and Dr Peverett were everywhere overseeing the process, not unlike the days in Sevastopol where they'd worked to treat the wounded. They fell into the old rhythms. He was easy to work with, giving clear guidance and being unafraid to ask for direction when he needed it.

At last, the men were settled. She and Dr Peverett strolled the rooms that had been set aside for the new arrivals, checking on the men one final time. Dr Peverett took the opportunity to introduce her to each one of them. It had been a long day and most were exhausted from the excitement of arrival, but they perked up at the sight of Dr Peverett, who had a story to share about each of them while Honoria laughed and made preliminary notes.

'Dinner is on the way, Peter.' The doctor gripped the legless man's hand at the last bed they visited. Dr Peverett smiled, but the man didn't smile back. 'What is it, Peter?' Dr Peverett was immediately alert to the man's concern.

Honoria glanced at the man, sensing his anxiety. 'I'll leave the two of you alone. Since we are done here, Doctor, I'll see about refreshment for us in the office.' She efficiently excused herself to give the man privacy and busied herself ordering tea and sandwiches. Dr Peverett probably hadn't eaten since breakfast aboard the ship, if that. She knew him—he'd have been occupied with disembarking. She'd seen him go all day without eating, wrapped up in his work.

She hummed as she set out the tea things on a low

table in the little room that functioned as her office. It would be nice to have him here if only for a few days. She'd been lonely since she'd returned in March. The friends she'd made in Sevastopol among the Sisters of Mercy had gone back to Ireland or their convents, back to old lives and other people.

Mary Seacole, who'd been her mentor, had prolonged her stay in the Crimea, hoping to recoup her financial investments from the supplies she'd imported, thinking the war would last longer. She had returned to England this autumn, but Honoria had lost contact with her. The thread that had held them together in the Crimea had been cut. Honoria missed the camaraderie with Mary and Isabella, two women who shared her passion for healing, as much as she missed the urgent sense of purpose that had infused each day.

She knew she was lucky to have found work at the Royal Hospital Chelsea, but she was an administrator here, an organiser, not a healer. She took care of the details no one else wanted to oversee. She was a glorified lackey. She was not a nurse, she was not saving lives, not making a difference. Her work was inconsequential here and thus she was inconsequential to people like General Sir Colin Haklett, who only required her services when there was something he couldn't be bothered to do.

She'd not been inconsequential in Sevastopol. She'd been essential there. Despite the Chelsea hospital being a home for military pensioners, there was no one here who understood what it had been like to do battle for men's lives every hour of the day, no one to commiserate with. Not that she wanted to relive the war. She definitely didn't want that. If it had been up to her, she would have got as far away from reminders of war as she could.

She'd have preferred to return to delivering babies as she'd done with her mother up until her mother had passed away, but a woman alone could not make a living doing that in London where doctors were male and had degrees from universities. A female healer was very much the anomaly here and very much alone. It would have been nice to have the company of someone who at least knew what it had been like. Hence the appeal of William Peverett. He knew. Neither she nor her experience were inconsequential to him.

'Ah, sandwiches, you read my mind.' Dr Peverett's pleasant tones had her turning around and wiping her hands on her apron.

'I assumed you'd be hungry. You probably haven't eaten all day,' she answered with a smile.

'You guessed right.' His gaze lingered on her as he returned the smile. 'It is good to see you, good to see a familiar face.'

'It's good to see you, too.'

Good to see someone who knows where I've been, what I've seen and what I've done, who knows what I am capable of.

'Come and sit, I'll bring you a plate and you can tell me all the news from Sevastopol.' She piled a plate with sandwiches and passed it to him before arranging her own. As she took a chair across from him, balancing her plate on her knees, Honoria felt a little less lonely, a little less disconnected. For the first time since she'd come back, it felt as if she hadn't simply returned, but that she had come home.

Chapter Two

❦

'This reminds me of your famous Crimean teas.' William smiled over the rim of his teacup, appreciating the memory as much as the food. 'How many nights in Sevastopol did I finish rounds, too exhausted to even think about preparing a meal for myself or going in search of one, only to have you sweep in with tea, a tray, and the determination to see that I eat when all my body wanted to do was fall on to a cot and sleep?'

Honoria laughed. 'Famous might be overdoing it, but definitely necessary. A doctor is no good to his patients if he starves himself.'

William nodded in agreement. There'd been days when he'd slept four hours to every twenty, eating as he treated the wounded, so short-handed were they compared to the need. In the summer of 1855, there'd been times when there were only three doctors to every two hundred patients. 'War was relentless, but so were we.'

William raised his teacup in a toast. 'Regardless, your teas were famous to me. You had the ability to make even the most meagre rations into a feast. I've no doubt they were the saving of me.' That and her company.

'You owe Mary Seacole's supplies for that, not me,' Honoria downplayed her own contribution. Mary Seacole had run the British Hotel, a place for officers to find a warm meal, the 'comforts of home' and, in some cases, somewhere other than the overcrowded field hospitals to convalesce. By the time the war ended, the British hotel was part 'hotel' and part 'emporium'. Every British soldier knew 'Mother Mary', as she was affectionately known, had everything from 'anchors to needles'.

'But I had your conversation, and I valued that as much as, if not more than, the sustenance.' He would not let Honoria get away with such a dismissal. 'I remember the first day I met you.' William smiled broadly. Did she remember?

'It was a day when we'd been besieged between an outbreak of fever and the Russian sharpshooters having improved their aim. You'd just arrived, but you saw our need instantly. You dropped your bag by the tent flap, donned an apron and went to work without unpacking.' He'd seen her competence immediately and had wasted no time persuading her to split her time between Mary's and the field hospital.

'There was so much to do and the need was apparent. Many of the doctors were off sick themselves,' Honoria said modestly.

'At any rate, it was the beginning of our friendship.' William sipped his tea.

'Misery loves company,' she joked.

'I wouldn't exactly call it misery,' he corrected. 'I'd call it consolation, comfort. Those are no small things during war time.' She'd given him far more than she realised. He had fond memories of ending his days with her, of creating a moment's peace before a quiet fire after days of blood and horror, men he couldn't save and perhaps men he shouldn't have saved.

Men like Peter Falkner, who was now concerned if his family would want him. There'd been days when the Hippocratic oath was more of a millstone than a bell-wether. There still were. Honoria McGrath had been someone he could talk it through with, someone who understood and did not judge him for his doubts and misgivings because she had lived the day, too, right beside him.

He let her refill his teacup, his eyes following her feminine movements before he asked solemnly, 'How are *you*, Honoria?' Their eyes held before her gaze slid away. She would know what he was really asking. Any-one who'd been to war and had seen what they saw knew.

Did she, like him, still dream of those bloody days when she closed her eyes? What was life like for her now that she was home? Had she found the peace she was looking for? He found himself hoping she had. She deserved it. He wanted that for her. And for him-self. Perhaps if she had peace, there was hope he might find it, too.

'Yes,' she replied softly. 'I still see them. Each one of them. I wish I didn't. I tell myself we did our best. It helps, a little.' She gave a rueful smile, a sense of con-nection rippling between them. He would have spared her the memories if he could. They were not pleasant ghosts, yet there was comfort in knowing he wasn't alone, that she knew.

William selected a ham sandwich from his plate. 'I

admit to being a little surprised at finding you here. When we last talked, I was under the impression you were hoping to find a different sort of post.' Her specific words had been that she was done with sick men, done with war. She'd wanted to get as far away from it as possible. She'd been angry and heartbroken. Silence rose between them, each of them remembering that night, the night she'd cried in his arms after they'd lost Samuel Lowell, a young boy from Oxfordshire. A death that should not have happened but had, due to poor nutrition and preventable circumstances despite their best efforts.

'A girl such as myself must take what is available.' She gave another rueful half-smile. 'I needed work right away when I returned and this place needed help which I was qualified to give.'

The word 'qualified' was sardonically said and William didn't miss the edge beneath the word. She wasn't a nurse here, though. She was an administrative assistant, spending her talents on paperwork instead of people. William furrowed his brow. 'You are wasted here. I've never met a finer nurse.' There was very little nursing to be done here with the temporary exception of the new arrivals. But they would all move on. And she would not.

He understood why in hindsight. The reasons were twofold: she was a woman alone. She had no one to count on but herself when it came to wages. There was no one to cover rent while she looked for a position that was more appealing to her, more suited to her passion. She was a fine nurse, a genuinely compassionate soul, caring not only for patients but for all those around her regardless of the hour of the day or how long she'd already been on her feet.

That was the second problem. The Honoria McGrath William knew was all heart, long on compassion, short on certification. Like her mentor, Mary Seacole, Honoria had *not* been formally trained in any way recognised by British medicine unlike the Sisters of Mercy or Florence Nightingale and her elite nursing corps. A corps that had, in fact, Honoria had confided to him during one of their late-night talks, turned both her and Mary's applications down. The corps had discounted Honoria's training in midwifery and basic triage at her mother's side as well as Mary's Caribbean background in regional herbal medicine. Mary's experience treating yellow fever epidemics had been repudiated outright by Florence Nightingale.

Such rejection had not stopped them. Mary and Honoria had come anyway under their own power, overcoming initial rejection in order to answer the desperate call for nurses in the Crimea. William had found such commitment admirable since that service required putting themselves in harm's way. Their service came at the endangerment of their own lives.

Once she and Mary had reached Sevastopol, skill had ceased to matter. The willingness to serve had been enough. Formal training hadn't mattered when lives were on the line. But home in England, the lack of recognisable training was no doubt posing a barrier to Honoria pursuing a nursing career. The double standard now being applied seemed exceedingly unfair, a poor way to pay back someone who'd put personal comfort aside for the welfare of others. 'You deserve better,' he said quietly.

She set her teacup down with a shake of her head. 'It's just how it is here. I'm used to it. I've been on my own since I was eighteen. I know how to get by.'

Annoyance flared within him. He wanted her to do more than get by. Getting by wasn't living, it was struggling. London in winter was difficult. 'I will put the word out,' William offered. 'I have brothers-in-law who have large families. Surely they will know of someone in need of a genteel companion.' It was the least he could do for her, although such a position would make little use of her best skills. A companion wasn't a nurse.

Her situation made him feel a bit guilty for delaying his return to Haberstock. She had no family to go to, but he had hordes of family waiting for him to return while he lingered in the city. He had everything to go home to, his future secure, while hers was anything but. William knew too well that, in society's eyes, an untrained nurse was viewed as little better than a whore for having exposed herself to the indelicacies of the male body without the benefit of marriage or the excuse of some minor education. Even a trained woman like Florence Nightingale struggled with that stereotype. While some might tolerate the discrepancy in order to nurse a family member, it was quite another thing to purposely expose oneself to care for a stranger's body. His sister Thea would say it was just one of the many hypocritical standards women were held to when it was perfectly all right for a male to expose himself to the bodies of strange females, the only difference being that he did it under the aegis of 'doctor'.

'That would be too kind,' Honoria demurred, the hint of a blush flushing her cheek, making her appear momentarily human and fallible like the rest of the world, like him. He liked knowing that she was human, too, that there was something he could give her, this woman who gave so much of herself to all those around her. William wanted to do more.

Honoria McGrath was the epitome of an angel of mercy in both looks and temperament: tender, selfless, a virtual paragon. Her soft touch had soothed many a wounded soldier as much as the sight of her had comforted them as she passed by each bed, her sincere blue eyes the shade of forget-me-nots, her straw-gold hair with its faint, teasing thread of red done up in a neat chignon, a smile on her lips as she wished them a good night, leaving a trail of summer lilacs in her wake.

That lilac scent had become her moniker. The Lady of the Lilacs, the men had taken to calling her, looking forward to her visits to the field hospital. Her mere presence had perhaps kept men alive when they might otherwise have given up and lost hope. William knew she had certainly kept him going against impossible odds.

'Tomorrow, we'll start looking through the patients' records and get them assigned to our staff,' Honoria said, turning the conversation towards business. 'You should be free to leave within a couple days. It's quite generous of you to delay. I'm sure your family is anxious to have you home.'

'I am happy to do it.' William rose, having finished his plate and becoming aware of the late hour. 'These men deserve all the comfort we can give them for having served their country so nobly in a not so noble cause.' This had not been a war about defending British borders but about defending British commercial interests far from home. It was a war about money and trade routes, profits the men bleeding and dying on the battlefield would never see. The men who did profit would never know Peter Falkner had given his legs for them.

Honoria's hand was soft on his sleeve. 'We shall see them well cared for. We can begin writing letters to their families tomorrow enquiring about next steps for their care. We'll get them home as soon as we can, although I doubt we can do much before Christmas, but we'll make Christmas special here.' For a moment the words surprised him. But of course she'd be here for Christmas. She had nowhere else to go, nowhere else she was expected. It would likely be a lonely holiday for her while she focused on making joy for others. A sense of protectiveness surged. He should do something about that as well. An idea nudged at his conscience, spontaneous and half formed and not well thought out, but before he could announce it, Honoria jumped up in a flurry of remembrance.

'Oh, I almost forgot! Dr Tresham left the key to his town house. You can use the place while you are here. It's just a few streets away. His housekeeper, Mrs Green, is continuing to look after the place while they're away. Your sister Rebecca stayed there a few weeks ago.' She went to the desk drawer, her skirts swishing with her characteristic efficiency, and retrieved the key before dismissing him as she had so many evenings before in Sevastopol. 'Get some sleep, Dr Peverett. I'll see you in the morning.'

* * *

The Tresham town house at Number Fourteen Cheyne Walk was next door to Tresham's practice, a very convenient set up that had William immediately envious. Despite his long day, he wasn't ready to sleep yet and he strolled through the town house, taking in his sister Anne's new life and learning about his new brother-in-law. Tresham had studied at Edinburgh, as evidenced by the diploma on the wall. Fine school, Edinburgh, one of the best. He, himself, had attended Cambridge, closer to home, as his father had.

William studied the front parlour approvingly. Despite being a duke's son, Tresham lived simply but comfortably. The town house was neatly kept, courtesy of Mrs Green, no doubt. Anne had never had much time for cleaning and polishing, not when there were herbs to be ground or salves to be made.

William helped himself to a small glass of Tresham's brandy in the parlour and settled beside the fire. Tresham and Anne were doing good work here in the city. He was proud of them even as he envied them the freedom to strike out on their own. William knew from Anne's letters that Tresham had a small fleet of medical wagons that journeyed through the low-income parts of the city, offering health care to those who could not or would not seek out a doctor on their own since to do so would require time off from work, a day without wages.

And for what? Any doctor the poor could afford or who would be willing to see them was likely to defraud them as opposed to cure them. But Tresham was changing all that, with Anne by his side. Tresham also had his practice and his work at the soldiers' hospital. Tresham had written a paper recently about the effects of war trauma on soldiers' minds, a subject William was also interested in.

He would enjoy speaking with Tresham about his findings. More than that, he would enjoy working *with* Tresham on his many projects here in the city. Together, there was much they could do for the returning soldiers. Here, he could be of use in a way he could never be in Haberstock.

William turned the tumbler, letting the cut-glass facets catch the flame. He'd have to convince his father of that first. His father had planned on them being partners as he slowly turned the Haberstock practice over to him. He would be disappointed to learn his son wanted to remain in the city, the partner of another man even if that man was his father's son-in-law. It wouldn't just be disappointment, it would be a betrayal not only of his father but of his ancestors, of everything Haberstock Hall stood for.

It was a difficult conundrum to be sure. By betraying his legacy, he gained his own happiness, but by being loyal to his legacy, that same happiness was sacrificed. He swallowed the last of his drink. He didn't have to decide tonight. There were patients to see, reports to write and rounds to make with Honoria McGrath before he had to tackle the issues of going home.

Chapter Three

December 22nd, 1856

Forty visits with patients and at least that many pages of notes later, the only thing preventing William from returning to Haberstock Hall was the lack of a train ticket, a lack easily remedied by simply showing up at the station and purchasing one. Yet William could not rouse himself to leave the warm comfort of the little office Honoria McGrath claimed as her own. He was quite content to sit beside the fire and gaze out the window on to the frost-covered grounds of the hospital sparkling beneath a rare day of winter sun.

At some point, he'd need to admit to himself that it wasn't just the lack of a ticket holding him back. He wanted to stay. With her, with Honoria. He glanced at the little clock sitting on the mantel of the small fireplace. Quarter to twelve.

'There's an afternoon train to Broxbourne at half past two.' Honoria divined his thoughts, something she'd proven to be quite adept in doing ever since he'd known her. 'You could make it if you left now. I have all I need to see the men appropriately cared for until their arrangements to move can be finalised.' Indeed she did. Along with the notes and final reports, they'd also written, with the men's help, to family members enquiring how best to proceed. For some families, those letters would be wondrous Christmas gifts—the return of a beloved husband, father, son or brother. But William was aware that for some, the letter would be the announcement of another burden for families to bear, families like Peter's. William worried what would happen next for the Falkners.

William smiled in her direction and gave a shake of his head. 'There's no need to rush. I had not planned on leaving until tomorrow, late. It's a tribute to your efficiency and thoroughness that we have finished ahead of schedule.' A whole half-day ahead of schedule. It wasn't even lunch yet and the afternoon stretched before him, an unexpected gift of time that wasn't already claimed by rounds, reports or train schedules. Although the latter could be, if he chose.

He felt the weight of Honoria's considering blue gaze on him from where she sat at the desk behind a stack of papers. 'You are not in a hurry to return home? I am sure your family is eagerly awaiting you. What a surprise it would be for them to have you for dinner tonight.'

He *could* make it. Broxbourne was an hour from London by train and then it was another hour from Broxbourne to Haberstock by coach. Barring any delays, he could be at Haberstock Hall by six, but he wasn't ready to leave for multiple reasons; he wasn't ready to face the future and the difficult discussions that would accompany it and he wasn't ready to leave her. This unexpected reunion with Honoria McGrath, the woman who had in many ways been his best friend in the Crimea, had been…satisfying. The word seemed inadequate. 'Tomorrow will be soon enough.'

He looked out the window, the cold, sparkling winter day energising him. He had an idea. Perhaps there was something he could give her, a small pleasure he could offer her out of appreciation for all she'd done for him these past few days. 'When was the last time you had an afternoon to yourself? No plans, no patients?'

Honoria gave a laugh. 'I can't remember. Perhaps in Sevastopol? But there was never anywhere to go except Mary's.'

William grinned, both of them remembering the iron house and wood outbuildings Mary Seacole had cobbled together to form the British Hotel. It had been rudimentary, the work of eager scavenging, but it had been a refuge and it had served its purpose. Now, he had a whole city at his disposal. 'I can't remember either. I'm not sure I know what to do with myself and yet the afternoon awaits. It would be a shame to waste it. Would you care to accompany me on some errands? It has occurred to me I can't show up at home without Christmas presents. I'd appreciate your help shopping for my sisters.'

He'd appreciate her company, too. While he had his own reasons for delaying his return home, it was not those reasons alone that had prompted the idea of a shopping trip. He was not ready to part with Honoria McGrath just yet.

Working beside her these past few days had been a

pleasure. Her efficiency was tempered with kind consideration for those she served. He liked watching her with the men, offering a smile and reassurances where needed. Even Peter Falkner seemed to blossom in her company. As he, himself, did. William was not unaware of her effect on him. She eased his own burdens by *sharing* in them, not merely waiting for instructions. She had a talent for looking ahead, for understanding what he'd need and having it ready for him. She made his job effortless.

The thought of shopping brought a smile to her face, lighting her blue eyes as she untied her apron and set it aside. William felt an absurd burst of pride at having put that smile on her lips.

'I haven't been shopping in ages. Give me a moment to make arrangements and get my coat. Have a cup of tea while you wait, Dr Peverett.'

'William. I think first names are safe enough.' He held her gaze for a long moment as she moved to leave, his boldness surprising even himself. Other than that first night over tea, they had maintained formal address between them, careful not to overstep themselves and make assumptions that their relationship was anything but professional now that they were on English soil.

'If we are to be shopping partners, you can't go about calling me Dr Peverett,' he teasingly explained. 'Today, we'll be William and Honoria, two friends shopping for gifts,' then added, for fear of having been too familiar, 'if you'll allow it?' He didn't want her thinking he was taking advantage of his position. In their occupations, he was her superior. It was her job to comply with his wishes. Today, he wanted to step outside those parameters, wanted to be equals, wanted to enjoy her company on its own merits, to give her something; a day away from the duty she did so tirelessly.

Another of her faint blushes threatened her cheeks. The request had flustered her just a little, as it had flustered him. He had surprised them both with his request. 'Yes, I'll allow it. Just for today, though.' She laughed as she passed. 'I'll hurry.'

If she hurried, she wouldn't stop to think about the folly of accepting Dr Peverett's—*William's*—offer. Hurrying meant only having enough time to think about what to do next: to tell Emily Sharp that she was stepping out to assist Dr Peverett and that Emily was in charge; to get her coat from the room the nurses used for their personal items. Telling Emily was easy. Her coat was a different matter.

Honoria paused as she draped the sorry garment over her arm. The dark blue wool was worn at the cuffs and elbows. She'd had the coat for several years. It had been the first garment she'd bought when she'd originally arrived in London. The coat hadn't even been new back then. She'd bought it second-hand. It had seen her to Sevastopol and back, but now it was showing its wear in ways she could no longer disguise. What would William think of it? She'd seen his coat when he'd arrived— a rich brown wool that brought out the deep chocolate shades of his eyes and a paisley muffler to match done in subtly elegant golds.

Just listen to her! Here she was thinking about William's eyes and concerned about the unfashionable quality of her coat. She would never have worried over such a thing during the war and she shouldn't worry over it today. He'd asked for her help, not for her to concoct fantasies about running errands. This was a simple outing between friends. Friends? Was she friends with the likes of William Peverett? Perhaps that was too audacious a claim. They'd been friends in the Crimea when crisis had overridden considerations of their station, but now? Did that friendship still exist? Or *should* it?

Once upon a time, as a gentleman's daughter she might have aspired to such a man as William. But she was a gentleman's daughter no more. She'd best remember her place. These days, she might have the manners she'd been raised with, but for all practical purposes she was a working girl while he was a gentleman's highly educated son.

She put her arms through her coat sleeves and reached for the knitted muffler and wound it about her neck. She gave her coat pocket a final pat, assuring herself she had her mittens. She patted her other pocket, feeling the small purse inside, and gave a rueful smile. She'd only be window shopping today. The few coins she possessed had to last until the next time the hospital paid her and she needed to eat.

Honoria tugged at her worn cuffs and hurried down the hall, scolding herself for giving self-pity the briefest of toeholds. A poor coat and little money were nowhere near enough to dampen her spirits over the prospect of an outing in the city with a friend. If the darkness and tragedy of Sevastopol had taught her anything, it was that moments of joy were fleeting and should not be wasted. They should be grasped with both hands and savoured to their fullest.

Since she'd been back in England, she'd not had a chance to do much seizing and savouring, but today she would. She would enjoy William's company and tomorrow he would leave, off to his family, and she would return to the hospital and her ordinary life.

'I'm ready,' she called out cheerily, returning to the little office. He was ready as well, dressed in his coat and paisley muffler. If he noticed the worn nature of her coat, he gave nothing away. He cocked his arm, inviting her to slip her hand through it.

'Shall we be off? I thought we'd do our shopping in Knightsbridge.'

Knightsbridge. She knew a moment's panic. Knightsbridge was more than a mile away. It would be a long walk in the pretty, glittering, but *cold* weather—a very long walk in her coat. She froze every morning when she walked to work from her boarding house just a few streets away. But the next moment the panic was gone, erased with his words, 'I'll hail a cab.'

It was an afternoon full of secret treats for Honoria: the cab to Knightsbridge, shopping among a middle-class crowd instead of the lower orders of Chelsea, the company of a handsome, interesting man, time to browse well-stocked shops bursting with goods for Christmas. She couldn't afford any of them, but it was fun to look, fun to pretend that maybe some day she could. She hadn't seen such luxury for years. Sevastopol had been a cesspit of deprivation and disease.

The afternoon passed in a whirlwind of stops: a trip to a small store called Harrods where William bought a special blend of tea for his mother, a bakery selling intricately decorated gingerbread men done in white icing, a brightly lit confectioner's for peppermints and other favourite sweets for his family and a street vendor's for a bag of hot chestnuts that the two of them shared while they listened to carollers on the street corner, William slipping a few coins in their hat.

The afternoon shadows were growing long when William stopped before the beautifully done window of an emporium featuring a dress form showing off a woman's coat and other outerwear accessories: mufflers, lined leather gloves in a variety of colours and half-boots lined with shearling. Just looking at the window made Honoria feel warmer. She could have stood there for hours, staring at the goods inside and imagining wearing the ensembles. What a luxury it would be to have a coat and muffler that matched one's gloves.

'Let's go in,' William suggested, his hand dropping to the small of her back as he guided her through the front door of the store. It was warm inside and crowded with good cheer. He ushered her to the glove counter and a neatly made-up shop girl in a dark dress came over to help them, smiling at William as she pulled out a tray showing a variety of gloves. But William was aware of the girl's flirtation. He turned to Honoria with a smile, deflecting the girl's efforts and making it clear who was in charge. 'You pick, we need four pairs.'

Honoria marshalled all she knew of his sisters to make her choices. She selected a dark blue for the quiet Rebecca, a vibrant red for the outgoing Thomasia, a forest-green for Anne. 'And this blue-violet shade for Thea. That's her favourite colour as I recall.' She'd heard so much about his sisters from William, she felt as if she knew them. She had looked forward to his letters from home as much as he had. Maybe more because she didn't take them for granted. There was no one to write to her.

'Your sisters will love the gloves. They're a thoughtful gift,' she assured William as the shopgirl swaddled each pair in delicate, protective tissue paper before wrapping them in brown paper and tying them with string.

William handed over payment and Honoria tried not to think about the sum and what it signified. The amount would have covered her rent for the month, but he didn't bat an eye. It was a subtle reminder of the difference between them outside the hospital. He was a gentleman's son, a man of means with an honourable profession. She struggled for rent while he bought four pairs of warm gloves for his sisters with no consideration for price.

On the way out of the store, she cast a final glance at the rack of coats, her hand trailing surreptitiously over the wool sleeves as they passed, a reminder that this was a moment out of time, a fantasy only. A reminder, too, that the best of the afternoon wasn't the things she couldn't buy but the company she'd kept. She'd known William Peverett, doctor. Today, she'd had a glimpse of William Peverett, gentleman's son and brother. The glimpse had not disappointed. His sisters were fortunate to have such a considerate man for a brother.

How different might her own life have been if she'd had a brother? Someone who would have watched over her when her parents died? Seen that she wasn't left to the caprices of fate? Then again, if she'd had such a brother, she never would have gone to the Crimea and she'd never have met William.

Today, William had shown her every courtesy, treating her like a lady, offering his arm, his hand at her back, consulting her on purchases. She would treasure this look inside his private world, treasure having been part of it for a day just as she had treasured those letters from home he'd read to her in the Crimea, making her feel like an honorary member of the family.

William hailed a cab to take them back to the hospital. He helped her inside and part of Honoria felt as if the clock was striking midnight. Her magical day was coming to an end. He settled across from her, his long legs crossed at the ankles. 'Did you have a good time? I did.' He smiled. 'Thank you for helping. I couldn't have managed without you.'

'It was my pleasure.' She was suddenly acutely aware of him, of being alone with him. It was an odd sensation given that she'd been alone with him before. In Sevastopol they had taken late meals together after a long day, shared his news from home. They'd sat with dying men and helped them pass. All intimate moments to be sure, but this was different. They weren't doctor and nurse just now. The silence stretched between them. She wasn't sure what to say—what should they talk about if it wasn't about work?

William spoke first. 'I was wondering if you'd be interested in a supper at the town house. Mrs Green will have left something delicious on the stove and then perhaps we could take in the performance at St Luke's tonight. A boys' choir is singing an excerpt from Bach's Christmas oratorio.'

He wanted to spend time with her. *More* time with her. Just her. The request wasn't wrapped in the pretence of needing help with a task, or wanting a woman's opinion. This was purely about wanting her company and it touched her. In truth, it moved her in dangerous ways that caused her earlier coat room fantasies to leap to life, as if he wasn't leaving in the morning, as if the day could be a beginning instead of an end. 'Yes,' Honoria said before she could think better of it.

Chapter Four

He should have thought it through better. They weren't in the Crimea any more where certain social protocols were relaxed due to their roles and the war. Where once it would not have been looked upon askance to walk with her in the stockyards of the British Hotel or take tea with her alone after a long shift, London society would indeed raise eyebrows at the two of them eating supper together unchaperoned at the town house.

He was doing her reputation no favours if anyone discovered what they'd done. There was some consolation in knowing that being found out seemed unlikely. Neither of them knew anyone in town at present. At the moment they were quite anonymous and William found that he liked the temporary freedom of not being beholden to anyone or anything beyond himself.

It seemed he'd spent most of his life being beholden to something: the Peverett family traditions, medical school and then the military. All were worthy causes. He regretted none of that. Each had been opportunities to further his education, his desire to care for others. But those opportunities had come with costs. During the war, his time had not been his own. Within his family, his decisions had not been entirely his own either. Always, there were others' needs to consider alongside his.

He sliced a loaf of the fresh-baked bread Mrs Green had left wrapped in a cloth on the kitchen table while Honoria set places for them. He liked the rhythm of them working together to put the meal on, liked the way she flitted about the kitchen, taking down plates and bowls and laying out cutlery, creating the appearance of domesticity. 'Are you sure you haven't been here before?' he teased, setting out a pewter bread plate with slices stacked on it. 'You seem to know your way around a kitchen quite competently.'

She smiled at him, tucking a loose strand of hair behind her ear. 'Most kitchens are intuitive.' She put her hands on her hips and looked about. 'What shall we have to drink?'

'Wine. My sister has mentioned her husband's brother sends over the most fabulous red wine. We should definitely try some.' William strode to a small cupboard and looked through it, finding a bottle. He brought it to the work table to uncork while she set out their plates. She'd moved a lamp to the centre of the table and its flame lent the space a cosy light as she ladled Mrs Green's beef stew into bowls. He poured the wine into glasses, letting the atmosphere of their little meal run away with his imagination.

He was no longer picturing Anne and Ferris and their life in the house as he had when he'd first arrived, but his own. If he had his own practice, he could afford a home like this, perhaps even a set up like Ferris's where his practice was next door. What would it be like to come home to such domesticity every night? To talk through the day at a softly lit table and hearty bowls of food with a wife who understood? A woman like Honoria McGrath, who not only understood but who might also choose to work side by side with him the way Anne did with her husband. He and Honoria would be a good team. He would not challenge her qualifications.

He let his imagination add a few tiny faces around that table as the years went by. He'd liked growing up in a large family. He was the oldest of five—he remembered most of his siblings being born. He definitely wanted children of his own—several, in fact. He was nearly thirty, it was time to get started on that dream, but it had to take second place until he had his career sorted out, and his head. It was time to rein in such a fantasy. Perhaps it was Christmas that was pushing such images to the fore, or the euphoria of an afternoon spent shopping in a lovely woman's company, or maybe it was simply the effects of being home, of knowing that for him the war was at least over in a very literal sense, even if it lingered in a more metaphoric one.

'The wine *is* good.' Honoria took a careful sip across from him. 'This is from the brother-in-law who is a duke's heir, correct?'

'Yes, Ferris's older brother is Viscount Brixton, the heir to the Duke of Cowden.' William tasted his own glass with appreciation not only of the wine, but her attention to detail. He could not have mentioned Brixton more than a few times to her as an addendum to a letter or news from home, yet she'd remembered just as she'd remembered his sisters' favourite colours this afternoon.

'You run in exalted circles, William Peverett.' Honoria gave a small laugh. 'Now that you're back home, you'll be too good for the likes of the hospital staff.' He understood what she meant. Too good for the likes of her. There she went again, classifying herself as ordinary when she was not, not in his eyes at least. To him, she was quietly extraordinary, something it had taken this brief reunion to see.

He frowned over his wine glass. 'Nonsense. I've never held with the idea that a man *or* woman is defined solely by their birth. My family doesn't see the world that way, it's far too limiting a vision.' It was a vision that had encouraged Thea, his twin, to pursue medicine even though women weren't allowed to study in England and to go to war alongside Florence Nightingale. A vision that had encouraged his sister Rebecca to invent medical devices that made life easier for people even though it was no easy feat for her to see them patented and brought to market because of her sex. A vision that had empowered Thomasia, his youngest sibling, to be a political activist on behalf of women's reproductive rights in a climate where men felt it was their prerogative to decide how women used their bodies.

'You're proud of your sisters,' she said when he'd finished.

'Yes, I am. They have purpose, direction. But more than that, they've each found the courage to bring that purpose to life.' He envied them that. He envied Honoria that even as he admired her for it. She'd found a way to nurse in the Crimea despite obstacles. Such courage was the one thing he seemed to lack.

'They're like you, then,' she complimented. The lamplight caught her features—she was lovely by flame light. He'd not realised before how physically beautiful she was. Perhaps that was best. He liked to judge a person's merit by their heart, not their looks. Honoria had both.

'Are they?' William gave her a considering look, the intimacy of the little dinner making him contemplative. He'd confided in her before on a professional and political level, back in the Crimea, about his worries over the sanitation for the men and the reasons behind the war. Why not confide in her now on a more personal level? He was in desperate need of a confidante and he wasn't sure of the reception his ideas would receive at home.

'Sometimes I think my sisters are far braver than myself. They knew what they wanted and they went after it. They faced plenty of obstacles. I think about Thea in Scutari with Florence Nightingale and the stories she'd write to me regarding the officers who refused to listen to their advice. She made them listen, she stood with them toe to toe, literally, every day and argued until she made her point.'

Honoria gave a small laugh. 'I remember those letters. They made me glad Florence had turned down my application. I'd like to meet Thea. She sounds like an avenging angel, fierce, loyal and determined.' Honoria paused and gave him a soft look. 'Although, I feel like I know her already by knowing you. I'm not surprised you're twins. You're a lot alike.'

William set down his wineglass. 'She waits for no

one while I dither in London because I don't want to face what waits me at home. My father expects me to take over the family practice, to be the next healer at Haberstock Hall.' To take his place in the pantheon of a centuries-old tradition.

'I know I should be grateful. I am male, I have no obstacles to being a doctor. My path is laid out for me. I don't have to fight for it like Thea and Anne have. I don't have to prove myself. I just have to step into the role and yet I am reluctant to take what is being handed to me on a silver platter. That is not bravery. That is cowardice.' He spat the last word, disgusted with himself. 'What sort of man walks away from family expectations, from tradition, from what he was raised to be?' Said like that, he felt foolish for even considering refusing his father.

Surely, Honoria would agree, but she said simply, '*Is* it your dream, though, William?'

He shook his head. 'No, not any more. I want to work with soldiers, especially those that come home with war-induced trauma. I want to ensure they have the best lives possible in exchange for the service they've given their country. I'd like to stay here in the city, close to the soldiers' hospital.'

She nodded solemnly, something indecipherable flickering behind her gaze. 'Then you have to tell your father what you want. Surely a man who has raised his children to be champions of social reform and health care will understand such a noble calling.' She cocked her head. 'Is that why you've delayed going home? Your worry over telling your father?'

William sighed. 'I worry over disappointing him.'
The Peverett legacy was nothing to scoff at.

'I don't think a father could ever be disappointed in
having a son like you, William.' She reached a hand
across the table and laid it gently on his arm in encouragement. It was a sweet gesture and it touched him almost as much as her unconditional belief in him to do
the right thing.

The image flared again of the two of them, partners
in life as they were partners at the hospital, and had
been partners in the war, fighting a continuous battle to
keep men alive. It was an image a man could get lost in
when it was accompanied by a pair of discerning blue
eyes. Did she understand what she did to a man? The
thoughts she could make him think? Were they thoughts
she shared? What would she say if he told her the very
thoughts running through his mind, put there by her
touch? What of her?

'William, you are miles from here. Whatever are you
thinking?' Honoria laughed and he decided to find out.

He offered her a slow, thoughtful smile. 'I was thinking about you, if you must know.' He watched one of
her blushes stain her cheeks. 'I was wondering if you
ever gave any thought to marrying?'

Did she ever think of wanting a partner? Children?
Someone to share her life with? Of putting an end to
the loneliness? Of course, but to no useful end. Still, it
touched her that he would ask. She'd not discussed her
dreams with anyone since her mother died. Her father
had not been interested in anything but his own troubles. And she could not recall the last time *she* had actu-

ally considered her own dreams. Even now, when asked directly, it was hard to find them in the recesses of her mind and dust them off, so long buried had they been.

She furrowed her brow, searching for the right words. 'Marriage is complicated. I used to dream of a home and family, but it's not a practical dream any more. It might have been different if my parents had lived and my father's circumstances had turned around,' she explained. 'Families and homes take money. I have little of either and I am not likely to meet a man who can afford such a dream.' The men at her boarding house were just as poor as she and just as limited in their occupations.

'You don't think you can live on love?' William asked in only partial jest, his gaze considering her as if he'd learned a new insight about her.

'No.' She was emphatic on that point. 'My father acquired a significant amount of debt and I watched the descent into genteel poverty destroy my parents' marriage. Then, after my mother died, it destroyed my father. If I'm meant to be poor, I will be poor alone. I will not risk dragging a child down with me.' A long silence stretched between them. She worried she'd been too blunt, said too much. In the past, she'd seldom spoken of her parents and her circumstances before the Crimea.

After a while, William spoke. 'And now? What do you dream of?' he prompted, his brown gaze narrowed in interest.

'Now it's best not to dream. I just want to get by.' A smaller dream, to be sure. To be warm in her tiny room at the boarding house, to have a full belly, to do good where she could, to be of help to others, to make a wage that allowed her to support herself. Those were dreams enough. *Are they enough, though?* For a while in the Crimea, she had lived her dream. Those dreams had been forcibly banked when she'd returned to England because necessity had demanded it, but having tasted them, they were hard to let go.

'Surely you dream of something more than paying bills.' William waited, his eyebrow raised as if he sensed she held something back.

'All right.' She relented when it was clear he would persist. 'I'd like to study nursing some day.' It was the dream her mother had encouraged when she'd been alive and seen her daughter's talent at midwifery, although her father had been rankly against it, saying it was not fit for a gentleman's daughter. But her mother had praised it, saying it was good and right to spend one's life caring for others in their time of need. But those dreams were in the past now because she hadn't the credentials or the connections required to pursue her calling further.

'You should do that. You are a splendid nurse,' William encouraged.

'Where? There are no formal nursing schools for women.'

William was not daunted by this announcement. Of course not. Nothing daunted him and his Peverett vision of changing the world when the world fell short. 'Thea thinks Florence might start a nursing school when she returns. You were in the war. Mary would write you a reference.'

Honoria shrugged, conscious of the difference between them yet again. Money was no obstacle to him. He could afford principles and aspirations. 'There would still be the issue of payment.' Practicalities always got in the way of her dreams.

William didn't argue. 'Still, it's a good dream, Honoria. Don't give up on it. Or on marriage,' he added. 'I don't think we, as humans, are meant to be alone. We're meant to love and be loved.'

'Why, William Peverett, I didn't have you down as a romantic.' She gave a soft laugh to cover the astonishment of the discovery.

'And I didn't have you down as a cynic.' He gave her an easy smile that said he didn't condemn her for it.

'Not a cynic, William. Just a realist. A good marriage is rare and precious. The odds are long.'

'My sisters all found good men.' He was grinning, enjoying baiting her, she realised. 'The Peverett girls are four for four. I think my odds are good.' They probably were. William Peverett had advantages she'd never have and any woman would be pleased to have William for a husband.

The clock in the hall chimed and Honoria rose, grateful for the distraction. The conversation had got away from her 'We'll need to hurry with the dishes if we don't want to be late for the concert.' She wasn't used to talking about herself so personally, but the damage was already done.

His questions had her thinking about old hopes, old dreams. But perhaps the damage had been done before that. Perhaps the pot of dreams had been stirred earlier today, with the shopping and shared laughter as they'd munched chestnuts and listened to carollers, as she'd picked out gloves in his sisters' favourite colours as if she were part of a family she'd met only in letters.

The pot was positively simmering as he helped her into her worn coat and offered her his arm as they set off for St Luke's as if they were a husband and wife out for a holiday evening of music.

This was what it would be like to be married to William Peverett, or a man like him, came the forbidden whispered thought.

Who was she fooling? There was no man like him, not where she came from. Men like Dr William Peverett with his family home in the country and his Cambridge diploma weren't for women like common, self-taught nurse Honoria McGrath. She could enjoy tonight, but in the morning she'd best remember that simple truth.

Chapter Five

Candlelight shone through the stained glass as they approached St Luke's, the light brightening the night as they completed the half-mile journey down Cheyne Walk, past the Physic Garden and on to Sydney Street where the Gothic tower of St Luke's soared into the night sky. A good crowd was on hand for the performance, William noted as he ushered Honoria inside, pausing for a moment to drop coins into the donation box. All proceeds tonight would go to benefit local charities at Christmas.

They found two seats towards the front and settled in, Honoria delighted by the stained glass and the reredos painting behind the altar. 'This place is beautiful,' she breathed in appreciation, her eyes alight as she took it all in.

'It is,' he replied, looking around. St Luke's was new to him as well. Even before the Crimea, he hadn't spent much time in the city and certainly he'd had no need to visit Chelsea prior to this. 'It feels like Christmas.'

Indeed it did. Large wax candles burned from evergreen wreaths swathing their bases, the silver chalice and plate gleamed on the white linen covering the communion table. To one side stood the Nichols organ and the chairs for the string quartet that would accompany the choir. To the other side, the choir stalls. Musicians began to file in and tune their instruments.

'The oratorio is usually performed in parts over six nights, beginning at Christmas, but tonight they're performing parts I and II.' William made small talk, reading from the printed programme they'd be given upon entrance. But such banter was a smokescreen only for his rising awareness of the woman beside him, an awareness that had been heightened with her revelations over dinner regarding her family.

He'd known from previous mentions that her parents had died when she was fifteen and then eighteen: her mother taken by a fever and her father in an act of reckless misadventure. Until tonight, though, he'd not known about the debt or how deeply her childhood had affected her outlook about her own future and marriage. Such revelations awoke the protector in him, the man who wanted to shield her from her cynicism, the man who wanted to show her it could be different.

There was another type of awareness growing, too, a physical cognisance of the lustre of her straw-gold hair, the scent of her—lilacs underlaid with vanilla, the promise of spring in the midst of winter—the inadvertent brush of her shoulder against his as they talked. She was comfortable to be with, but tonight it was not comfort that drew him. Tonight, he wasn't simply enjoying her company, he desired it, desired *her*, not as a nurse, a co-worker, but as a woman.

'Tonight can be our Christmas.' She offered him a quiet smile that turned the space around them private and made a man forget the sounds of tuning instruments and the milling crowd to focus solely on a pair of sparkling blue eyes. 'Thank you for bringing me, William. This is a very special gift indeed. The perfect way to cap off our day.'

Our day. Our Christmas. He liked the sound of that as long as he didn't think about those words in juxtaposition to the idea that there would be other days, another Christmas a few days hence and he'd be miles away, surrounded by the love of his family while she'd be here, watching over the hospital. For her, tonight might be all the Christmas she got. Perhaps he was being overly dramatic. Surely there would be a few hours for her to celebrate with…with whom? Whom would she pass the holiday with?

'What will you do on Christmas Day?' William enquired as the white-robed boys' choir began to file in.

She leaned close to be heard and he breathed deep of her lilac and vanilla scent. 'There will be a roast of beef for the men, plum pudding and perhaps an orange apiece.'

William shook his head. 'No, I didn't mean the hospital. I meant you, just you. What will you do on Christmas Day, Honoria?'

'I'll be at work, of course, making sure Christmas dinner is perfect for our returning veterans. They deserve that.'

His heart sank at the image. What about what she deserved? Honoria McGrath deserved better than spending a holiday doing what she did so tirelessly throughout the year, caring for others. 'Will you not take a few hours and visit with friends?'

'My friends have long since been scattered across England. I had thought to see Isabella Armstrong at Christmas—Isabella, like Mary Seacole, had established her own nursing headquarters in the Crimea. But she has opened a soup kitchen which keeps her busy.' She smiled, William thought, to ease *his* pain on her behalf. But he could hear the disappointment in her words over missing the chance to reunite with a fellow Crimean nurse.

The conductor stood before the choir and quartet. The audience fell silent around them in anticipation. He gave a rap of his baton and the first, vibrant, exciting swells of the opening movement reverberated through the high ceilings of St Luke's. There was a joyous quality to the first cantata which celebrated the birth of Christ. One could not listen to the choir, the organ, and not be caught up in the festivity created by the music.

William slid a sideways glance at Honoria. Did she feel it, too or was he being fanciful? He had a moment's gaze at her enrapt face before she caught him and cast a smile in his direction, her eyes shining with delight. Without thinking of anything other than sharing the joy of the moment with her, he covered her hand with his where it lay in her lap and an idea began to form.

His hand was still there an hour later when the two cantatas concluded, as was his burgeoning idea. They were in no hurry to leave the church. They waited until those around them had left before they rose and walked slowly back towards the nave and out into the cold night where yet another surprise awaited them.

'It's snowing!' Honoria tipped her face to the sky as they stepped outside, catching snowflakes on her cheeks. 'It won't last, but isn't it beautiful?' Enough snow had fallen to sprinkle the road white and to decorate the dark, bare tree branches. It would be gone by morning. Snow didn't stay long near the Thames, but for now it was as if Mother Nature had conspired to make an early Christmas miracle just for them.

He walked her home to her boarding house, located between the Chelsea Physic Garden and the hospital, loath to part company with her and loath to keep her outside longer than necessary. He'd not missed the way she'd reverently eyed the wool coats at the emporium today in Knightsbridge. Then he'd glanced at her own outerwear and seen the thinness of it for the first time.

He'd offered to hail a cab tonight, but she'd insisted on walking to the church instead and to the boarding house. She'd not wanted to miss a moment's joy of walking in the snow. For him, the walk was only a matter of prolonging his time in her company, but for her it was a matter of the weather. He hoped she didn't pay for such stubbornness by catching cold.

At the steps of the boarding house, he could prolong the day no further. Somewhere, a clock struck nine. 'Thank you for today. You were more than generous with your time,' he said, feeling his words were inadequate for what he really wanted to say.

Thank you for making me feel alive today, for letting me feel like a man and not just a doctor. Thank

*you for listening to me, for not expecting me to have
all the answers.*

'Thank *you*, for all the treats. Cab rides, chestnuts,
a dinner and a wondrous concert.' She blew into her
mitten-covered hands and he could see that she was
chilled. If he meant to broach his idea with her, he'd
best do it quickly. 'I suppose this is goodbye again—'

'Does it have to be goodbye?' he interrupted, grasp-
ing her hands in his in the hopes of warming them
even as he hoped her touch might settle his own nerves,
aware that his question was a prelude to moving their
friendship to a new level and perhaps beyond *if* she
was willing.

She gave a little laugh, her breath turning frosty in
the night air. 'You are off to Haberstock, to your family and your future.' From another woman, such words
might have been perceived as a coy lure, a subtle beg-
ging for attention and reassurances. From her it was
merely facts. She was not angling for anything, which
made the opening all that more precious and he took it.

'Come with me.' His grip tightened on her hands as
he gave voice to the idea that had settled on him during
the performance. Why should she languish in the city
alone when he could give her a holiday surrounded by
family? 'Come to Haberstock for Christmas.'

'Come with you?' She involuntarily took a step back-
wards, tugging at her hands trapped in his grasp. He
did not let go, demonstrating some of his trademark
tenacity. Perhaps he'd anticipated her reaction would
be to run, as well she should. The notion was insane.
One did not simply go home with a man for Christmas.

'Why not? You said yourself you feel as if you know

my sisters already. They will adore you and you're a healer, too. You'll fit right in.' William gave a broad, persuasive smile, one that would have had the nursing corps swooning for a week. Only her common sense kept her knees from buckling and her resolve.

Did he truly not see the reason for her resistance? 'If you show up with a woman by your side, your family will have expectations, they will draw conclusions.' She gave him a meaningful look. 'About us.' She could not spell it out any clearer for him.

'That we are friends from the war who have reconnected in London?' William's dark eyes danced. 'Would that be so bad?' Was it really as harmless as he made it sound? Was that all this was to him, a reunion? Perhaps she had misread him, let her imagination run away with her despite her best efforts.

'But the war is over, William. Things and associations that were acceptable in Sevastopol are not acceptable here. Your family will not approve.' They would not want a simple nurse for their son. Surely he was not naive enough to not understand how outward appearances would look if he showed up with a female guest for Christmas.

'I think you misjudge them and me. I would not set you up for failure,' William answered sternly, the seriousness of his response underscoring how resolute he was on the issue and just how close to dangerous territory *she* was. To go home with him for Christmas would allow the fantasy to continue, it would tease her into believing in the old dreams he'd stirred to life tonight. It would be terribly difficult to come back to reality after a Christmas at Haberstock, a Christmas with him.

He tipped her chin up with his gloved finger to meet his gaze and for a moment she had the odd sensation that he might kiss her, one more fantasy to add to the growing list. She would be lost if that happened. She opened her mouth to protest. 'Even so, it isn't possible,' she stammered, gathering her arguments. 'There's the hospital to think of, a thousand things I need to do before I could leave. Besides, you don't really want me there. Christmas is a private affair, it's not for strangers interloping.'

William pressed a finger to her lips, silencing her list of obstacles. 'You needn't worry about being a stranger any more than I do. I've been gone so long, missed so much, I'll feel like an outsider.' It was the next words that did her in, that and a pair of pleading dark chocolate eyes.

'It would be a help to me to have a friendly face beside me, Honoria, someone that I know. We can meet the new babies and the new husbands together.' To be of help, to be able to do something for this man who had done so much for others and asked so little for himself in return. How could she refuse to do this act of kindness for him?

'Well, if you're sure I won't be intruding or making difficulty for you?' he asked one last time.

He smiled, perhaps sensing that victory was his. 'Trust me, Honoria. All will be well. I'll call for you at twelve. We'll take the afternoon train, that will give you plenty of time to make arrangements with Emily Sharp for the men.' He raised her mittened hand to his lips and kissed it. 'Thank you, for this. I'll see you tomorrow.' He stepped back, releasing her hands and melted into the snowy darkness before she could recoup her reason and change her mind.

There was nothing for it. The decision had been made. She was going to Haberstock for Christmas, a realisation that sent a trill of excitement through her even as her mind warned of the dangers.

Careful, it cautioned. *Nothing can come of this. You will have to come back and be ordinary Honoria Mc-Grath again. This is only make-believe.*

Chapter Six

December 23rd, 1856

Who would have believed that when she'd first met William Peverett in the Crimea, she'd be going home with him for Christmas? Or that the family he'd so generously shared with her from his letters would suddenly become real? It was the latter part Honoria found amazing as the Peverett family coach bore her and William towards the snow-tinged village of Haberstock, with its church spire gleaming white in the fading afternoon.

'Don't tell me you're nervous.' William smiled at her from his seat opposite. The big coach had been waiting for them at the station, the coachman pleased to be the first to welcome William home. It had made the transition from the train to the next part of their journey effortless. Yet another way she didn't belong to William's world. William nudged her foot with the toe of his boot, teasing, 'It's not as if we haven't spent this holiday together before.'

'True.' She answered his smile with one of her own,

their gazes holding in a shared, silent communion of Christmases remembered. Those Christmases in Sevastopol had been spent half working, half celebrating with the staff and patients, making merry as best they could. Despite the war, it had been a good Christmas for her. For the first time in years, she hadn't been alone.

'You shared your Christmas pudding with me,' William recalled. She remembered that, remembered William dragging himself into what passed for a canteen at the British Hotel hours after the meal had been served because he'd been taking care of patients who'd come down with a fever that had swept through the field hospital a couple days before. He'd looked dead tired, but there'd been compassion in his eyes when he'd given her the updates on patients they had both treated. Not once had he complained about his own lack of food or sleep.

His gaze was soft on hers. 'You always watched out for me.' The reciprocity of the current situation was not lost on her. Now they were home and he was the one watching out for her, ensuring she had somewhere to go for Christmas. But this felt different from holding back a portion of pudding.

In Sevastopol, there'd been the context of work surrounding them, creating a means by which to understand her gestures of kindness. Now that context was gone, swept away in the wake of yesterday's shopping spree and an intimate dinner coupled with private conversation and an evening out together, none of which was required by work. Their friendship was changing, progressing, extending itself beyond the bounds of work.

For her, it was both worrying and exciting. Honoria

had not forgotten the warm strength of his hand as it had held hers through the concert or that moment outside the boarding house when his gaze had lingered on her mouth and she'd thought, *wished*, that he would kiss her. In some ways it would have been the perfect end to a perfect day and in other ways it would have created complications. Perhaps he'd sensed that, too, and had cried off at the last.

She was glad he had. She could not have accepted his invitation otherwise. Somewhere between the beginning of the day and evening, they'd crossed over from being reunited co-workers to being firm friends. Those were boundaries enough to cross for one day without throwing a romantic wrench into the works.

Although one might argue that given the things they'd weathered together—saving men, losing men, enduring rations and dodging disease—they were friends already, bound together by mutual hardship, but nothing else. Theirs was a friendship that had existed away from England's shores and there were those who would argue it should stay that way, something best confined to the past and explained away by unique circumstances. Nothing good ever came of men and women being friends. It wasn't possible. Such a friendship was an uncommon arrangement for a reason.

You'd best remember that, her inner voice counselled.

She'd been far too careless these past two days with letting her fantasies wander down impossible paths and allowing old dreams to stir to life. She was setting herself up for disappointment.

William leaned forward, looking out the window. 'See the church? That's where Becca was married recently. We'll have Christmas Eve service there. The bells ring at midnight and it's quite beautiful.' He nodded, encouraging her to look out, too.

She took in the neat snow-layered village with its brightly lit shops glowing in the dusk, the people bustling home for supper. In the early evening, the village looked serene and inviting. Just the sort of place where she imagined finding relief from the war, where she could be away from its daily reminders, reminders she couldn't escape at the Chelsea hospital.

This is his home, not yours, came the caution of her far too alert inner voice. *You have no home, no place to call your own. You have a job, a room in a boarding house and that's it.*

On that sobering note, she sat back in her seat.

'The Hall is only a mile from here.' William reached across and squeezed her hand, misinterpreting the reason for her sudden retreat. 'I'm glad you're here. Thank you for coming. I did mean it yesterday when I said I was in want of a friendly face. There are strangers in my family now.' He cocked his head in contemplation, a little smile teasing his mouth. 'Do you think I'll like my sisters' husbands?'

She heard the unspoken worry behind the words and hastened to assure him. 'They'll like you just fine. I read somewhere that women often marry men who remind them of the males in their family,' she offered, laughing, but that was not the totality of what he was asking. He was wondering if there'd be a place for him in this new, expanded family. His family had grown and changed in his absence. It would not be the same one he'd left.

Would there still be a place for him or had these new men filled the gap he'd left?

Perhaps, too, Honoria speculated privately, William feared his father now had four new sons where before he'd been the only one. For the first time in his life, perhaps William felt he had competition for his father's affections, especially given the controversial nature of what he wanted to discuss with his father during his visit.

'Your family will be so proud of you,' she offered, feeling the platitude was inadequate to the situation. But what could she say that would matter? That would have any credibility behind it? She did not know him or his family well enough to speak to that deeper issue.

They passed a blue-shuttered stone cottage and the coach turned from the road on to a long, tree-lined drive. Tall chimneys came into view, dark columns against the dusky sky. They were nearly there—the fabled Haberstock Hall. Honoria felt her stomach clench with nerves as the Hall took form. It was far too late to turn back now. The coach circled before the front steps and halted. Light spilled through long windows in invitation.

'You're sure they won't mind a surprise guest?' she asked as William handed her down, the firmness of his grip offering her courage.

'My family love guests and surprises.' He gave her a broad smile and tucked her arm through his just as the front door was thrown open and warm chaos poured out into the evening borne on a cacophony of joyful exclamations, of 'William!'

'You're home!'

'You're here at last!' and even a few 'What took you so long?' and 'It's about time.' Then they were surrounded by sisters, some with toddlers on hips, everyone trying to hug William at once and laughing as they tripped over one another. There was more chatter. 'William, who have you brought?'

'A guest, how delightful!' There were hugs for her as well although she'd not even got her name out amidst the hubbub.

'William's brought a guest!' Someone with coppery curls and a squirmy toddler on her hip—was that Anne, perhaps?—called out as the exuberant tide of Peverett siblings carried the reunion into the front hall. The great hall stole what was left of Honoria's breath as she glanced around. It was decked out in Christmas glory with evergreen swags and red bows draping the oak banister, and, she noted with a careful eye, boughs of mistletoe interwoven among the garlands over door frames to catch out the unsuspecting.

She would need to be on her guard. Nothing changed relationships faster than kisses. A welcoming fire roared in the fireplace, a large relic left over from Elizabethan times. It was the perfect image of a country house Christmas, but appreciation would have to wait while there were people to meet. William's parents were there, exclaiming over their son and embracing him in a manner that brought tears to Honoria's eyes to witness it, such was the love in his father's gaze.

'Welcome to Haberstock Hall, my dear.' His mother turned some of that love in Honoria's direction, laughing as she wiped her eyes in joy over her son's return. 'Forgive us our unorthodox antics. I'm Catherine Peverett and this is my husband, Alfred.' She slipped her arm through Honoria's, detaching her from William's side as William made a hasty introduction.

'This is Miss Honoria McGrath. She was a nurse at the British Hotel and in my field hospital in Sevastopol. I was pleasantly surprised to discover she was working at the Chelsea hospital when I arrived.'

A tall, dark-haired man stepped forward with a laugh. 'Miss McGrath, all this time you never said a word about knowing William!' He took the squirmy toddler from his wife and the little boy settled down immediately in his father's arms.

'Dr Tresham.' Honoria blushed. 'It took me a while to work out the connection through your wife and once I did, there wasn't a chance to bring it up.' It was the truth. She'd not even realised Anne Tresham was Anne Peverett until a few months ago and she seldom worked alongside Dr Tresham when he visited. She was consigned to paperwork these days and they had no pre-existing relationship that invited such intimate conversation.

'Ah, so you're Tresham.' William stepped up and shook the man's hand. 'I've been looking forward to meeting you. I've been making free of your town house these past few days.'

'Good.' Tresham took Anne's hand in his, his affection for his wife evident in his gaze. 'We're glad you did.' He juggled the boy in his arms. 'This is Benjamin, your nephew.'

Honoria watched William bend to the boy's level and smile with genuine affection at the child. 'You're a fine lad. How old are you?'

'One and a half,' Anne supplied proudly when the boy buried his face in his father's chest.

'Oh, Anne, I'm so happy for you.' William's words were infused with brotherly warmth.

By now, the rest of the family had organised themselves into the semblance of a receiving line and Catherine Peverett moved her through it skilfully with William beside them. 'This is my daughter Thea and her husband, Leopold,' Ah, the Earl and the Countess, Honoria added silently, although apparently such titles held no sway here.

There was no mistaking Thea as William's twin. They shared height and chocolate eyes. There was a round of handshakes between the two men and a hug for Thea. Honoria heard William whisper to his twin, 'How I missed you! We're both home now.' The two of them had shared everything, even the war, although they had served in different locations.

'These are our newlyweds, Rebecca and Jules, or Mr and Mrs Howell, if you prefer,' William's mother went on, beaming with pride at the couple who were still clearly enchanted with each other and with the idea of being Mr and Mrs Howell. Jules Howell was tall and dark haired, with friendly green eyes.

Honoria was noticing a trend. Rebecca and Thea had indeed married tall, dark-haired men like their father and brother. But the last man in the line, while also tall, broke with that pattern. Shaw Rawdon sported a thick, wavy head of bright auburn hair as he stood tall and broad next to his very pregnant wife, Thomasia, whose hand had surreptitiously moved from her belly to rub at the small of her back. A blonde little girl—who must be two? Three?—stood between them, swinging on their hands with a wide, happy smile.

'Any day now?' Honoria asked the expectant mother sympathetically.

Thomasia gave a rueful smile. 'Any day would be fine. Tonight would be wondrous. I haven't seen my toes for weeks now.' She laughed, but Honoria could see that she was miserable, poor thing.

'We have a pot going on when it will be.' Dr Tresham strolled up. 'I think Christmas Eve, but Anne thinks the twenty-sixth.' He winked good-naturedly at his wife.

'I could live with Christmas Eve.' Thomasia rubbed at her belly. 'The sooner the better.'

'It could be Christmas Eve. I'm sorry, Anne. I have to agree with Dr Tresham,' Honoria put in.

'I like those answers better, anyway, Anne.' Thomasia rested her gaze on Honoria. 'How do you know such things?'

'My mother was the closest thing to a midwife in our part of the county when I was growing up. As a consequence, I've done a bit of unofficial midwifery in my time.' She knew the signs of imminent birth and they were present. That worried Honoria, actually, but Thomasia was surrounded by two doctors, two herbalists and an exceedingly talented nurse in her sister Thea. Surely if there was anything to worry about, they were aware of it.

She felt William's hand at her elbow. 'You've met all of us now, Honoria, and you haven't run for the door. I'll take that as a good sign we haven't overwhelmed you entirely.'

She shook her head. 'I'm so pleased to be here, everyone,' she said, looking at the group that had formed a haphazard half-circle about them, their faces still glowing with the joy of having their beloved brother home. 'It sounds silly to say it, but I've heard so much about you from William's letters that it's almost like having characters from a beloved book come to life before my eyes.' That made them all laugh and Catherine Peverett took her by the arm.

'Let's get you settled in a guest room. You've had a long day and you'll want to rest before dinner.' Catherine fixed her daughters with a mock look of sternness. 'None of you are to sneak in and disturb her, you hear? Now, come with me, dear, and let's get you unpacked.' Honoria cast a final look in William's direction, reluctant to leave her one security, but he merely flashed her a smile and a shrug that said his mother's word was law in these parts. One disagreed at one's own peril.

Upstairs, Catherine showed her to a room done up in shades of pale blue and white, a colour combination that managed to look beautiful year round. In the winter, it matched the stark, white outdoors. In the spring, the blue would match the flowers. 'This is quite the nicest room I've had in some time,' Honoria confessed, trailing her hand across the thick blue and white counterpane. White curtains framed the long window and a warm fire burned in the small grate of the fireplace.

'The maid will be up to help you unpack and to bring hot water for washing. If you need a dress pressed before dinner, just let her know. But don't worry about anything fancy. We dress simply for supper.' The last put Honoria at ease and when Catherine smiled at her, a strange thickness gathered in Honoria's throat and tears threatened in her eyes. 'We're very glad you're here, dear.'

All Honoria could do was nod, so overcome was she with emotion. Meeting the family had not overwhelmed her, but being surrounded by their outpouring of love and attention had. When the door closed behind Catherine, Honoria wiped at her tears. This was what she'd been missing all these years and now she'd found it in the one place she absolutely could not stay because it belonged to another. It felt bittersweet to be here: sweet because it filled the lonely ache within her and bitter because she'd have to give it up.

Chapter Seven

It felt good to be home, a goodness he felt all the way to his bones, a goodness that ran so deep William could not stop smiling as he looked around the long supper table, the Peverett dining room filled with the faces of his sisters, his new brothers-in-law and niece and nephew. At last, he felt the emotions, the elation of homecoming that had eluded him on the journey and in London. Perhaps because homecoming wasn't at all about coming to a physical place but to the people one belonged with, an interesting idea given the state of his own dilemma about what to do next. He belonged with these people, but did that limit him to belonging only in Haberstock?

Jules, seated on his right, passed him the platter of thin-cut roast beef. William offered a serving first to Honoria. 'One piece or two? I might recommend two,' he advised teasingly. 'It will be a while before the platter makes the rounds again.' He flashed her an appreciative smile.

She was holding up well, taking the Peveretts' exuberance in her stride, and he found that pleased him.

She'd changed for supper into a dress of dark blue wool with a scooped neck into which she'd tucked a white lace fichu and she'd restyled her hair into a fresh chignon that lay loose at her nape, a few errant curls allowed to frame her face. She looked pretty and fresh. More than that, she looked like a Peverett.

She looks like she belongs here, among us, came the thought.

She more than *looked* the part. She certainly fit the part as well. She not only listened to the conversations swirling about the table, but engaged in them, asking questions and offering insights. The determination, straightforwardness and empathy she demonstrated at the field hospital served her well here. Perhaps this holiday would strengthen her ties with Tresham and Anne and there would be some help for her in that. But even as he thought it, William felt a twinge of jealously at the thought of others helping her. He wanted to be the one.

Her wine glass was empty and William reached for the carafe set before them and refilled it for her. *He* wanted to help her, support her, give her the things she dreamed of, whatever they might be. He was learning more about her every day and with each new item learned, she became more interesting, more multi-faceted than he'd guessed and more intriguing.

The more he knew, the more he wanted to know of her even as he acknowledged her dreams were different from his. She wanted to be away from the war whereas he wanted to study it, to help men cope with it. Well, some of their dreams were different. Not all. They both dreamed of having a family—at least she'd once dreamed of that. Surely that gave them something in common.

'Ahem… William, the gravy boat, please,' Thomasia scolded playfully from Honoria's other side, drawing him out of his thoughts to realise the gravy had made a second circuit around the table and come to an abrupt stop before his plate. 'I'm eating for two,' Thomasia reminded him and everyone at the table laughed.

William passed the gravy to Thomasia and caught his father's eyes on him. His father smiled, his face full of pride and what could only be described as abject happiness—happiness at having his long table full of his children once more, at having his son home safe from war. William smiled back, refusing to spoil the moment with thoughts of the conversation that must come. That conversation would be difficult for them both. He didn't want to upset his father.

His father looked older than William remembered. His posture was still straight, but his hair was greyer and there were more lines at his eyes and his mouth. He'd be sixty in the spring. He'd served the Haberstock community diligently for thirty-five years. His father deserved a child to follow in the family footsteps. He *could* do it and William knew he *would* do it out of love for his father if it came to it. But didn't he deserve happiness, too?

Beneath the table, he felt Honoria's hand close warm and supportive over his as if she'd followed the direction of his gaze and knew the thoughts that gaze had prompted. There was strength in her touch that comforted and consoled and he was grateful for it.

Further down the table, his nephew sent up a plaintive cry at being denied something. Anne whispered to her son, but William's mother rose from the foot of the table with a kindly look for her daughter. 'He'll be tired, dear. It's a late night for the little ones.'

A maid moved forward to take each of the children by the hand and lead them from the room to settle them for the night. His sisters all stood to follow their mother from the room and he felt Honoria slip her hand from his. He reluctantly let her go. She flashed him a look that only half teasingly said *Good luck*. He slid her an answering glance: *You, too*.

He watched Thomasia loop an arm through Honoria's as they all trooped off to the music room and hoped his sisters wouldn't interrogate her. Although he didn't hold out too much hope when he heard Thomasia exclaim in friendly tones, 'Oh, good, now we have you all to ourselves.'

The friendly interrogation took place in the music room with its cream striped wallpaper and blue damask-covered furniture grouped invitingly about the white marbled fireplace. This room, like the rest of the house, was decorated for Christmas with an evergreen swag caught up at the mantel tied with bright blue ribbons. Chased silver candlesticks sat atop the mantel at either end with a clear glass vase filled with decorative sprigs of mistletoe between them in pride of place.

It was a lovely arrangement that caught the eye and soothed the soul with its seasonal beauty, or at least it would have if Honoria had been an ordinary guest, an expected guest. But she wasn't. She was an interloper, an outsider who'd shown up with their beloved brother and taken them unawares and now their curiosity must be appeased.

She sat beside Thomasia on the sofa and looked about the cluster of her would-be interrogators in their wool gowns not much different than her own except in the quality of fabric; Dark-haired Thea, the female image of William, sitting regally in a wing-backed chair; Anne perched beside her sister on the arm of the chair, her coppery curls burnished by firelight; Catherine Peverett in the chair opposite Thea, Rebecca at her feet, Rebecca's dark head leaning against her knee. It might have been a familial tableau, so comfortably were they arranged in their perfection.

How many nights had they all sat thus before their marriages? Reading or sewing, or talking together? For a fleeting moment, it called to mind evenings she'd spent before the fire with her mother in happier days, their heads bent over needlepoint. But she would not think about that loss tonight. She'd need her wits for other things like Thomasia's questions.

'So, you met William in Sevastopol and you've reunited the moment he returned? He stepped off the ship and came straight to you.' Thomasia's sherry eyes sparkled with the unspoken words *How romantic.* 'That sounds quite…'

'Likely,' Honoria put in hastily, before Thomasia could say the 'r' word out loud. 'I work at the Chelsea hospital which is putting up the men while they connect with their families. It was a lovely coincidence, I assure you.' It wouldn't have happened at all if she'd found a different post when she'd come home. 'When I left the Crimea, I had no intention of seeing him or anyone,' she quickly added, 'again. But the only work I could find was at the soldiers' hospital.'

Thea leaned forward, more interested in the comment about work than she was in her sister's line of questioning, much to Honoria's relief. 'Does such work not suit you? You were with Mary Seacole in Sevastopol. She was a marvel. She was to Sevastopol as Florence was to Scutari.'

'Mary Seacole is a phenomenal woman, I learned much working for her,' Honoria said, 'but to be honest, I'd like to put the war behind me in all ways. However, I've been unable to do that so far in terms of work. I've enquired about positions for companions and such, but nothing has turned up.'

'No nursing? I am sure the Gentlewomen's hospital on Harley Street could use you,' Thea kept probing.

'I am acquainted with the hospital,' Honoria said quietly, fighting the urge to look at her hands instead of holding Thea's gaze. 'But they are not interested in me. I haven't the formal training,' she said boldly, not flinching from Thea's stare. She would not shirk from the fact that she was a nobody, a girl who'd learned her nursing by doing, first by following her mother around, then by following Mary and the doctors about Sevastopol and taking avid notes, learning as she went. Even Thea would have to admit defeat on that front.

Thea drew a breath. 'This is exactly why we need Florence's nursing schools, a chance to formalise nursing education. It's positively hypocritical to press women into service nursing when the need arises, then, when a woman wants to pursue her career, refine her knowledge and receive formal recognition for that learning it is simply too much to ask.'

Anne reached for Thea's hand from her perch on Thea's chair. 'We'll change all that, Thea, we *will*. Our daughters will have choices.' A look passed between the two sisters and Honoria recalled William saying how much it bothered Thea that she had studied beside their father as William had, but she could not go on to medical school with him, that for her, the journey had limits. Now, that she'd met Thea, Honoria could see especially how those invisible chains must chafe. To be a countess, to be a peeress, a woman of rank, and yet not be able to pursue her heart's desire even when she possessed the intelligence and skill to do so simply because she'd been born female.

'Change is too slow in England,' Thea answered Anne, a slow smile curving on her lips. She fixed the room with her gaze. 'Leopold and I have news.' Beside her, Honoria felt Thomasia's hand move to her belly in anticipation of a certain announcement.

Thea laughed and shook her head, catching her sister's gesture. 'Not that kind of news. *My* kind of news. I'm starting medical school in Germany for spring term.' The room erupted into questions and congratulations.

Anne was hugging Thea and laughing. 'Oh, my dear girl, you're going at last!' she cried.

'Only because Dorothea Erxleben did it first.' Thea wiped at her eyes. 'I'll be attending the University of Halle, just as she did.'

'Your namesake.' Anne squeezed her sister's hand. 'You've waited so long and now it's finally going to happen for you. I was so disappointed when you didn't go this autumn.'

'We had good reason to delay. We wanted to be sure the war was truly over. We didn't want to be travelling while the war was on and while there was a chance Florence still needed me here,' Thea explained. 'Besides, I wanted to be here if and when William came home, and I wanted to be here for Thomasia's baby.' She smiled fondly over at her youngest sister. 'I didn't like missing Effie-Claire's birth.'

'We? Then Leopold is going with you?' Becca asked.

'Yes, he's already commissioned a yacht to carry us to and from the Continent. He's going to study music and work on his piano playing. We'll be home in the summers so he can spend at least some time in Parliament and tour the estates. His mother can handle the estates while we're gone. It will only be for a year and a half.'

Honoria felt Thea's gaze pick her out. 'The university is willing to acknowledge my experiences in the Crimea and my training with my father.' Honoria nodded. She understood what Thea meant to say: *If I can do it, you can do it, too. The path is being carved right now.* But the cynic in Honoria was quick to quell the swell of hope. Thea Peverett was the Countess of Wychavon. She was Honoria McGrath, she was nothing.

'We should celebrate.' Rebecca reached for the bell pull. 'I'll have Mrs Newsome bring up some eggnog.' Within minutes, everyone had a punch glass in hand filled with a foamy white confection topped with a dollop of cinnamon-sprinkled cream.

'It's not really eggnog because there's no rum in it,' Rebecca explained as Honoria studied the drink. 'Father counsels against excessive spirits when one is expecting, so we all defer when we're together. Except for wine at dinner.' Rebecca winked.

Of course they did. The Peveretts were all for one and for a few days Honoria got to be surrounded by all that love and caring. Her throat clogged and tears stung at her eyes. By bringing her here, William had given her so much more than a place to simply spend the holiday. He'd given her a family for a short time and that gift was priceless.

Anne raised her punch glass. 'Here's to dreams coming true,' she toasted her sister with genuine affection shining in her eyes as they all drank. She gave her sister a one-armed hug. 'I'll miss you, but I am so happy for you. This is turning out to be the most amazing Christmas ever. William is home, we're all together again, Thomasia will have a holiday baby and you're going to medical school. You're going to be a *doctor*, Thea!' She laughed out loud. 'They're going to have to change the Hippocratic oath when you graduate.'

Honoria watched everything happening around her. Amazing was indeed the right word. It was amazing that she was here, toasting the impossible with these women who welcomed her, who'd included her in the joy of their celebration, who saw their victory as *her* victory. They wanted for her what they wanted for Thea, for women everywhere.

She'd never met such people. They weren't just dreamers. They were dream-makers. This time, when doubt arose, it was hope that overpowered the cynic in her. She dared to entertain the thought… If such lofty things were possible for Thea, what might be possible for her?

Don't. Don't dare to dream or you'll be disappointed...dreams are not for you.

Her inner voice was trying to protect her, but tonight she didn't want to be protected, didn't want to be warned against disappointment. She wanted to bask in the achievement of the impossible, wanted to be part of the marvellous circle of Peveretts.

Chapter Eight

The music room door opened and the men traipsed in, William among them, slapping Leopold on the back as if they were old friends. No doubt they'd been celebrating the news. Even among the tall, handsome Peverett husbands, William stood out to Honoria's gaze. Not because he, too, had some height and build, and shiny dark hair, but because there was something indefinable about him that drew the eye as it drew her eye now.

He radiated an inner confidence, a calmness that said even in the midst of a storm, he was untouched by its chaos, always steady. And yet such steadiness had not left him without emotion as was often the case with others. Along with confidence, he radiated a genuine good will for those around him.

He caught her gaze and raised a brow in question. *Have you survived?*

She smiled back with a nod and raised her empty cup of eggnog as William made his way first to Thea with congratulations and then to her to take up a post at her side. 'It is wonderful news about Thea, is it not?' she said.

'The very best. She's wanted it for so long.' William smiled. 'You look intact,' he teased.

'It wasn't so much trial by fire as it was trial by one bright burning ember named Thomasia.' Honoria laughed. 'But I've handled worse. Doctors, you know.' She rolled her eyes and William chuckled, taking her hand in his in an easy gesture that had become far too commonplace between them in the last two days. Was he even aware he did it? She certainly was aware of each touch, aware of each gaze, of where he was in a room or when he was *in* the room, and acutely aware of her body's reaction to his presence. It was one more path she ought not let herself walk down and yet her feet insisted on putting one foot in front of the other until she could not ignore the direction she was headed.

William's voice was low at her ear, the scent of his evening toilette filling her senses. 'Brace yourself, we'll have music next.'

She looked up at William and laughed. 'I've heard so much about musical evenings here at the hall, I should hope so.' There'd been many evenings in Sevastopol when she'd listen to him tell her about his family, about how his father believed music was good for the soul and insisted all his children cultivate some kind of musical skill. It would be the perfect end to a perfect day. Such days were rare for her, but here at Haberstock Hall they were plucked from life as easily as low-hanging fruit was plucked from a tree in spring.

No sooner had William warned her than Dr Peverett announced, 'We must have music tonight. Thea and William, you shall play first.' He gestured to the two cellos standing at the ready in the corner.

* * *

Dr Peverett might have wanted his children to cultivate musical skill, but they were more than skilled. They were talented and Honoria found herself enjoying the evening from a state of perpetual amazement. Thea and William's cello duet was followed by the tea trolley so that the family could enjoy sweets along with the music. Thomasia and Shaw were next, Thomasia accompanying him on the piano as Shaw sang an energetic rendition of 'God Rest You Merry Gentlemen'. Rebecca played a duet she'd arranged with her father that incorporated a medley of popular carols.

Then the evening turned more serious. Rebecca accompanied Jules who sang 'Jesu, Joy of Man's Desiring' with surprising sophistication. The evening ended with a Christmas composition of Leopold's very own. It was no wonder he was eager to study music while his wife studied medicine. Honoria had never heard the piano played as he played, evoking such emotion and passion that she found herself wiping at tears when she concluded.

'I think that was even finer than the boys' choir at St Luke's,' she whispered to William. It was also the perfect note to end the evening on. Couples began to rise and say their goodnights until only Catherine and Alfred were left.

'Are you coming up?' Catherine asked her son as she and the doctor prepared to go up.

'Soon,' William promised as his mother came to plant a kiss on his cheek, the look in her eyes saying it all. *I am so glad you are home.*

Honoria turned away and studied the banked fire before her emotions could betray her.

'Well, you've survived your first evening among the Peveretts,' William joked after his parents went up.

She turned from the fireplace. How did she tell him what tonight meant to her? 'More than survived. Your family is exactly how you described.' Warm. Welcoming. 'They're the source of your strength, I see that now.' All those days in Sevastopol when she'd nearly despaired of being able to make a difference, he'd been a steady rock for all of them, caregivers and patients alike. She'd never met a man with that kind of strength. It had amazed her and now she saw the very source he drew on. Instead of having the source diminished through revelation, it became that much more desirable, that much more intoxicating.

'I'm glad you like them,' William crossed a long leg over a knee, settling into a chair. She liked them too much, she feared. It would be hard to leave. 'You fit in, like you belong here.' He was looking at her again in the long considering way of his, the way he'd seemed a lifetime ago, yet it was only a couple of days, yet another way in which Haberstock Hall was all-consuming, making one forget about the world beyond it.

Oh, she was headed for a bad fall! 'It's kind of you to say so.' Honoria struggled for a way to restore a semblance of reality, a reminder for them both but especially for her that she was just a guest here, invited by a friend who didn't want her to spend Christmas alone. Nothing more.

'It's not kindness, Honoria. It's the truth,' William replied drily in a tone that put her on alert that there was perhaps more to his earlier comment. 'Do you not agree?'

'No, not entirely. Your family has been welcoming, but I'm not like them, not any more. I have no family, William. I belong nowhere.' It hurt to say the words, to be reminded of her loneliness after an evening surrounded by such warmth. Honoria held his gaze. He needed to understand his folly before it became perilous for them both. She was not the sort of girl a man like William Peverett married.

'I don't believe that.' William calmly disagreed. 'No one is nobody. You are somebody to me.' His chocolate eyes rested on her, dark and penetrating, sending a delicious shiver through her, a shiver she ought to ignore.

'We are friends, William.'

'Are we only that?' His gaze turned dangerous. 'Do you ever think we might be something more? That there is a reason I found you again in London?' He sounded like Thomasia now and she had to tread carefully. She could not lose this argument and yet she'd never wanted to lose more. He was boldly giving words to the fantasies in her mind. She wanted him to be right, wanted him to lead her down this impossible path.

'I would not want to lose this friendship over conjecture.' Honoria rose from her chair, marshalling her last defence. She could end this conversation by leaving the room and in the morning light he would thank her for it, for saving them both from the twin embarrassments of mistletoe and midnight. But William rose with her, unwilling to cede his ground.

'You do not think much of our friendship, then, if you think it cannot survive a few growing pains.' William was challenging her. 'Friendships are not static things, they grow and change over time as the people in them grow and change.' But how much change and how fast? Their relationship had changed rapidly since his return just a few days ago.

She placed a hand on his sleeve, a common enough gesture and one she'd made with him before. But in the late hour of a long day, it seemed more intimate than she intended. 'William, it's the emotions of the day talking, not you. It would be easy, amid the excitement of homecoming, of seeing your sisters and their families, to get caught up in wanting that for yourself and reaching for whoever is near.' Goodness knew she found herself caught up in it. She *knew* how easy it would be.

'You *are* right. I *do* want those things: a wife, children, happiness, all of it.' William's voice carried a note of hoarseness to it as he tugged her close. 'But you're wrong about you. You are *not* merely a convenience to me, Honoria. You are a woman I admire, who has captured my attention with her strength and caring, and I believe I have captured that woman's attention, too. Can you deny that? If so, I will stop right here and ignore the dictates of the mistletoe.'

He meant to kiss her. Her breath caught, giving her away. She shook her head. She could not deny it. 'I don't want to ruin anything between us.' His friendship was too important to her to throw it away on a whim.

'Not acting could be just as ruinous,' William argued gently, the back of his hand skimming her jaw in a soft gesture that sent her pulse skittering. 'To not know, to never know, would be akin to throwing away happiness with both hands.' He had her face in his hands now, his eyes intent on her. He'd always been braver than she and he was the brave one now. 'We survived a war, Honoria. We will survive one kiss. We can always blame it on the mistletoe.'

Yes, she thought as she leaned into him and felt his lips claim hers, they would survive it, but it would change everything no matter what they blamed it on.

She tasted of cinnamon and cream, of holidays at Haberstock Hall, of Christmases past and present, of hopes for the future, of nutmeg from the girls' frothy eggnog, a promise of sweetness fulfilled. Her arguments overcome, he felt her lean into him, her mouth open fully to his, her arms slip about his waist, drawing her close against him and sending a bolt of hopeful desire through him. It seemed the most natural response in the world to deepen the kiss, to drink and drink from the never-ending well of her, to fill himself up in a way he'd not been filled before. To be with her like this was instinctively desirable…selfish. The word inserted itself even in the midst of his pleasure.

Was it fair to her to take what she offered? What he wanted? Without being sure of what he could offer in return? He'd cavalierly whispered such audacious words as 'trust me'. But was he worthy of that trust? Had he started something he wanted to finish but perhaps could not? And yet he still wanted her, wanted this, and that was the selfish part. He knew better, but did not hold back regardless.

William drew back, his mouth reluctantly relinquishing hers, but not his touch, not her touch. They stood together, rooted in each other's embrace, her arms still wrapped about him, her face still framed in his hands as they stared down the aftermath in each other's eyes. Adam and Eve in the Garden. They'd eaten from the tree of knowledge.

'Now we know,' Honoria whispered. There were secrets no more. Now they knew they could make one another burn with want, that they were more than friends. There were pretences they could hide behind no longer, there was no more protection for their hearts. They were like deer in a field, out in the open. Exposed.

William brushed a curl back from her face, delighting in the soft warmth of her skin beneath his fingertips. 'Yes, now we know what heaven feels like,' he murmured, stealing a kiss that overrode the asking of what came next.

Chapter Nine

December 24th, Christmas Eve

'What are your intentions towards Miss McGrath?' At his father's words, William's hands halted on the instruments he was sterilising. Up until now, they'd passed a peaceful morning in the familiar comfort of his father's surgery, a place where William had spent hours learning medicine beside his father and Thea.

This place is the birthright you refuse to accept, his conscience whispered.

It had been doing a lot of that—of whispering, of cautioning, of challenging him, since he'd stepped foot off the ship. He was not used to such intrusive prodding. He was generally a man who knew his own mind without fail, but since leaving the Crimea that had not been the case.

Or rather you do know your own mind, you're just afraid to speak it.

There his conscience went again, confronting him.

'Well, my son, do you mean to marry her?' his father pressed, stopping his own tasks to study him.

'Were you this direct with my sisters' husbands?' William joked, hoping for distraction. He wasn't prepared to discuss Honoria, not after last night. That kiss had rendered all of his pre-planned explanations regarding their relationship moot at best and untruthful at worst.

His father chuckled. 'Well, with Jules I was. He hasn't much of a father of his own. He needed direction.' His father smiled and wiped his hands on a towel, but he wasn't deterred from his original question. 'You've brought a girl home to meet the family, to be taken in by the family. Surely you've given some thought to what that means.'

'I think any conclusions are hasty,' William said slowly, taking time to gather his words. His thoughts were all topsy-turvy today. He could no longer explain Honoria as just a friend who needed a place for Christmas. To do so would be to demean what had passed between them beneath the mistletoe last night *and* it would be a lie. He did not make it a practice to lie to anyone, particularly his father. Yet he wasn't sure he had a grasp on what the truth was at the moment.

'I've been in England for five days. I'm barely out of the military. Leaping into marriage seems highly precipitous.' It certainly was when explained that way. To marry a woman on a five-day acquaintance the moment one returned from war sounded like the height of folly. His father knew him better than that. He was not a man who rushed into things. He was careful, methodical. At least he had been. Kissing Honoria made him want to be none of those things. He wanted to be reckless with her, the very last thing he should be when entrusted with the quality of her friendship.

His father picked up a scalpel and began to wash it. Beyond him, outside the window, the sky was grey, promising more snow by evening. It would be a white, boisterous Christmas by then if that was so. This morning was supposed to be the calm before the storm of celebrations broke.

While the women were all gathered in the house making preparations for the open house at the Hall that would last until midnight church, he'd been looking forward to time with his father. He would not have 'the discussion' with his father today. He wouldn't deliver that disappointment on Christmas Eve, instead, he would take the time to enjoy his father's company, time to enjoy being home and perhaps recapture a little of the old days. 'But it's not just a five-day acquaintance,' his father corrected. 'You've known her for a year in close quarters.'

'But it has also been nearly a year since I've seen her without even the exchange of a single letter,' William added pointedly. So much for the calm before the storm.

His father gave him a censorious stare. 'Are her parents comfortable having her travel alone with you? Having her spend Christmas among strangers neither she nor they have ever met? It does surprise me somewhat, given that her manners speak of her being of gentle birth.'

'Her parents have passed,' William supplied.

'She's all alone then, poor girl.' His father nodded his head sadly. 'Then you must be doubly careful with her for both your sakes. You've done right in bringing her here, of ensuring that she's not alone for Christmas, but don't mistake pity for love, William. She will not thank you for it.'

William wanted to correct him, to tell him that it was most definitely not pity that had urged him to invite Honoria home for Christmas. But to say that would feed right into his father's initial question: what were his intentions? One did not invite a girl home to the family without having them. True, he'd not liked the idea of her being alone for the holiday, but more than that, he'd not liked the idea of himself being without her at Christmas. He'd wanted her here with him, at the one place in the world that was more important to him than any other, with the people dearest to him. But to what end? That was what he had to figure out.

To do so required knowing his path and hers. What did Honoria want from life? From him? He wasn't sure. He knew only that she, like him, wasn't where she wanted to be. Once they found their own paths, would there be room for each other on them? She wanted to get as far from the war as she could, but he wanted to work with veterans. She wanted to live in the countryside while he wanted to live in London close to the hospitals and other experts.

'I see I've given you something to think about.' His father smiled kindly, as if he guessed at and understood some of the dilemma brewing in his son's mind. 'It's good to have you home, William. I've missed working with you.' He turned back to his task, continuing to talk. 'Everyone will want to meet you at the open house today and welcome you home. We'll do unofficial rounds on Boxing Day and you can meet those who couldn't come. We'll have you up to snuff on the parish in no time.'

So that they could begin the transition of transferring the health care of the area into his hands. It would be a slow, gradual transition as people accustomed themselves to William and his new role. William nodded and said nothing, but his father's plans were a reminder that he had to decide soon. That had become complicated after last night. It was no longer his needs alone that bore consideration.

He needed to talk with Honoria. He was well aware as he and his father finished their washing and returned to the house that if he was serious about her, he had the ability to give her dreams to her. He could take up the mantle at Haberstock Hall, give her a home here, a family here, the life in the country far from reminders of war and all those they'd lost. He could please her and his father in one move and in part he could please himself. He could marry her, build a life of service and caring with her.

It was not an unappealing option, but it came at no small expense to himself. To do so would cost him his dreams, his goals. What would happen to men like Peter Falkner who counted on him? How long would his own personal happiness survive under such circumstances? His father was right, there was much to ponder.

How long did happiness last? Honoria fought the urge to pinch herself as she stood with Thea in the great hall, surrounded by festive good cheer on all sides. At one end of the room, the enormous fireplace held a roaring yule log tugged in by a hearty, ruddy-faced group of villagers earlier that afternoon and presented to Dr Peverett. At the other end of the Great Hall, a long table positively groaned under the largesse provided by Haberstock Hall.

There was ham, ably carved and proudly served by Cook, a lightly glazed apple cake made from Haberstock apples, trays of beautifully iced ginger cookies in various festive shapes, a silver epergne piled high with a tower of oranges, a tureen of hot soup and a punch bowl filled with a warm mulled wine. To the side were kegs of local apple cider distributed by Jules and his brother, Winthrop, who'd recently moved to the area.

Honoria was keenly aware the afternoon was a glimpse of Christmases past when her own family had once entertained in happier times, as well as a tantalising glimpse of Christmases future. Both brought with them a bittersweet mixture of joy and sadness, a complicated blend of memories and hopes, each impossible in their own ways.

'Are you overwhelmed yet?' Thea asked when they had a break from guests wandering by to greet them.

'Never.' Honoria smiled, handing Effie-Claire off to the nursemaid who'd come to claim the little girl for her nap. Effie-Claire had been her constant companion today as they'd prepared for the open house and Honoria had loved it, loved having the bright, curious child at her side, chattering and 'helping' in her own way. 'This is what Christmas should be like. Neighbours together, food aplenty, decorations and a roaring fire. A day without want. It's magical.'

Thea nodded. 'I agree. I love the Christmas Eve party. Last year was the first year the Hall didn't host one. It was an…awkward…year. I was with Leopold's family for our first Christmas together, William wasn't here. Anne and Ferris were with his family celebrating the return of his brother. Thomasia was newly and quietly returned home with Effie-Claire. A discreet Christmas seemed the best choice.' Thea gave a soft smile. 'You're good with the children, by the way. Effie-Claire adores you and even shy Benjamin has taken to you. Not everyone has the patience for toddlers.' Thea paused, clearly waiting for her to say something.

This was definitely an invitation to discuss her own desires for children and family, but Honoria did not allow herself to be drawn in. Thea let the moment pass with a sigh and returned to the conversation. 'Having missed a Haberstock Christmas last year and the one before that because I was in the Crimea, I will never take it for granted again. This is a special day, a moment out of time when all can be right in the world.'

'Exactly. It will be hard to go back to London after this.' Honoria smiled to mitigate the sadness the words engendered. How could life ever be the same after this? After knowing that there was a place where her dreams came alive? That the things she wanted weren't just fanciful imaginings? They did exist, they could be created and had been created here in Haberstock.

Thea's brow furrowed. 'You'll go back?'

'Well, my job is there,' Honoria gently reminded.

'It's just I thought perhaps you and William might make an announcement.' Thea shook her head. 'Forgive my bluntness, it's not my business, although Thomasia thinks it's hers.' They laughed together and Honoria's liking for this woman grew tenfold. In a different time, they could have been sisters.

'Thank you, by the way, for running interference last night. Your news certainly called off the hounds.' The more time she spent with Thea, the more she liked William's twin. The woman was intuitive and sensitive to those around her. 'William and I are…friends.' Even as she said it, she felt transparent as if Thea could see right through the lie. Friends did not kiss like they had. She'd lain awake most of the night, reliving that kiss and forcing herself not to think about what it might or might not mean.

'William is a good friend. He didn't want me to be alone for Christmas.' Such a friendship would be enough, she told herself. To hope for more would be to hope for too much, to reach too high, to come too close to her dreams. Yet her gaze drifted to where William stood near the cider keg in conversation with Dr Tresham. The two of them had been talking for a while.

'Any idea what they're discussing?' Thea asked as Leopold returned with cups of mulled wine for each of them.

'Probably Dr Tresham's paper about post-war trauma and its effects on the mind.' Honoria thought it likely they were discussing more than that, like the possibility of William working at the soldiers' hospital with Tresham—the one place she wanted to escape, and the one place William wanted to be above all else—but she could not discuss it with Thea. That was private information William had entrusted her with. It was not hers to share.

'Hmm,' was all Thea said, but Honoria was aware

Thea was watching her carefully, a faint, knowing smile hovering on her lips.

There was a brief, brotherly embrace between Tresham and William, before William turned his gaze towards her and started across the room, purpose in his stride, in his dark eyes, and it was all directed on her. Honoria flushed at the realisation that it was she who drew him, she whom he wanted to speak with out of all the people present, people he'd not seen for years. He'd been quite popular earlier this afternoon, everyone swarming about to greet him. But now, he was making it clear he wanted only to be with her.

Thea turned to Leopold. 'I think we'll be *de trop* in a moment, darling.' She gave a little smile over the rim of her mug. '*Just* friends, Honoria? Are you sure?' She looped her arm through her handsome husband's and they moved off a discreet distance. No, she wasn't sure. She'd not been sure of anything since that kiss last night except that William's kiss had awakened her, as a woman, as a dreamer, as a person of hope and passion, the person she used to be. She wasn't sure she wanted to be awakened. She'd buried such feelings long ago because they were flames and flames warmed, but they also burnt. She did not want to be burnt again by disappointment, by overwhelming loss.

'You look beautiful, red becomes you,' William complimented, placing a quick kiss on her cheek. She could almost hear Thea's laughing challenge—*Just friends?* She wouldn't be able to claim such status now. But she couldn't be angry. She liked how he'd crossed the room to her, liked that he'd noticed the time she'd taken with her appearance. It was one of Thomasia's old dresses from her pre-pregnancy days that no longer fit and the girls had insisted she wear it. *The girls*. Just listen to her. That was dangerous, a sign of how close she'd allowed all this to become in such a short time.

'Careful,' she warned. 'You don't want anyone jumping to conclusions.'

William grinned, his dark eyes dancing. 'Let them jump. Come with me, I want to show you something, and talk about something.' She cast a look around, wondering if they could sneak away without being noticed by anyone but Thea and Leopold.

'Games will be starting soon, it will be chaos,' William assured her. He took her hand and led her through the crowd, down a quiet corridor away from the party, grabbing a cloak for her from a peg as they went. Using a back door, they slipped out into the dusk. Afternoon had come and gone, evening was settling in, the dark punctuated by silvery white snowflakes. William draped the cloak about her shoulders, the heavy garment as welcome and warm as the hands that lingered at her shoulders.

'Where are we going?' She gripped William's arm to keep her balance on the frozen ground and hoped the journey outside wouldn't ruin the little slippers that matched the dress.

'Not far,' he promised. 'Just to the barn. It will be quiet and private, and we can talk without interruption.'

The way his eyes glittered when he said the words 'private' sent her stomach to fluttering as it had last night when he'd kissed her. What would he ask her? How would she answer? Was she ready for William's question, whatever it might be?

Chapter Ten

They didn't make it to the barn before he pulled her into his arms and kissed her hard beneath the snowy skies. 'I've wanted to do that all day.' He laughed and spun her around. She felt good in his arms, right, as if they'd been made to hold only her, as if she belonged in them, the way she belonged here.

She belonged at Haberstock Hall. She belonged with him. In his home.

The depth of that realisation hit him hard as he set her down, taking in her cheeks, bright with the cold, eyes sparkling with her own laughter. He brushed a snowflake from her nose with his thumb. 'It's cold out here.'

'I like it.' Honoria's breath came in frosty gasps.

'Haberstock agrees with you,' She fit here effortlessly, like one of the perfectly tailored gloves they'd bought in Knightsbridge—tight about the fingers, leaving no gap. Honoria had fit in seamlessly with the Christmas excitement. His mind was filled with bright images of her as she'd been last night when he'd entered the music room to find her surrounded by his sisters, laughing with them as if she were already one of them.

The sight of her today in the kitchens when he'd come back from the surgery, a smudge of flour on her cheek while she'd baked and filled trays alongside Anne and Becca for the open house, the ease with which he'd caught her toting Effie-Claire on her hip throughout the busy afternoon—for a woman who said she eschewed marriage and thoughts of family, she was entirely too comfortable with children. It would be a pity for her to miss having some of her own simply because she thought they were beyond her.

Yearning struck him hard and without warning. He wanted to show her such things—children, a family— were possible for her. They were within her reach, with him. He could give her what she secretly craved and outwardly denied. All he had to do was stay. The earlier thought returned, pulsing more determinedly now. He could do it. He could stay for her, for his father, for the family he had now and the family he would have later…with her. Maybe this was real courage, to be brave enough to embrace his destiny instead of subverting it.

'Haberstock is wondrous.' Honoria twirled in a circle, arms outstretched, white snowflakes dotting the hood of her cloak as evening fell in full about them. 'It's even better than your tales made it out to be.' She stopped spinning and pinned him with her blue gaze. 'It's magical here,' she said in all seriousness. Her hood fell back, revealing gold hair glistening with melted snowdrops. 'It's the trees, the river, the fields. Jules tells me there's a waterfall.' He'd seen her in deep discussion with Jules earlier today. So, that's what they'd been talking about. He'd wondered.

She lowered her voice and gripped the lapels of his jacket as if she were about to impart an important secret. 'Jules told me coming here changed his life. He was broken, aimless, and then he came here and found himself again. Wychavon, too, tells a similar tale. Haberstock Hall was the saving of them.'

William stared down at her with admiration. Was there a more genuine person in the world? She had spent her time, patiently listening to two men who were virtual strangers to her up until yesterday just as she'd listened to the soldiers under her care, and in return Jules and Wychavon had spilled their inner thoughts to her. This was why he loved her—yes, *loved* her. She was selfless and caring.

Perhaps she was right, there was magic at Haberstock Hall. Maybe, even now, it was working its soothing power on her and on him, helping him to see the possibilities of life here. Or maybe it was the magic of Christmas Eve, a night of hope and new beginnings. He'd always thought it odd that a celebration of such overwhelming newness happened at the end of the year.

'Jules told me about a dog you saved. I want to meet him,' she said, tugging him towards the barn.

'You mean Thomas?' They ducked into the warmth of the stable. 'He should be around here somewhere.' William led the way down the centre aisle, peeking in stalls until they found Thomas curled up in a pile of hay. He raised his greying muzzle at the sight of William, tail wagging in recognition. William made the introductions and they sat down, one on each side of the hound. Honoria stroked the dog's head and William felt a moment's jealousy. As much as he liked Thomas, he wanted those hands on him and was not inclined to share.

'We called him Thomas for Doubting Thomas out of the Bible,' William told her the story. 'He didn't trust us at first. He'd convinced himself he was better off alone, that he didn't need anyone,' William let his eyes linger on Honoria's, willing her to see the allegory. She needn't court loneliness out of the need for self-protection. He would protect her.

'But we changed his mind. We earned his heart and he's been loyal and true ever since.' William chuckled. 'He runs these stables now. He barks when the stable-boys are too lazy. He trots at my father's heels when he goes out on rounds. The whole countryside knows him and he knows them.' It would be like that for Honoria if she would let it.

He reached a hand out to stroke Thomas's neck and brushed Honoria's fingers, the unintentional gesture sending electric awareness sizzling through him, an awareness born of his intentions with her and for his future. The die was cast. He would stay. He was meant to be with her, to give her all of this, her very heart's desire. She looked up, their gazes holding. 'We could be happy here, Honoria. We could have a life here.' A certain peace settled on him as he said the words, a new peace, a different peace.

'We could,' she whispered softly, brushing an errant piece of straw from his hair. It would be a wonderful life, a family, surrounded by the magic and purpose of Haberstock Hall. Perhaps this new peace he didn't quite understand came from having made the choice, know-ing that he was consciously choosing to embrace the

Peverett legacy. Perhaps the problem had always been that he'd felt the legacy was choosing him, not him choosing it, that it was being thrust upon him without his permission. Perhaps now it would be all right because he was the one doing the choosing, the agent of his own choices, his own destiny.

Thomas chose that moment to leave them. He rose up from the hay to conduct his self-appointed evening rounds of the stalls. It was all the encouragement William needed to reach for her, or was it her reaching for him? Did it matter? They were falling together into each other's arms, into each other's promises, the sweet hay bower surrounding them, keeping the world at bay. His mouth found hers, embarking on a longer, extended version of their kiss outside, want and desire flaring hot between them. Today and every day forward would all be worthwhile as long as Honoria was beside him. Or beneath him, as the case might be.

Honoria stared up into William's dark eyes, her breath catching in excitement and realisation. This was not going to stop with kisses as it had last night. Although perhaps she ought to stop it, came a quickly squelched whisper of caution. She was *not* going to stop this even knowing this could lead nowhere beyond the moment, but she *would* claim that moment with *this* man for herself. One selfish moment against a lifetime of giving. Surely that wouldn't be so wrong. Not wrong, but it was certainly not safe. This was reckless, this left her open to disappointment. But it was necessary. There could be hope without disappointment and no disappointment without hope. Tonight, she wanted hope, if only for a little while. She wanted to believe in the pictures painted by his words.

We could have a life here.

William *did* mean it. She did not doubt his sincerity, but such things came with a cost. One or both of them would have to pay for such things. For now, her body said, there was no price, only pleasure: the pleasure of his mouth at her lips, her neck, her throat; pleasure in the way her pulse leapt when he touched her, his warm hands slipping beneath her skirts to the hot wet core of her where her desire throbbed in answer to his caress, where her body begged for release, but not yet. Not until they could be joined. 'With you,' she breathed. 'I don't want it alone.' She'd been alone too long.

'And you shall have it,' he promised, his own tones hoarse with unmistakable desire as his body settled between the welcoming vee of her thighs, his shaft at her entrance, a hard juxtaposition to her softness, a softness she wanted conquered, a softness she offered up freely for his possession at least for tonight. And then she was alone no longer. He slid into her, completion and pleasure riding them both hard until it overtook them, wrapping them in release.

'Have you spoken to your father?' she spoke softly in the quiet aftermath. How long had they lain here? How long had they gone without the need for words? That bliss was passing, and in its wake a suspicion had formed. She knew now the price for tonight, for the vision he'd promised her. He was the one who was going to pay it. She knew now how he dared promise those things to her, things he would never promise blithely.

'I don't know that speaking with him is needed any longer,' His long fingers ran down her arm in an idle caress. He was still drowsy, but she was fully alert now and fully alarmed.

'Why is that?' She was certain she knew why, but she wanted to hear him say it.

'I've been thinking that coming home is the right decision for me, after all, that I've been stubborn.' He came a little more awake. 'I can give you everything you want, everything you believe is out of your reach. A home, a family, a partner for life.' He levered up on one arm, facing her, excitement radiating from him. 'Think of it, Honoria. You can live in the country. You can practise medicine beside me. No one here will care about your credentials. You can study with me or with my father if you like and when the time comes and there are nursing schools, you can go. I will not hold you back and you'll be ready. Your dreams are here, Honoria, every one of them.'

If he'd been the snake in Eden, she would have eaten the apple and asked for seconds. William Peverett, up close and personal after lovemaking, was a persuasive power nonpareil. How did a girl argue with any of that? What girl turned that down? A girl who did not want pity. It was her only defence. 'I don't need you to save me.'

'This isn't about saving you, it's about loving you, loving what we can have together. Everything we want is right here.'

But not everything *he* wanted. 'Except your men,'

she pointed out softly. How like William to overlook that when he was busy putting others first. She could not allow it.

He nuzzled at her neck, 'I'd rather have a lifetime of you, a lifetime of this.' In those words she saw the dilemma he'd grappled with since returning home, a dilemma she'd not aided in lessening, but abetted in enhancing. She had only made it worse. What had once been simply the dilemma between returning to Haberstock or staying in London had become entangled with other considerations. Returning to Haberstock fulfilled her needs while returning to London did not. Returning to London allowed his work to move forward while it impeded hers. But here in Haberstock there were no soldiers for him to care for, the one thing that weighed in the balance against all else.

Perhaps for another man such a consideration would seem a small trade indeed, but for a man of William Peverett's tenacity and integrity, it was no minor matter. She'd seen him labour over men for whom there was no real hope until the last scrap of hope was gone—to do less was in violation of his oath as a physician. She could not let him give all that up. Not for her, not because of her. She could not live with that. Such a compromise would tear a man like William Peverett apart as assuredly as poverty had torn her father and family apart.

William's nuzzling was becoming more insistent as was the hard pressure of him against her leg. There was tonight, only tonight. They would make the most of it. She hitched a leg about his hip and levered herself atop him with a wicked smile. 'My turn.'

Chapter Eleven

They missed the dancing, but not the chaos. By the time they returned to the house, a fine new layer of snow coated the grounds of the Hall and guests were bundling into wagons to make the short trek to the village for the Christmas Eve service. Midnight was little more than an hour away.

'There you are!' Thea drew them aside, worry in her expression. 'I've been looking everywhere for you.' The scold was for William, but her gaze encompassed them both, giving Honoria the impression she knew exactly what her twin had been up to. 'Thomasia has gone to her room. She's not feeling up to church.' There was a meaningful look behind the words and Honoria had no difficulty reading between the lines. The baby was on the way. 'I offered to stay behind, but she won't hear of it. Shaw's with her, but he's no doctor, he's a politician.'

'We'll stay,' Honoria spoke up, already turning to fetch William's bag from the surgery. She was keenly regretting not bringing her own things, but she'd not thought she'd need them for the short trip to Haberstock. William's hand gently stalled her.

'You should go to church. You were looking forward to hearing the bells.'

She shook her head. 'Absolutely not, I am staying with you. You might need an extra hand.' Especially if her concerns bore out. She still hadn't liked how large Thomasia was.

'Then it's settled.' Thea gave her an approving smile. 'I'll feel better with you both here.' Thea leaned forward conspiratorially. 'Her last birth was difficult,' she told Honoria. Her gaze rested on her twin. 'I won't be far away, if anything…'

William put his hand over his sister's and offered the strength Honoria had seen him offer so many patients in the past. 'With seven healers on hand to assist, Thomasia will come through just fine.' Seven. Honoria felt a flush of pride when she realised he'd included her in that number. This was what life at Haberstock would have been like if it had been possible: being included in the care of others. Honoria swallowed hard. It was difficult enough to give up the man, but it would also be difficult to give up the dream. 'I'll get your bag and be right up,' she said around the tightness in her throat.

Thomasia was pacing the bedchamber when Honoria arrived with William's bag. She was dressed in a white nightgown and loose robe and sweating despite the open window and the snowy breeze. Her husband, Shaw, was in shirt sleeves, watch in hand, studying his wife nervously.

'Tommie, you should have said something sooner,' William was scolding sternly, only to be rebuked in return.

'You were nowhere to be found, Will.' Thomasia gave a grunt and gripped the mantel of the fireplace as a spasm rippled through her enormous belly. 'But it didn't matter,' she continued once the spasm passed. 'They stopped and I didn't want to ruin the party.'

'But now they're back, fast and furious.' William stripped out of his jacket and rolled up his sleeves while Honoria poured hot water into a basin for washing. She'd wash after he did. One could not be too clean when it came to delivering babies. 'How close together, Shaw?'

'Two minutes, or slightly less. Is that bad?' Shaw looked up from his watch with concern.

Honoria went to him, remembering this was his first birth. Effie-Claire wasn't his biological daughter. No wonder the poor man was nervous. He'd not been through it all yet. 'It's perfect, it means the child is on schedule and due shortly.'

At her words, Shaw seemed to relax until Thomasia said somewhat peevishly, 'Effie-Claire took thirty-six hours. It won't be fast.' Another spasm took her, this one nearly knocking her off her feet and it would have if Shaw hadn't been there to hold her.

'Time for bed, Tommie,' William insisted, helping Shaw to guide her to the big four-poster.

Honoria washed her hands and fetched William's stethoscope from his bag. No one argued with a mother in labour, but she was certain Thomasia was flat-out wrong. This baby wasn't going to wait much longer. She approached Thomasia. 'May I have a listen?' With Thomasia's consent, she placed the stethoscope to her belly and turned to William with a smile. Now she understood the reason for Thomasia's ungainly largeness. 'Listen, tell me what you hear.'

William listened and straightened in surprise. 'Tommie, get ready to work—you're having twins, likely within the hour.'

Willa Honoria Rawdon was born in the last two minutes of Christmas Eve, followed five minutes later on Christmas Day by her brother, Alfred, both of them in possession of a lusty set of lungs that nearly drowned out the peal of the bells from the village. Honoria could not imagine a more perfect way to herald in Christmas than with a babe in her arms, standing beside the man she loved, knowing that her efforts had safely brought not one but two lives into the world on the night that the world celebrated the birth of unconditional love.

'It might have gone differently if we'd not known to expect two,' William said softly. They were standing at the now-closed window with the newborns, offering Shaw and Thomasia a moment's privacy while Shaw helped her into a clean nightgown.

'The second heartbeat can often hide and remain undetected during an exam. It's easy to miss and it will remain so until we have stronger stethoscopes.' Honoria adjusted the sweet little bundle in her arms. Alfred was a bit smaller than his sister, which wasn't unusual for twins, but he seemed to exhibit no immediate ill effects for being born second. He would bear watching over the next few days, though, just to be sure.

'Well, anyway, thank you. I'm glad you were here. I needed you.' William's eyes were soft as their gazes met over the infants. She knew what he was thinking—it was a variation on her own thoughts downstairs when Thea had summoned them. This was the beginning of their life together, of what life would be like at Haberstock for them. And he was convincing himself that it would be enough.

He looked good with a babe in his arms, a natural father. The thought brought tears to her eyes and she quickly turned away. She had to be strong. She couldn't give in to the temptation that maybe it would all turn out right, that maybe she could stay. She had a few days in Paradise, that was all. It was more important than ever to set him free when this was over. That way, only one of them would be disappointed.

It was well into Christmas morning before the house retired. There'd been the excitement of returning from church to meet the latest arrivals to the family. Everyone had wanted a turn to hold the twins, to hear Thomasia's account of the birth which was full of lavish praise for Honoria's part in it. The attention, quite frankly, put her to the blush.

Thea hugged her. 'I knew I could count on you, Honoria,' William's twin said joyously, drawing her aside as the initial excitement died down.

'William deserves a lot of credit,' Honoria protested humbly.

Thea gave her a cryptic look that put Honoria on alert. William's sister wanted to discuss more than the birth. 'I am counting on you there, too. William's been very closed since he's been home. I know him and there's something weighing on his mind, something he doesn't want to discuss.' She peered at Honoria with intent brown eyes. 'Do you know what it is?' It was the second time Thea had asked such a thing, but Honoria's answer was still the same.

She did know, but this was not a position she relished being in, caught between the new friend she'd found in Thea and the loyalty she owed William, but there was no question of her answer. 'I could not say.'

Thea gave a knowing smile. 'I thought that would be your response. Loyalty is an admirable quality. Most of the time,' she added wryly. 'I hope William appreciates your discretion.'

From the bed, Thomasia began to yawn and Shaw subtly began the process of shuffling new grandparents, aunts and uncles from the room so that his wife could rest. Honoria stopped beside the cradle where the twins lay side by side for one last peep. 'Sleep well, little ones,' she whispered, feeling William come to stand beside her, his hand resting easily at her back. She gave a contented sigh. 'Is there anything more precious?'

'All life is precious, in all its forms, all its moments,' William answered solemnly as they stepped quietly from the room and shut the door behind them. He was thinking about his men, no doubt, and contrasting their situation to this one. The babies were taking their first breaths while so many of the men they'd served in the Crimea had breathed their last. There'd been preciousness in that as well, to be with someone in the last moments, the last breaths of their life.

'I think I like these moments best, though. It felt good to deliver a baby again,' She smiled softly as they made the slow stroll down the hall to her room. 'These last few years have been more about endings than beginnings.' Not just the losses of war for her, but the losses of family and home. She was tired of it, tired of losing, tired of the hopelessness that came with constant struggle. Too much of the war had been about loss.

William's arm was about her shoulder. 'Your mother would have been proud of you tonight, delivering twins.'

'*We* delivered twins,' she corrected. 'But, yes, my mother would have been proud because I was doing what I was meant to do.' And what she was meant to do was to let him go so he could pursue his own calling. That was a bitter pill to swallow. She could not let him sacrifice his calling for her. They'd reached her door, but she was not ready to let him go, not when she knew time was running out, that the one night she'd promised herself was nearly over. 'I don't think I'll sleep just yet,' she said.

'Me neither.' William smiled. 'I'm too awake, too alert.' It was always like that after a big operation, or a successful day when one felt one had accomplished something. Physician's Euphoria. She felt it, too. They might as well use the opportunity and the privacy to talk. There were things that must be said and they would be best said before it became harder to dislodge the ideas William had given life to in the barn, before her resolve could be tested further.

The Fates were probably laughing at her as it was. The moment she'd decided there could only be one night with William, Fate had promptly thrown the twins in her direction, showing her quite vividly a glimpse of Christmas future, of what life would be like with William—of them delivering children side by side, of being surrounded by a family who embraced her, who filled the gaps inside her left by her mother's death. What had been lost to her had been found here at Haberstock. All she had to do was claim it. 'Why don't you come in and we can talk?'

'Talk?' William teased naughtily, his eyes glinting with serious flirtation. 'Is that what we're calling it?' He stole a kiss in the dark hallway and her resolve faltered. He was devastating like this, playful and teasing, his guard down in a rare moment of not worrying over patients.

Perhaps if you stayed, you could make more moments for him like this, whispered the devil on her shoulder, proof of how badly she wanted to stay, how badly she wanted to ignore the price behind his offer in the barn.

It would be so easy to pretend everything would be all right, that William would be happy with his decision, that she could make him happy. She knew full well that happiness was the domain of the individual. No one could be responsible for another's happiness. That was an illusion.

She fumbled for the door handle behind her and they stumbled into the room, kissing and teasing, desire rising fast between them. She tried one last time. 'We have to talk about the things said in the barn, I'm serious, William.'

William laughed between kisses, 'I'm serious, too. I'm serious about getting this dress off you at last. Whatever it is we have to discuss, we can discuss it naked.' There was probably a flaw to that logic, but she couldn't find it at the moment. Getting him naked would take little effort on her part. He'd already discarded his waistcoat and jacket for the delivery and not bothered to put them back on. It was easy work to pull his shirt over his head and not bother with the buttons.

'Not fair!' William groaned, frustrated to discover the red dress laced at the back.

Not fair indeed, Honoria thought as she dropped his shirt on to a chair. How was a girl to concentrate, to keep a level head when faced with William Peverett's well-sculpted torso? And shoulders and arms? Sweet heavens, but he was a man who knew how to keep himself fit which was no small matter given the rations they'd faced in the Crimea. While there was no ounce of fat on him, there was plenty of muscle, likely hard-earned from hauling men from the battlefield, lifting them on to stretchers and tables.

Doctoring required a certain amount of physical strength. It was one of the reasons female nurses were dubious commodities. They might offer 'tea and sympathy' in the sickroom, but they hadn't the strength for battlefield triage no matter how much skill they possessed. William Peverett, though, was the whole package of physical and intellectual excellence. Not that she was focused much on intellectual anything at the moment. She was preoccupied with making an anatomical study of the rounded musculature of his upper arms, the symmetrical precision of his rippling stomach muscles and, lower still, the lean, chiselled structuring of his iliac girdle which disappeared into the waistband of his trousers.

'Give me your back, let me have a go at those laces,' William groused playfully.

She made a pout as she turned. 'Now I can't look at you.'

'I'm glad you saw something you liked,' He nuzzled her neck as his competent hands worked the laces and then the petticoat tapes and corset stays. 'I've been dying to get this dress off you all afternoon. I wanted to see you naked in the barn, to touch your skin, to feel *you*.'

His hands stilled, signalling that he'd completed his tasks. She stepped back and turned, clutching her loosened layers of garments to her for one more moment until she had the full attention of his gaze. 'And now you can.' She let them fall, leaving her only in her cotton chemise, a garment she could dispatch by herself.

Honoria pulled the thin garment over her head, a gesture she made every night as she prepared for bed, but this time she was aware of how provocative the simple gesture was, how the act raised her arms over her head, how it pushed her breasts into taut, high relief as the firelight played over her skin, highlighting the intimate valleys and planes of her body for his gaze alone.

William exhaled raggedly. 'Good lord, you're beautiful, Honoria. I want to explore every inch of you, with every sense I possess. I want to lick you, taste you, touch you, listen to you moan your pleasure as I do.' His words sent a damp heat to her core. She'd like that, too. Too much. It would be one more way in which leaving would become more difficult.

'Your turn.' She gestured to his trousers. 'The feeling is mutual, you know.' He was not the only one want was running away with. There was an erotic quality to watching him remove his trousers, working his fastenings with those long, slender hands, his gaze riveted on her the whole time.

I am doing this for you, putting myself on display for your gaze only.

Just as she'd done for him.

He kicked his trousers aside and stood before her gloriously nude, letting her gaze take him in from stem to stern and what a stem it was. The eye could not help but be drawn to the centre of him where his phallus rose healthy and strong from a dark nest of hair in physical reminder that whatever talking was going to take place would happen later, much later.

'Come to bed with me, Honoria,' His hand reached out in invitation and she took it. It seemed more important at the moment to indulge their senses, to taste and to lick, and to revel in the pleasure they could give one another. After all, what she had to say could not change, the outcome of their lovemaking would not change, what she had to do. She had to let him go. Where he saw tonight as a beginning, she saw it as an ending. This was not a celebration of their first breath, but their last.

Chapter Twelve

The Peveretts celebrated 'Second Christmas', as they'd taken to calling their late rising the next day, around noon; their 'first' Christmas having been the celebration of the twins' arrival. As a result, no one had risen until after ten and it had been another hour before everyone had found their ways downstairs to the dining room, Honoria and William included.

If anyone noticed that William had not awakened in his own bed, no one said anything. He had, however, awakened precisely where he wanted to be—in Honoria's arms, in Honoria's bed. Soon to be their bed, he thought to himself, a private smile teasing his mouth as he seated her beside him at the long table.

Waking beside her had been a quiet glory. They'd made drowsy love with the light of a snowy morning drifting through the window. In their haste last night, they'd not drawn the curtains and snow on the ground made for a bright start to the day despite grey skies. The room had been warm, her body had been warm and he'd been loath to rise from the blankets to put on clothes, although he thought his family would probably prefer that he did. Only Thomasia was allowed to wear her dressing gown to breakfast. He was pleased to note that she appeared to be well considering she'd delivered twins twelve hours prior, twins that were being gently passed about the dining table to willing aunties so that Thomasia and Shaw could focus on making the late morning Christmas meal special for Effie-Claire.

'This is a feast!' Honoria proclaimed beside him as someone handed her a platter of honey-baked ham. She leaned towards Jules. 'You should make a painting of this, it's just like a picture.' Then she turned her beaming smile in his direction and said quietly, 'William, such a meal is the stuff of Christmas dreams.' He could see from the shining appreciation in her gaze how moving she found the scene: the ham, the sticky buns with white icing, the bowls of fluffy, scrambled eggs mixed with cream from the Peverett dairy, rashers of bacon and racks of toast, underlaid by the aroma of strong coffee on account of the late night.

You can give her this every day. She will never want for a beautiful meal again. This is worth what you're giving up.

Across the table, Thea was looking at him queerly. Leopold leaned forward with a gentle smile. 'This beats Christmas in the Crimea, doesn't it?'

'Hear, hear!' Ferris raised his coffee mug. 'Well said. A toast, to safe homecomings, old and new.' It was a perfect toast, William thought, one that included his own return and the arrival of the new babies. Beside him, he felt Honoria's gaze on him, studying, considering. Whatever she'd wanted to discuss had never come about. Perhaps for the best. He'd decided on his course, he'd taken her to bed and not lightly. He was set on his path now and gladly so. He loved her. Whatever it took to be with her, he would do. He'd told her as much and his word was good.

After breakfast, the family trooped into a sitting room that had been set aside as the Christmas tree room this year where a tall, proud fir stood, decorated with little glass ornaments, the presents beneath the tree sending Effie-Claire and Benjamin into squeals of delight. William thought he saw Honoria surreptitiously wipe a tear from her eye.

It was too much. Honoria felt her throat constrict at the sight of the tree, her resolve waver perilously at the sight of the children in raptured alt. This was a fairy tale come to life. She felt as if she had a role in a play. This was too good to be true. It could not last. And it wouldn't. She already knew that. Like a play, the curtain would come down here, too. Tonight, she would tell William she was leaving. She would set him free. It was the right thing to do although it wouldn't be easy. All of this could be hers for the rest of her life. William was offering it all to her. She needn't be alone.

There was no more selfless gift than what he was giving her.

Do you want a family? Have mine. Do you want a place where you can pursue your nursing? I will give you a village and instructors in my father, my mother, my sisters Thea and Anne. Do you want a Christmas morning of the sort you've only dreamed of? Do you want a lover who will be true to you, who will treat you with the reverence you deserve? Come with me, I will fulfil all your dreams and more. I will worship your body and I will show you your true worth.

All it would cost was one man's life, a good man's life, who was willing to throw away other ambitions all for her, a man who was willing to give up his happiness in order to ensure hers.

You should let him. You will never get a better offer, never get a better chance. You did not make him do this. He loves you. He wants to.

She loved him, too. Not in return. That implied love was a commodity that could be spent in exchange for other goods. She didn't love him because of all he offered her. She would have loved him anyway, even if he'd been a poor man. She loved him because he was good, because he was admirable. She loved him and that meant she had to ensure his happiness if he would not ensure it for himself. That was how love worked.

Everyone took up a seat and it was time for presents. Ah, this will be a bit of reality, she thought. This will be a chance to ground myself in the reminder that I'm not one of them. I was a surprise guest. There will be no gifts for me. But she was wrong. Ferris and Anne began the gift exchange, handing out bottles of expensive brandy, acquired through his brother's connections, to the men and sweet-smelling soaps, hand-made by Anne, for the ladies. To Honoria's great surprise, there was a bar even for her. She held it to her nose and inhaled. 'Oh, this is delightful, I will be sure to save it for special occasions.'

'Or use it every day.' Anne laughed, pleased by the appreciation. 'I will make you more.' Honoria smiled politely. Anne might make more, but she wouldn't be here to receive it. She felt William's gaze on her, studying her much as she'd studied him at breakfast. She had the distinct impression that despite their outward smiles, they were both dancing around the question of their relationship. Was he already regretting his promises? Or was he still trying to convince himself that he'd made the right decision to stay in Haberstock? She hated that she was at the heart of each of those scenarios.

There were more gifts. From Thea and Leopold there were books beautifully bound in leather for each according to their tastes. 'This is an old journal of mine,' Thea said, presenting her with the gift. 'It's empty. I thought you could use it for your own notes about nursing. I started you out with a few notes of mine here on the front pages.'

'Thank you,' Honoria stammered, grateful for the comfort of William's hand squeezing hers, otherwise she would have burst into tears at Thea's thoughtfulness. There were little watercolours painted and framed from Jules and Rebecca, each about a subject dear to the recipient's heart. For William, they gave him a painting of Haberstock Hall.

'Thank you—' William nodded his head '—it's beautifully done', but Honoria did not miss the sudden tightness of his jaw. A gilded cage was still a cage. She would not be the one to lock him in it.

When it was time for their gifts, William let her do the honours. 'Honoria and I picked these out,' he said as she presented the girls with their gloves. 'She knew everyone's favourite colours.' She flashed him a look of gratitude. It was one of the countless ways he'd ensured she'd fit in, feel a part of the magic. And she had. It would be hard to walk away, especially now that she'd had a taste of him, of the life that could have been if they weren't so different. If she didn't want to leave the war behind. But where he needed to go, she could not follow.

There were toys for the children and Ferris and Shaw sat beneath the tree entertaining Effie and Ben while the others talked quietly and took turns with the infants. 'Happy?' William asked as they sat together looking through the medical text Thea had given him.

'I cannot recall another afternoon I've enjoyed more,' she said truthfully. Perhaps it was because everything was more precious when something was ending, when it would never be again. She held his gaze, 'William, we need....'

Mrs Newsome, newly returned from her sister's to make sure that dinner got on the table promptly at six, bustled into the Christmas tree room. 'There's a boy here with a telegram from the village. He's in the kitchen waiting for a reply. It's for Dr Peverett.'

Both William and his father rose out of habit. His father laughed and sat down, realising his patients didn't need to send telegrams. 'I'll have to get used to my son being home,' he joked, pride shining in his eyes as William rose to take the note.

Honoria's eyes were glued to William, watching for any sign. A telegram couldn't be good news and yet she couldn't read his expression. She saw his head bend, saw his hand clench the paper. Bad news, then? She resisted the urge to go to him, to put her arms about him regardless of his family watching.

But he wouldn't want that. It wasn't how he processed bad news, if this was indeed bad news. She'd seen him after losing a patient, after delivering bad news. He would need time. Yet she wasn't convinced this was that, that it wasn't all bad. But something in that telegram had triggered dismay.

He looked up for a moment, searching the room for her, his gaze finding hers. 'One of my patients has written, Peter Falkner.' William tried for a smile, attempting a brave face. 'His wife has arrived already and they are joyfully reunited. They are not sure what the future holds for them, but they are together.'

Honoria saw the dilemma immediately. It was not Peter Falkner's happiness that upset him. That was all William had wished and worried for. It was what came next. How long would that happiness last for a man with no legs? Who could not provide for his family in the traditional sense? William would feel responsible for that, not just for Peter, but for all the men he'd saved. What had he saved them for if their lives were destroyed none the less? How could he walk away from them when they needed him? His jaw worked as his eyes lingered on her, his voice hoarse. 'I'm sorry, excuse me, I need some time alone.'

I'm sorry. Those words had been for her. There was a wealth of meaning in those two words as he exited the room. Sorry that he could not give up his calling after all, sorry that he'd made promises he had to break. She was sorry, too. Sorry she hadn't told him he was free, sorry she had let him believe that she would *allow* him to give up his calling for her. That had been selfish, all so that she could enjoy a few days. But she could make it right. She could set him free to go back to his men, his dreams and the prospect nearly broke her. How would she find the strength to do it?

Thea was beside her, taking William's seat. 'I know what you're thinking. You're thinking it's impossible, the two of you being together.'

Honoria felt tears break through, refusing to be held back at last. 'It *is* impossible. If I let him go, I'll lose him. But if I take what he's offering and keep him, I'll lose him in another way, perhaps in even a worse way.' She did not want to sit down to supper with a ghost every night.

'I don't pretend to know what has passed between you or what sort of understanding you might have, but I do know this. What's impossible for one person to solve is better handled together. You have all of us and we've got considerable experience in handling impossible situations.' She nodded towards her blonde husband. 'Leopold didn't even have his own name when we fell in love, no memories of who he was. Ferris was threatened with the loss of his career if he married Anne. Jules walked away from the corruption of his family for Becca and, in doing so, helped his brother to freedom as well. And Shaw risked his seat in Parliament to stand up for what was right even though society has made it difficult for him. But we all found a way through, together, and we'll find a way through for you and William, too. Give it time and don't give up. Love will prevail—you just have to believe.'

Honoria glanced about the room. Did she dare? Or would believing in the impossible, empowering the impossible instead of allowing herself to be defeated by it, only make it worse when that defeat came? Perhaps it wouldn't hurt to believe one last time. For William's sake.

Chapter Thirteen

He couldn't do it. He couldn't leave his men, his patients. William sat in the garden glider, head bent, his body racked with sobs, howls really, as he shook with the futility of it all. How could he walk away from Peter Falkner and men like him, men that he himself had saved? He'd played God with their lives in that field hospital, taking limbs in exchange for life, and then said, *'Go and live that life, although I'm not sure what it will look like.'*

Peter's wife had come. There was joy in that, but it would fade in the wake of the reality they would have to face. What sort of life would they build? William's military orders said his obligation to those men was done. He'd saved them. But his Hippocratic oath demanded he do no harm, to treat the ill to the best of his ability. In his professional opinion, he had not done the latter, not yet, not until he could give each of them a life back that was worthy of them. Those men needed an advocate. He could not be that advocate, that supporter, tucked away at Haberstock. He couldn't stay here. He was needed in London.

The new peace he'd felt last night dissipated, like mist evaporating, giving way to bright sun which brought certainty at the expense of destroying the fuzzy cocoon of fog. He saw his way clearly now, but not obstacle-free for all its clarity. There would be difficult conversations to have. They could not be avoided. Perhaps there'd never been another choice, another way. If this was where his heart lay, he had to pursue it, had to tell his father, had to tell Honoria.

Desperation swept him anew. He was going to lose her over this. He could not be a decent husband to her, racked with guilt over not following his path. He could no more give up his calling to work with veterans than he could give up Honoria. Therein was the futility. He'd not fully understood until now.

Before, it had been simply the dilemma of choosing one or the other. But now, he saw that no matter what he chose, it would be more than that. Giving up either would be a blow against his happiness. Any happiness would be utterly incomplete and incomplete happiness was impossible by definition. This, he recognised, was the real seat of his desperation, the true font of his grief.

But grief has the unique ability to be a crucible of clarity that burns away the unnecessary until only the essentials remain once that grief has broken a man down so that he is only the core of who he is. At that core, William knew one thing in that cold, crystal, Christmas night. He wanted both Honoria and his calling. He was unwilling to part with either.

So don't, came the answer from the depths of his core. *Your problem has been that you thought you had*

*to choose. Choose to have them both and solve the prob-
lem from there.*

In his darkest hour, an idea began to form and along
with it hope began to carefully unfold, Honoria's words
coming back to him.

*'It's magical here...it's the trees, the river, the fields.
Coming here changed Jules's life. He was broken, aimless, and then he came and found himself again. Wychavon, too, tells a similar tale. Haberstock Hall was the
saving of them.'*

Last night, he'd been too wrapped up in seeing her,
with snow in her hair, but tonight, he saw the vision of
her words. Why not bring the men *here*?

'William?' Honoria's voice came through the darkness. The last of the afternoon had fled. Lost in his
thoughts, he'd also lost track of time. He heard half-
boots crunching on the snow and looked up. She'd
brought a lantern and a coat was draped over one arm.
'I've found you at last. Thea thought you might be here,
but I tried the barn first.' She smiled, but her face was
splotchy as if she'd been crying. That was his fault.
He'd given her cause for tears and even though he'd
made her cry, she'd brought his coat, thought of him
and his needs.

She held out the garment and draped it about his
shoulders. 'You'll be freezing by now.' It was a scold
for having been out so long, for bearing his troubles
alone without her there to shoulder part of the burden.
He shrugged his arms through the sleeves. The warmth
felt good.

She slid on to the glider seat beside him, tucking the

cloak about her. Her fingers came around his. 'You're worried about Peter's future. About all of their futures.'

'The government won't care for them, won't find them jobs, won't save their families from poverty. In bringing him home, I feel I have failed him just as if he'd died in the Crimea. I want to do more for them.' He paused, gripping her hand, understanding that he had come up with a solution, but he could not force her to be part of it. The potential to lose her was still there. Everything hinged on the next few minutes.

'While I've been out here, I've come up with an answer.' He gave a soft chuckle. 'Actually, it was you who gave me the idea with your words last night. I want to bring recovering veterans here: amputees, those with lingering mental trauma from the war, those who need a place to go. The men would have peace here. They could hike, fish, ride, swim. There's a lot of physical activity they could engage in to strengthen their bodies.' He could hear the excitement in his own voice. The more he thought about the idea, the more he gave words to it, breathed life into it, the more powerful it became, the more possible.

'And they leave when they're well?' Honoria furrowed her brow, her quick mind working to wrap itself around the project.

'They don't need to leave,' He was ready for her. 'We can model it after the Royal Hospital Chelsea. Some can choose to stay here as pensioners, although payment can be based on whatever they can afford. This can be their home. Those with mental distress can be here for Ferris and I to help and to observe. Others, like Peter, can stay here as well.'

'People who live here will need purpose. Men cannot be idle.' Honoria tested the idea. 'They will need income and they won't be alone. Peter would want his wife with him.'

'We can have work for them.' William nodded. He'd thought of this, too. 'My sister Becca needs people for her toymaking venture—people to paint and assemble her soldiers. The men can be taught as part of the assembly line, not just for her toys but for her other inventions. Jules and Winthrop can likely keep a good number of men employed at Winthrop's cider press.'

'And where would these men live?' Honoria was smiling in the darkness and it gave him hope.

'There are some empty cottages on the property we can use to start with and we can build others. Men who come early can build more cottages for the others. I am hoping Shaw might be persuaded to leverage his connections in order to get funding from Parliament and, if not from Parliament, perhaps he can encourage the Prometheus Club to invest.' Jobs, homes, a quiet place to recover, to be near doctors and the care that could restore a quality to a life that had been, if not wrecked, altered. It was…possible.

'You wouldn't be in London, though, with other experts.' Honoria's question moved the discussion to other, more personal considerations. 'Would you still take on the legacy of being the Haberstock healer? That would be a lot, even for you, William. Too much, I'd say. All that work would wear you to a nub in no time and you'd be no good to anyone.'

'It would be too much for me alone.' William nodded, touched by her concern for him amid all the upheaval of the day. 'That's where Thea comes in. She'll have her diploma in a year or two. She can focus on being the healer at Haberstock Hall.' He ran his thumb over her knuckles in a thoughtful motion. 'It's what Thea has always wanted, to be the healer here. More than me. But until now, it was always beyond her reach because of her gender, that the best she could hope for was making rounds with our father. Always the tag-along. Never *the* healer. But now, both Thea and I can have what we want. Thea as healer takes the pressure of my father's legacy from my shoulders while ensuring the legacy of a Peverett healer in Haberstock continues.'

'It will truly be a family affair then.' Honoria snuggled against him. 'Thea as healer, Jules and Becca offering employment with their manufacturing, giving men purpose; Shaw and Thomasia along with Anne and Ferris lobbying for funds and investors to build cottages; Ferris working alongside you to help men recover from the mental and physical ravages of war. You've been busy out here, William Peverett,' she murmured appreciatively. 'From the ashes of despair and impossibility, it seems a phoenix has arisen,' she said softly.

'There's one more question you haven't asked, Honoria, and that is what your part is in all this?' She wouldn't ask. She was too selfless to ask such a bold question, so he asked it for her. 'I've designed this not only for my dreams, but for yours as well.' He squeezed her hand, forestalling a quick answer.

'Listen to me first, Honoria. I know you don't want to be surrounded by reminders of the war, but here at Haberstock you can pursue your own nursing preferences. You could work with my mother. My mother misses Anne now that she's in the city most of the time. She'd love to have someone come alongside her. You could be a midwife to the local women and if there are nursing schools that open, as Thea predicts, we'll send you if it's what you want. I promised you, Honoria, we'd build a wonderful life here together, only tonight that life looks a little different than it did last night. Will you come alongside me?'

They sat still and quiet in the glider for a long while, hands interlocked in the winter night until Honoria spoke at last. 'It seems Thea was right. She told me that love prevails, we just have to believe. It seems we've both been on a journey of sorts this afternoon. When you left the house, I thought I would have to give you up after all so that you'd be free to follow your passion. Even in the barn, I knew something wasn't quite right.'

'You were going to leave?' His fingers clenched about hers and his heart broke anew with love for this woman. He'd said nothing and yet she'd known the dilemma that had lain on his heart even as he'd uttered promises about the life they'd make together here. How did a man earn such a woman's love? If she would stay, he would spend his life figuring out how.

'Yes, but not any more. Thea helped me to see that love builds ways and new worlds, William, not walls. You and I were too focused on the walls, I think.' For the first time since the telegram had brought him to his knees, William felt a flicker of hope flare deep in his chest at her words. 'I couldn't lose you, William. You unlocked my dreams. With you I came alive again in ways I haven't been for years. I want to return the favour and unlock your dreams, and together we will unlock the dreams of others according to our gifts and abilities.'

William felt his chest loosen, felt himself draw a full breath. He was overwhelmed, not with despair that had driven him out here, but with hope, with the power of love, that Honoria brought alongside him.

'This is not just for you, remember. It's for us, for men like Peter Falkner.' Honoria guessed the trajectory of his thoughts. He nodded with a smile and raised her hand to his lips. Stars came out overhead, bright in the wintry sky. Snow sparkled about them on the ground, nearly as bright as Honoria's smile.

'There's only one thing left to do then,' William said solemnly. He went down on one knee in the snow, her hand still in his. 'Honoria McGrath, you have been the saving of me more than once. You've given me hope when I was hopeless and courage to go on when I couldn't find the way. Now, will you give me your hand in marriage? And I will endeavour to make you the happiest woman in the world every day for the rest of my life.'

She was crying again, gasping and laughing all at once, tears glistening on her cheeks. 'Yes.' At her words, he rose and swung her about in his arms and their laughter was like the peal of Christmas bells in the night.

'Now, shall we go tell your family?' She laughed up at him. How he loved the sound of her laughter, loved knowing he could make her laugh. He would devote his life to making her laugh.

'No, now we shall go tell *our* family and then, after they've celebrated, we'll tell them we're putting them all to work.'

'*Our* family. I like the sound of that. I've been without one for too long.' She smiled up at him as they began the walk back to the house where lights glowed through the windows, beckoning them to their future. At the front door, they stepped inside and stood still in the great hall, looking and listening to everything about them: the clatter of dinner being prepared in the kitchens, the cry of the twins from upstairs, the piano in the music room playing carols.

'Merry Christmas, Honoria.' William took advantage of the mistletoe over the door and placed a swift kiss on her cheek. 'I brought you here to give you a Christmas, but it's you who has ended up giving me the greatest gift of all.'

Honoria wrapped her arms about his neck. 'Merry Christmas, William…' she pressed a kiss to his mouth '…and welcome home.'

At last, the sense of homecoming he'd waited for, been craving since the ship had put in, flooded him. 'I *am* home indeed.' In the place he loved, with the woman he loved in the very season of love itself.

Epilogue

December 25th, 1858

'We have two more presents, but we'll all need to go outside for them,' Catherine Peverett announced as the Christmas morning gift giving came to an end. The Christmas tree room was a merry tangle of toys and children, some mobile and the most recent additions—Rebecca's son, Elliott, and Anne's second son, Arderne, named after one of Britain's first surgeons—held lovingly on laps and in the arms of their aunts and uncles.

'Are there more birthday presents?' Willa asked precociously, tugging on her grandmother's hand, eager at the idea of going outside.

Catherine bent down to her two-year-old granddaughter with a bit of grandmotherly mischief in her eye. 'There just might be. Get your boots and coat.'

There was much laughter as everyone—a family of eighteen now—bundled up to go outside. 'We're quite an unruly mob these days.' William laughed, holding Honoria's coat for her—a beautiful, rich brown with a mink collar and cuffs for warmth. Never again would his wife worry about the cold.

His wife. After nearly two years of marriage, the word still sent a thrill through him. They'd married two weeks after his Christmas proposal, having acquired a special license so that they could wed before Thea and Leopold left for Germany. The service was performed by long-time vicar the Reverend Donnatt who had also married Becca and Jules. 'A wonderful winter tradition,' the man had joked merrily.

It was a day William would remember all his life, the marking of a new beginning. The church had been decked out with fresh winter evergreens and smelled faintly and wonderfully of winter spices, courtesy of his sisters. There were tall white wax candles at the altar and Leopold at the church organ playing Mendelsohn's wedding march as Honoria walked toward him on his father's arm, his father just as proud to give her away as he'd been to give away his other four daughters. But despite the beautiful surroundings, William's attention was all for Honoria, dressed in a white gown made here in Haberstock village, adorned only with a bright blue ribbon at the waist. White for new beginnings and blue for loyalty she'd told him.

We must be unbreakable. You and I. For ever.

His wedding day was the gateway to that forever, something he'd not forgotten each day since.

Some people preferred summer weddings, but William thought winter the best time to wed and to hunker down like the seeds in the fields and the animals of the forests, tucked in their nests waiting and planning for spring. He'd certainly enjoyed that first winter—long mornings in bed with Honoria and afternoons spent planning the soldiers' facility.

It hadn't been all play. There'd been a lot of letter-writing, there'd been a few trips to London to talk with investors and to make arrangements, and to visit those of his patients who were still at the Royal Hospital Chelsea, chief among them, Peter Falkner. His was a story of a man who deserved more than he'd had in life. But his story was also a lodestar that kept William and Honoria motivated to see their project through. He would see Peter today, in fact.

Later this afternoon, he would make the rounds of the fifteen men he'd been able to settle here since the centre had opened last summer. Peter had been the first to take up residence, along with his wife. They'd become important leaders in the veteran community at Haberstock Hall.

William and Honoria followed the family out into the cold December morning. There was no snow this year, but everyone's breath steamed in the air as they walked towards the surgery, Catherine and Alfred in the lead. They stopped before the door, a cloth covering a square hanging on the wall beside it. His father gestured to Thea. 'Daughter, come here, this first gift is for you in acknowledgment and congratulations on your graduation from medical school. Go on, take off the cloth.'

Thea removed the cloth, astonishment and tears forming in her eyes as she read the bronze plaque out loud. '"Dr Thea Peverett, MD. Haberstock Hall Surgery. Est. 1640".' Her usually assured voice trembled at the end and Leopold slipped an arm about his wife to steady her.

'She's part of the legacy now, just as she wanted to be,' Honoria said quietly beside him. William noted his wife's eyes glistened just a little, too. Honoria and Thea had become close through correspondence during Thea's time away in Germany studying. It seemed right that his wife had found not only a sister but a friend and a fellow healer in his twin, the person he'd shared his life with from his first breath.

'Your diploma is inside. It came a few days ago. Forgive us for keeping it a secret. We wanted to frame it and hang it in its proper place for you.' His father opened the surgery door and everyone filed in, crowding the space to gaze at Thea's diploma and all it meant—a woman doctor. She had done it and anyone with enough determination might do it, too. Change was coming. Thea would be the healer. Dr Peverett would ease into retirement at his leisure, although being a grandfather was bound to be an active second career for him. And, William suspected, there would be a role for his father at the Haberstock veteran's centre as long as his father wanted it. A good physician never truly retired.

After a while, they all moved outside again, making a short walk to the road at the end of the drive to the Hall. A group of men were gathered there that William quickly recognised as the veterans who'd taken up residence, Peter Falkner among them, standing on the two prosthetic legs Becca had fashioned for him upon his arrival. 'It's a miracle,' William whispered to Becca who'd come up on his other side. 'Every time I see him upright, I think about what your invention has done for him.' She'd thrown herself into creating tools that would help the veterans and had developed prototype prosthetics she was hoping to patent. Peter had been the benefactor of such efforts and the inspiration.

'He's one of my best painters,' Becca confided with a smile. The toy production was going well, too. Her toy soldiers had been in stores for the first time last Christmas and orders had doubled this year.

'What is he doing out here, though?' What were they all doing out here? It was cold, they should be indoors enjoying their fires.

'You'll see.' Becca moved off to join Jules. The little minx, she knew. In fact, William had the impression the whole family knew. His father cleared his throat as everyone gathered around the object in the road.

'William and Honoria, this is for you, and veterans, this is also for you, in celebration of the Christmas two years ago which marked the beginning of this new centre. William, come do the honours.'

William pulled the tarp off another plaque, this one embedded in a monument marking the entrance to the drive. He read it out loud, his voice catching with emotion. 'The Peverett Veterans' Recovery and Pensioners Community.' He squeezed Honoria's hand even as she wiped tears of joy from her own eyes. He looked about the assembled men. 'Thank you, everyone, for making this dream of mine come true.' They were entirely inadequate words, but they were all he had at the moment.

Peter came forward. 'It's us who are thanking you, Dr Peverett. You've made it possible for us to rediscover our lives.'

William clapped Peter on the back. 'This place is due

to all of you as much as it is due to me. This is what is possible when people work together for the common good.' Over the last two years, they had indeed built a new world and torn down old walls to make a place of hope for those who had none, who walked in constant despair. He and Ferris had devoted themselves to the study of the mental effects of war and how best to treat men who suffered from their experiences. They had made some progress, but there was more to make. The dream was underway, but it was not complete. He looked forward to the continued challenge of his work.

He glanced at Honoria who gave him a nod. It was time to move on to the last surprise, this one for the children. 'Effie-Claire, Benjamin, Willa, Alfie, come lead the group with me to our next destination,' he called out, he and Honoria taking them each by the hand. He and Honoria had been up late last night, called to the barn shortly after they'd returned from Christmas Eve service.

The barn was warm as he led the four children to a stall at the end of the aisle and let them look inside. It took the children a moment. Effie-Claire gave a gasp. 'Uncle Will, it's puppies! The puppies are here!' Eight black and tan balls of fur lay curled up against their mother in the hay.

He nodded. 'Born early this morning, with your aunt's help.' Old Doubting Thomas's last litter, sired just before he'd passed at the end of October from a sudden case of pneumonia.

'Can we hold them?' Effie-Claire asked reverently.

Their mother was an even-tempered dog and didn't mind human intrusion. William knelt down in the hay, the children beside him. He scooped up one of the puppies and carefully handed it to Effie-Claire. 'Hold it like this, with a hand at his bottom. Hold it close to your body so he stays warm. Very good, you're a natural, Effie.' She loved animals and they seemed to have a natural affinity for her as well. She'd taken losing Thomas quite hard. He handed another one to Ben and then he and Honoria helped the twins hold their own with much assistance.

His gaze held Honoria's over the heads of the children. This is a perfect moment, that gaze said. Something twinkled in his wife's eye. 'What is it?' he asked quietly.

'I was just thinking it's a good thing you're so talented with children,' she whispered, a conspiratorial smile playing on her lips.

He answered with a slow smile of his own. Was this going where he thought it was? 'And why is that, my love?'

'Because while old Thomas was siring a brood, you may have been, too. In fact, I am sure you were.'

'That unseasonably warm day at the waterfall, perhaps?' William's smile broadened as he thought back to where they'd been two months ago in October.

'Or the night of the cider press ball.' Honoria smiled back. 'Or the night…'

'I get it. We had lots of opportunities,' He laughed, leaning over the children to kiss her. 'We are going to be parents.' Then he paused. 'Are you happy about it? It's not too soon for you?' He was ecstatic, but did this fit her plans?

'Yes, it's perfect timing. Thea says the Nightingale

Nursing School at St Thomas's won't be accepting applications for two more years. It's in the early stages now. Time enough for me to have this child and still see to my schooling.'

'You'll have help,' William promised. 'You won't have to do it alone.'

'I know,' she said softly. 'And that's the greatest gift of all.' They held each other's gaze, their hearts speaking in the silence of quiet children and sleeping puppies, both symbols of the promise of futures to come. Where there was love, no one walked alone.

* * * * *

*If you enjoyed this story, be sure to read the other
books in Bronwyn Scott's miniseries
The Peveretts of Haberstock Hall*

Love Harlequin romance?

DISCOVER.

Be the first to find out about promotions, news and exclusive content!

f Facebook.com/HarlequinBooks

Twitter.com/HarlequinBooks

Instagram.com/HarlequinBooks

Pinterest.com/HarlequinBooks

YouTube.com/HarlequinBooks

ReaderService.com

EXPLORE.

Sign up for the Harlequin e-newsletter and download a free book from any series at **TryHarlequin.com**

CONNECT.

Join our Harlequin community to share your thoughts and connect with other romance readers!
Facebook.com/groups/HarlequinConnection

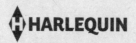

Get 4 FREE REWARDS!

We'll send you 2 FREE Books plus 2 FREE Mystery Gifts.

FREE Value Over $20

Both the **Harlequin® Historical** and **Harlequin® Romance** series feature compelling novels filled with emotion and simmering romance.

YES! Please send me 2 FREE novels from the Harlequin Historical or Harlequin Romance series and my 2 FREE gifts (gifts are worth about $10 retail). After receiving them, if I don't wish to receive any more books, I can return the shipping statement marked "cancel." If I don't cancel, I will receive 6 brand-new Harlequin Historical books every month and be billed just $5.94 each in the U.S. or $6.49 each in Canada, a savings of at least 12% off the cover price or 4 brand-new Harlequin Romance Larger-Print every month and be billed just $5.84 each in the U.S. or $5.99 each in Canada, a savings of at least 14% off the cover price. It's quite a bargain! Shipping and handling is just 50¢ per book in the U.S. and $1.25 per book in Canada.* I understand that accepting the 2 free books and gifts places me under no obligation to buy anything. I can always return a shipment and cancel at any time by calling the number below. The free books and gifts are mine to keep no matter what I decide.

Choose one: ☐ **Harlequin Historical**
(246/349 HDN GRAE)

☐ **Harlequin Romance Larger-Print**
(119/319 HDN GRAQ)

Name (please print)

Address   Apt. #

City   State/Province   Zip/Postal Code

Email: Please check this box ☐ if you would like to receive newsletters and promotional emails from Harlequin Enterprises ULC and its affiliates. You can unsubscribe anytime.

> **Mail to the Harlequin Reader Service:**
> **IN U.S.A.:** P.O. Box 1341, Buffalo, NY 14240-8531
> **IN CANADA:** P.O. Box 603, Fort Erie, Ontario L2A 5X3

Want to try 2 free books from another series? Call 1-800-873-8635 or visit www.ReaderService.com.

---

*Terms and prices subject to change without notice. Prices do not include sales taxes, which will be charged (if applicable) based on your state or country of residence. Canadian residents will be charged applicable taxes. Offer not valid in Quebec. This offer is limited to one order per household. Books received may not be as shown. Not valid for current subscribers to the Harlequin Historical or Harlequin Romance series. All orders subject to approval. Credit or debit balances in a customer's account(s) may be offset by any other outstanding balance owed by or to the customer. Please allow 4 to 6 weeks for delivery. Offer available while quantities last.

Your Privacy—Your information is being collected by Harlequin Enterprises ULC, operating as Harlequin Reader Service. For a complete summary of the information we collect, how we use this information and to whom it is disclosed, please visit our privacy notice located at corporate.harlequin.com/privacy-notice. From time to time we may also exchange your personal information with reputable third parties. If you wish to opt out of this sharing of your personal information, please visit readerservice.com/consumerschoice or call 1-800-873-8635. **Notice to California Residents**—Under California law, you have specific rights to control and access your data. For more information on these rights and how to exercise them, visit corporate.harlequin.com/california-privacy.

HHHRLP22R2